FROM THE
WORLD
OF
GALLIZE
SHIFTERS

CORBIN

Wild Wolf Pack

DIANNA LOVE

DEDICATION

This is for Tina Rucci, who has been a great asset and friend during my writing journey. Thank you for all you do.

DEAR READERS:
   This is Book 2 in the new *Wild Wolf Pack* series, which is a spinoff from the League of Gallize Shifters. If you've read the League of Gallize Shifters, you'll know how this new wolf pack happened and who is alpha. If you haven't read the Gallize series yet, that's fine.
   This series stands alone.

   Thanks for reading my books.

Dianna

   PS: **I do not use AI for my writing**. I still write every book the same way I wrote my first one, which won a RITA® award. Writing is not easy, but I find the creative story and character development that goes into every book a rewarding experience. Thank you for reading books written by real authors.

PRONUNCIATION GUIDE

Ares – *AIR ees*
Corbin – *KORE ben*
Eirene – *eye REEN*
Givenchy – *zhee VON shee*
Kesa – KEE suh
Ladrón – *lah DROHN*
Leszek – LEZ ick
Sully – SULL ee

CORBIN
Wild Wolf Pack

Both secretly hiding their shifter identities when younger, Corbin fell for Eirene then was captured by Eirene's security in the middle of the night and sold to a Romanian mafia leader. Her betrayal cost him everything, but he found a way to escape. Corbin is now running from the Romanian leader who will stop at nothing to bring him back. A celebrated shifter singer, Eirene secretly risks her life and freedom to help rogue female shifters in trouble.

Having joined a wolf pack, Corbin is offered a chance to secure his place by working with the alpha and her mate on a high-profile shifter security detail to uncover who is killing members of the security team. The top suspect is the celebrity – Eirene. Corbin is all in on finding the woman he believes destroyed his life but begins to question if she's truly the murderer as someone tries to kill her.

With one bad decision, Eirene and Corbin land in the wrong place at the wrong time, facing jackal shifters stalking them. Could it be shifter law enforcement trying to entrap Eirene for aiding rogue shifters or the Romanian leader hunting Corbin? They both have secrets to protect and need each other to survive, but can they trust again?

Note:

**All the Wild Wolf Pack
are stand-alone paranormal romances.**

Please join Dianna's newsletter at
https://authordiannalove.com/connect
to stay up on all her releases.
For signed books, bookplates, and swag, visit
www.DiannaLoveSignedBooks.com

Chapter 1

FIFTY-NINE MINUTES LEFT.

The damn time kept disintegrating faster than his patience.

If Corbin and his pack mates were late to the rescue … they might find only a few body pieces.

Sweat streaked down his face and pooled around his neck despite cool air in the sixties. He lowered himself, carefully feeding out the nylon rope a few inches at a time. Decent summer temperature for rappelling down a difficult face in the Blue Ridge Mountains of Virginia … if he did this sort of thing for fun.

Not in this lifetime.

He'd been an idiot to say he'd done a little mountain climbing in the past. Being a wolf shifter made it damn near impossible to lie to other shifters, but saying he'd done it before had been true. Although he'd failed to admit he'd been forced to climb and rappel in the past with zero professional instruction.

The climbing rope slipped in his hand, yanking him back to his priority of staying alive. His heart tried to blast out of his chest. Was he doing this correctly? He gripped both ropes like he'd been shown, took a breath, and kept easing his way down, or he'd never get to the base of this almost vertical drop. Agreeing to join Adrian and Ladrón on this mission had sounded like a good way to secure his place in a pack where he could hide from worse dangers than falling off a mountain. Mated to their female pack alpha, Adrian had asked for volunteers for this operation.

Offering to go didn't make Corbin special, just stupid.

He flicked a quick look left, but he could not see Ladrón, aka Ghost, who rappelled thirty yards away out of view due to a bulge of mountain between them. Being a better-trained person at this, Ladrón had to be lower down the face than Corbin by now.

Get going. If you fall, I'll heal the body, Ares bragged telepathically.

Yeah, I bet you will, Corbin muttered back at his arrogant wolf.

Ares snorted.

That offer might sound reassuring and supportive, but his beast would bust free and go homicidal if Corbin ever ended up unconscious. He spent most of his waking and half-asleep hours keeping Ares locked inside. As insurance, he wore a braided metal collar when he needed to sleep hard. If he allowed the wolf to go on a rampage, Corbin would lose his sanctuary and very likely his life.

You too slow. Get off this mountain, Ares demanded, as if he expected Corbin to jump when he shouted in his head.

Still feeding out the rope to keep moving, Corbin sent back a reply lacking any patience. *You want me to shift and let you figure out this rappelling bit or have you learned how to fly?*

Silence followed for a moment, then his wolf muttered, *Shut up and get us down.*

Another day in paradise with a combative wolf.

"Ladrón, check in." Adrian's tense whisper came through Corbin's tiny earbud with minimum distortion. The device had been specially crafted for their sensitive hearing. They were all three on the same channel.

Mild cursing came back first, then Ladrón said, *"This mountain sucks."*

Corbin perked up. Could the pro climber be having difficulty? Petty of him to feel a little smug, but with his background, he rarely got that opportunity.

Adrian snapped, *"What's wrong?"*

"The trailing rope is bound. Caught in a crack."

"Shit fire!" Adrian roared softly. *"How'd that happen?"*

"I slowed to move around an outcropping. Could not see the wide fissure in so little light."

That's all Corbin had to hear to convince him not to slow down.

Adrian had skills based on what Corbin had seen on their way climbing up the backside of this mountain. He sure moved like an expert. Corbin had gained minimal climbing experience while trying to stay alive under the thumb of his Romanian mafia captors. He knew enough to comprehend Adrian and Ladrón's instructions but wouldn't pass a test on terminology.

The main problem was that none of them had prior experience with this mountain range.

Attempting this during daylight when they began the ascent on the opposite side of the peak had been fine. That all changed once twilight had settled in at the top of the mountain and cast a dingy glow over everything. This sucked.

"What about you, Corbin?" Adrian asked next.

Breathing hard more from stress than physical strain, Corbin admitted, "I'm still descending, but I'm not the fastest at this." He felt the need to point out, "We're running a little behind on time."

Fifty-two minutes to go, to be exact.

Adrian had quieted. Clicks and thumps sounded as if he were rigging up to descend.

Glancing over his shoulder, Corbin considered the tall evergreens soaked in dark shadows far below and sighed. He'd only volunteered for this crazy stunt to build goodwill with Adrian in case Ares did something stupid.

None of that mattered now. Corbin had to admit the obvious. "Since I'll land before you two, I'll take off to locate the kidnapper's shack."

Cursing burst in his ear from Adrian and Ladrón arguing about his point.

He whisper-shouted, "Too loud. Cut it out."

Both quieted.

Adrian grunted something, then came back to say, *"I'm on my way down to free Ladrón. We don't know what we're going up against with this bear shifter, Corbin. He could be a behemoth grizzly."*

Corbin's nylon rope made a soft whirring noise as he kept dropping at what felt like a fast pace, but in truth was more steady than quick. "I'm going to get as close as I can and then wait near whatever structure he's using to hold the woman captive."

Damn bear shifter had a human female he'd threatened to kill and eat if her family did not pay the ransom of a million dollars. A private security firm had advised her father to contact Adrian's boss, the Guardian, for help because he couldn't get his hands on even half that much cash.

Ladrón spoke up. *"Is good idea, Adrian. You and I would do the same if we landed first."*

Coming from a military background where Adrian had probably led his men into battle, he'd stayed back at the peak to make sure Corbin and Ladrón descended safely first in case someone ran into a problem.

Like the one right now.

A frustrated Adrian agreed. *"Okay, but don't engage. I didn't bring you here to be a sacrifice."*

No, that had not been the plan, but they'd had little time to plan at all for more than one option. The bear shifter had holed up in an old shack in the valley below and would likely expect a threat to come from the lowlands spreading outward from his position.

Not the mountain Corbin had just descended.

"I know you didn't, Adrian." Corbin chugged deep breaths and kept his boots moving against the mountain with every foot of rope he fed out. "We volunteered knowing we were going up against a bear." Corbin would not regret his intention of paying it forward because of the support he might need later. He still had a deadly group of

Romanians hunting him. If they ever found him after this, Adrian and Ladrón might fight to help him survive.

That was more than he'd expected the day he crawled into the compound.

On the other hand, Adrian's mate, Jaz, might kill him herself if he brought a deadly threat to the pack.

"Be careful and watch out for booby traps," Adrian sent back between harsh exhales. He had to be dropping at a fast rate.

"Roger that." Corbin sharpened his focus on making it off this mountain without breaking bones.

Ladrón added, *"Cuídate, amigo."* Take care, friend.

"Thanks." Corbin smiled to himself. His Spaniard pack mate had barely spoken to him when they'd been paired up to train in mock battles. Adrian worked daily to teach the pack how to win a fight without shifting from human form to wolf.

Corbin won the last match-up with Ladrón, leaving the bruiser puzzled.

Keeping both hands busy, Corbin began considering places he might encounter traps. If the kidnapper anticipated an attack from between the cabin and the mountain, anything was possible.

His feet slid too quickly over a smooth section. He scrambled to prevent losing his footing where he might land in a worse situation than Ladrón. Stupid mountain. Drawing in a deep breath to calm his nerves, he tossed another quick look over his shoulder. Damn, he hadn't thought the trees would grow so close to the base of the mountain.

Two directly beneath him were forty feet or more tall with an umbrella of leaves preventing him from seeing any opening to the ground.

How was he supposed to get down through that?

"One more thing, Corbin," Adrian said in a tight voice. *"If Ladrón and I don't make it in time before the bear calls her father ... try to draw him away from the structure if you can but stay ahead of the bastard."*

"Roger that," Corbin muttered, fingers and arm muscles burning from gripping the rope for so long. He slowed his erratic pace and began a more controlled descent to avoid getting tangled up in tree branches with a backpack adding to the size of his upper body.

Stupid idea to climb mountains, Ares pointed out, since his wolf had nothing better to do than provide commentary.

I'm not getting into this argument again, Corbin sent back. Trying to calm his chaotic pulse, he pulled in deep breaths of crisp air filled with the fresh scent of pines.

Undeterred, his wolf argued, *I can sneak up on any bear. Not very smart shifter. Easy to kill.*

What an asshole. Corbin wished counting to ten, or even a hundred, would help. *You think everything is easy to kill. I'm sick of killing unless we're trying to survive.*

Must kill to survive. Ares lived to get the last word.

Corbin's back ran up against a bushy branch. He stopped and felt behind him with his boots for a branch that would hold his weight. Nope. No way past these trees unless he could fly twenty feet to either side.

Hanging on tight as he let out rope, he lowered one foot at a time through a mass of branches and searched blindly for a thick limb. He began squeezing his body through the crisscross of branches while death-gripping the ropes. Leaves smothered him in darkness when he sank lower.

His boot thumped against skinny branches that rattled.

Finally, his knee whacked one solid enough to not move. Shit! That hurt.

Ares snarled, *Stupid!*

Just once, Corbin would like to get his hands on that wolf's throat and shake some sense into him. Moving his arms through this living gauntlet took all his effort. Bending his knee, he lowered himself to sit on the branch and shook out one cramped hand at a time.

A couple of deep breaths, and he was back in his element.

With a new surge of energy, he tested the branch before creating slack in the rope. No sound of cracking. He made fast work of shedding his climbing gear, then dropped it to the ground before lowering himself all the way until he touched solid ground. He tied his gear as high as he could on the trailing rope.

For the first time since getting on the back side of this mountain, something felt natural.

Even in the dark, he made it down the tree with ease and leaped to the uneven ground.

His wolf growled and pulsed angry energy through his body.

Corbin pulled the vinyl cover off the face of his digital watch. Thirty-eight minutes left. He should be able to reach the cabin in twenty to twenty-five minutes, right? He pressed the flap back in place.

Adrian and Jaz had given them great equipment.

Shrugging off the comfortable backpack that Jaz had stocked for each of them, Corbin checked the contents. She'd sent a lightweight tranquilizer pistol to stop the bear, and a change of clothes should theirs get shredded. Where had their people gotten tranqs that packed enough punch to stop a bear? Having to be within seventy feet to discharge the tranq dart left little room for mistakes.

Flexible metal rods had been built into the looped straps of the backpack for holding it off the ground so a wolf could step through the opening and wear the pack.

That had been an irritating negotiation with Ares.

Corbin got what he wanted in the end, having only surrendered one token agreement he hoped not to regret.

Give me body! Ares shouted.

Corbin grabbed his aching head. *Stop yelling. I'm almost ready.*

Too slow.

Ignoring that, Corbin reminded Ares, *We have an agreement. Wait for my directions and for me to approve any killing.*

Keep talking and there will be no one to kill.

That had been the one concession Corbin had made. Ares could kill the bear shifter if Corbin's team failed to contain the kidnapper. Adrian wanted to keep the kidnapper alive, if possible, to find out who else might be involved.

Corbin should be able to make that happen with the dart gun. Adrian and his people were hoping the undependable cell reception in this area meant a shifter holed up this deep in the woods would be delayed in learning from a partner if the money got dropped. Unless the kidnapper waiting with the woman had a satellite phone like Adrian's, the odds were good they'd reach the cabin before he found out he'd been screwed.

But any gambler would say odds are never dependable.

A niggle of worry argued with Corbin's confidence, but he had no time to kick this around. After stripping down, he tucked both his boots and clothes into the backpack. He dropped onto his knees and hands, then called up the shift.

Ares needed no help. His monster wolf intentionally blasted out of their skin fast to punish Corbin for making him wait. It felt like hot needles stabbed into every muscle.

The minute Ares shoved his head and paws into the backpack openings provided, he wiggled his body, moving the pack to where he wanted it, and got serious.

Corbin always did his best to leave his wolf alone when on the hunt.

He only hoped Ares could keep his head screwed on in the right direction.

Ares dropped his snout to the ground, sniffed a couple of places, and took off at a steady trot. He'd covered twenty yards when he paused, lifting his head and sniffing. Then he lowered his head, continuing to scent everywhere as he moved more slowly.

Minutes ticked away too quickly in Corbin's mind. He remained silent. Pushing his wolf to run could get them caught in a trap or killed.

Ares suddenly paused and abruptly backed up.

What is it? Corbin asked.

Trap. Hole in ground. Bear scent heavy a few steps forward, but skunk scent dripped in a line going out to left and right. Sniffing faster, Ares made his way around the boundaries of the hole, which was well-camouflaged by brush and very likely armed with vertical spikes. Ares had a talent for sorting scents and quickly determining if any seemed out of place.

The skunk scent should be more concentrated in one spot, not dribbled in a straight line.

Smart move by the bear shifter, though. Where a natural animal would more likely change directions and avoid the area, a shifter hard on the hunt would leap over the stench to keep moving forward and land in the pit.

Not Ares.

He and Corbin had learned about traps the hard way over the years.

Without access to his watch, Corbin had no way to be sure of time, but it felt as if they were down to less than ten minutes. Ares paused again and lifted his head. Looking through his wolf's eyes, Corbin spotted a tiny flicker of light through the trees.

He urged his wolf, *Keep moving but without making a sound.*

You insult me. Ares started forward, avoiding downed branches and anything else dead that would make a snapping sound to alert the shifter kidnapper. Forty yards from a small shelter that had once been a decent shack, Ares hesitated again. *Bear scat everywhere.*

Corbin had caught a whiff, but the lack of sounds in the cabin worried him more than a shifter right now.

Were they too late?

He told Ares, *Let's move closer.*

We are upwind, his wolf argued.

True. The wind had shifted while they headed this way. Regardless, he had to know if the woman still lived. *Be careful and get close enough to hear if one of them is speaking softly.*

No argument this time. Ares had all but tiptoed a short distance when a woman screamed, *"Noooo! Don't touch me!"* Sobbing followed.

A loud roar came next that should have shaken the old wooden shack into a pile of rubble.

Ares stepped behind a thick bush and held his nose up to catch scents.

Corbin had to get to the young woman. He couldn't handle seeing any female being abused. *Give me the body.*

No. Ares lowered his head and backed out of the pack he'd been carrying. He wanted to fight.

Give. Me. The. Damn. Body, Corbin shouted at Ares internally.

Wait. Bear coming out in human form.

Before Corbin could argue another word, a bull of a man stepped from the shack with a rope in his hand. The other end was tied around the waist of a skinny young woman. She looked more like sixteen than nineteen as stated on the report.

She limped on a bad ankle or a broken foot. Her ripped pale-yellow shirt and dirty white shorts showed the least of her mistreatment. She'd lost her shoes. Blond hair tangled with sticks and leaves fell to her shoulders. Scratches ran down her arms, some with dried blood.

The bear shifter dragged her to a tree and tied the rope around it, leaving little slack.

She yanked back and cried, "Let me go. He's wrong. My father paid. I know he did."

Ah hell. No, her father had not paid because he had expected Adrian's team to save his daughter before the payment was due. Even if he had paid, the kidnappers would have killed her.

"No, he didn't, bitch. You humans think you're smarter than a shifter. He's going to find out what happens for lying to Dagger." He yanked off his gray T-shirt and started unbuckling his belt—a true wacko who spoke of himself in third person.

She fell to her knees, hands clawing at the rope. "Please don't do this."

Come on, Ares. We can't let him rape her.

You let me kill him?

Son of a bitch. Ares would pull that card now. Corbin said, *Let me have the body so I can shoot him with the dart gun.* He might have to give in to Ares if this went on too long.

Ares grumbled, *Asshole.*

The shift came hard and fast again. Corbin ground his teeth through the pain and got ready to act. The moment he had human arms and legs, he dug the gun from the pack. It already had a dart chambered, and he grabbed a second one.

Cursing the whole time, the bear shifter shucked his jeans, leaving him naked.

The woman's wild eyes dropped to Dagger's groin area. She screamed a gut-wrenching sound.

Just as naked, Corbin ran out and ordered, "*Stop!*"

That froze the bear shifter long enough for Corbin to get a shot into his rump, the only part of that body that didn't look carved from a tree trunk.

Corbin ejected the dart and jammed a second one in as the bear shifter turned on him and started changing. Shit. He pointed at the man's neck and discharged the gun again. Luck was with him. The shot struck true.

A black bear, Dagger lifted his hand with claws ready to slash, stood a moment, then slid down to his knees. His eyes rolled up, and he fell forward.

Corbin wanted to help the woman, but she'd been terrified already, and he'd make it worse heading over with all his male glory hanging out.

He called over, "Give me a minute and I'll free you."

Every pack also held a few medical supplies and an extra-large black T-shirt for the female. Jaz had prepared Adrian's team for the possibility that the victim might be in any condition. Rushing, Corbin snatched a pair of loose warm-up pants, stepped into them, and then ran to the woman.

She stared at him open-mouthed. Okay, she was in shock. He had to go slowly. "I won't hurt you. I'm here to save you."

Then she started shaking her head and talking between sobs. "There's … there's … another—"

A much deeper roar shook the air, then a massive brute with thick brown hair hanging to his shoulders and a bushy beard to his chest stomped out of the cabin.

This guy looked at the shifter on the ground, who might not be Dagger after all, then pointed at Corbin. "You're dead."

With his next blink, the kidnapper began shifting into a … grizzly. Of course.

No time to get another dart. Corbin shed his warm-up pants, telling his wolf, *Showtime, Ares. You're off the leash. Do what you want to him.* Adrian's people would have the other shifter to interrogate.

Ares and Corbin could shift as quickly as that bear when they worked together, but multiple shifts were beginning to strain them.

The grizzly stood on his hind legs and let out a furious roar. That might be the last sound Corbin and Ares heard before this monster cut them to pieces with sharp claws longer than Corbin's human fingers.

Ares stood six feet at the point where his thick neck met a wide pair of muscular shoulders. He snarled a vicious sound. Corbin had been going deep into the woods on the pack compound to let Ares run so the others wouldn't see the abomination he kept hidden. His wolf stood a head taller than any wolf shifter he'd ever seen in animal form.

Except for Adrian's red wolf. Another monster.

Scratching the ground with both front paws like a bull ready to rip prey apart, Ares growled low and menacing. They'd fought a damn polar bear shifter once and almost lost, saved only by the Romanians who shot the bear in the head with titanium rounds.

Adrian and Ladrón weren't here yet.

No one to save them now.

Dagger's bear dropped down to all four legs and lowered his head, opening a wide set of jaws packed with vicious fangs. He wasted his time trying to put fear in Ares.

Corbin's wolf had only feared one thing, and dying wasn't it.

The grizzly charged in a loping run, which meant he planned to launch his bulk and leap on top of Ares—Slam dunk. Dead wolf.

Corbin sensed adrenaline flooding his wolf's body. They'd been in battles before where he hadn't expected to survive. They might not win this one, but he and Ares had never backed down. This was the only time they functioned as a team.

If they lived, Ares would go right back to being a jerk.

Right now, Corbin would welcome that possibility.

The bear dipped low in the front and leaped.

Ares ran forward, dropped low, and lunged.

Still in motion, the grizzly's eyes rounded in disbelief at the aggressive move.

Ares twisted as he went airborne, his jaws wide open, and latched onto the side of the bear's throat. He let his body drop to hang like dead weight. The grizzly rocked his head from side to side and lifted a paw, trying anything to knock off Ares.

Corbin felt the jarring yank that should have ripped Ares' jaws open but didn't.

Dagger's bear hit the ground and batted Ares away with an arm as thick as Corbin's body. Ares had unlatched his jaws before they reached the ground and bounced away with blood slinging everywhere.

Pain seared Corbin's senses. The bear had gouged Ares across his ribs. They were bleeding, but so was the grizzly. The gash in the grizzly's throat poured out a river of blood, but the bear pushed up. Adrenaline would fuel him for a bit longer.

If Ares could race around and dodge strikes to keep the grizzly moving, the bear would bleed out fast.

Corbin hoped.

Ares stood tall, but Corbin struggled to breathe along with his wolf. His side and lungs burned from the clawed wound.

Functioning on rage alone, the bear charged Ares.

Corbin advised his wolf, *Just stay out of reach.*

I will kill this one, Ares replied.

Well, they wouldn't last long against a damn bear.

Even bleeding out, that grizzly could barrel into Ares and knock him off his legs. With one deep swipe across his soft underbelly, the bear would drag Ares' entrails out.

Game over.

Dagger's bear attacked, and Ares evaded a strike but put no distance between them. He instead ran around and bit down on the bear's lower leg, ripping tendons when he jerked his head.

The grizzly kicked out with his other rear leg, catching Ares in his right side.

Mother, that hurt!

Damn wolf kept jumping back and forth, jaws open to find another spot he could tear open.

The grizzly had been on the ground, defending himself. He lifted his head and shoulders as Ares came at him, then swung another humongous leg, hitting Ares like a tree limb gone mad. Corbin's wolf went flying into a jarring roll.

Corbin saw stars. This was it.

Ares could hardly breathe and fought to stand. He would not die lying down.

Corbin clenched against the pain they suffered.

They'd survived the worst life imaginable growing up. Daily inhumane treatment at the hands of their Romanian captor, while forced to kill other shifters who murdered for fun had savaged his soul. No innocent humans or shifters were killed, but even a justified death cut deeply into Corbin's soul.

Was this how it all ended? He'd gotten his hopes up for a new life. A real life where maybe they could mend the damage done over so many years.

Ares pissed him off every waking minute, but Corbin didn't want him to die this way. His wolf had reason to hate everyone, including Corbin.

Through blurred vision, he watched the bear struggle until he lifted all that weight off the ground. He took a step forward and went down on his front legs. Blood oozed from his jaws with every snarl.

He shoved up again and came like a drunken elephant for Ares.

When the grizzly got within two feet of striking, Corbin prepared to feel the final blow. He told Ares, *You did your best.*

I am not done.

Corbin would have laughed if he'd been in human form. Arrogant son of a bitch.

Standing still, the grizzly stared down at Ares. The skin around his bloody mouth pulled back to a vicious grin. Blood soaked the coat below his throat. How was that bear still moving?

The bear's uninjured rear leg gave out, dropping him into a lopsided sit.

Ares returned the grin by pulling the skin back along his jaws and showing off his own bloody fangs. He acted as if his life fluid did not flow from the wound on his side.

Grin gone, the grizzly lifted a paw and pulled it to the side to swing with all his might for the killing blow.

Ares tried to move backward, but he couldn't. His legs started to buckle. He widened his open jaws, ready to bite that claw.

The bear's arm hung in the air, then moved forward. Halfway to Ares, that mountain of brown fur crashed over on its side.

Hell. Corbin told his wolf, *Damn good fight.*

I know.

Hard to compliment an egotistical wolf. Corbin said, *Give me the body.*

Safer with me.

Miserable wolf! Corbin suffered the physical hurt along with Ares and had run out of patience long ago. Whimpers near the tree reminded him that the woman he'd come to rescue had to be even more traumatized after that battle.

Ares glanced over. She hugged her legs against her chest and sobbed.

Corbin couldn't take much more of this. *You can't help her, but I can. Give me the body!*

Ares snarled. *We will not shift again soon. You kill us both.*

Yes, they'd pushed too many changes too quickly. They'd have to wait an hour or more to shift again or risk not completing the change.

Corbin had no choice. He had to take that woman to safety, anywhere but here. *I didn't question you when I handed you the body.*

Because I am superior.

Right now, the only superior skill that wolf had over Corbin's human body was faster healing. Ares could not carry the woman anywhere. The cut on his wolf's right side had stopped bleeding and begun to close enough for them to shift without adding even more damage to what they suffered.

Corbin and the woman could move out as soon as he returned to human form and determined if she could walk at all.

With no idea how much time they had to put a mile or more between them and the slumbering bear shifter, Corbin gambled and began forcing the shift. If his wolf refused to help, Corbin could end up falling to the ground with a mix of wolf and human parts. Then they'd both be in dire straits.

Ares needed his energy as much as Corbin needed his wolf's.

He had not seen other shifters stuck in a change, but Ares had tried taking the body once when Corbin refused to let the wolf out. He shuddered to think back on that nightmare.

Ares yelled in Corbin's head, *Who stuck me with a stupid human half?* In the next few seconds, he thankfully pushed energy to force the change along faster.

As soon as Corbin became fully human again, the pain ratcheted up to a new level of misery. He sucked in air as he hurried to grab his pants and boots from the backpack. With those on, he found the long-sleeved green pullover he'd tossed aside earlier. Lifting his right arm sent pain racing through his banged-up ribs, but having the shirt on might help stanch the blood flow.

When he reached the woman who sat like a ball of shivering arms and legs, he spoke softly. "Hey, there. Let's get you out of here."

She'd been staring ahead but stopped moving.

They had to get going quickly, but he needed her cognizant of her surroundings first. He dropped down on one knee. "I'm Corbin. I'm with a team here to rescue you."

She looked at him with confusion. "Are you … human?"

Seeing any woman in shock and terrified hurt him. He'd like to soothe her with the words she wanted to hear, but he made a point of not lying to females. He could not promise she'd survive this if he didn't. Men were another story. He had his own set of rules for life. "I'm a shifter in human form *now*, but the wolf you saw fighting the bear is part of me too."

The best part, Ares interjected.

He'd give her twenty seconds, then he might have to drag her out of here. Adrian and Ladrón could come back to figure out this mess. He had no idea if there were more kidnappers in this ring, and every second sitting here sent dread crawling up his spine.

She blinked hard as if trying to wipe away the horror clouding her mind. Pale blue eyes stared at him with confusion. He'd once fallen hard for a girl with unusual aqua-blue eyes.

He'd never seen that color since.

A cursed color that starred in his nightmares.

Twenty seconds were up. "I'm going to cut the rope loose, okay?"

No response.

He withdrew a switchblade that had been strapped inside his pants pocket with elastic and thanked Jaz for her forethought again. He first cut the rope end tied to the tree, hoping the idea of being free would lessen the grip terror had on her. With no words from her yet, he slowly reached for the rope around her waist. He slipped his finger between the coarse rope and her torn shirt to give him room to cut without harming her.

She flinched, and he felt sick to his stomach.

He'd never frightened a woman. "I'm sorry." She might believe him if he hadn't sounded irritated. He couldn't help it. If any more shifters showed up, he could not hand Ares the body again yet.

Tears ran down her face. "No, I'm sorry. I'm, uh …"

Relieved at her talking, he supplied, "Shook up? That's understandable. You've been through an awful time here, but I'm getting you out of this place. What's your name?" He knew her name but wanted to keep her distracted with easy-going dialogue. He finished slicing through the rope and pulled it away from around her waist.

She whispered, "Judith."

"I'm Corbin. Nice to meet you."

Ares casually said, *Bear waking. You want to fight this one?*

What? Corbin swung around to find the first bear shifter still lying on the ground with claws poking out of his meaty hands covered in black fur from where he'd stopped in mid-shift. His distorted mouth moved, and he clenched his jaws.

Ares snickered.

No. Don't wake up, Corbin silently begged the universe. He stood and reached for the woman's hands. "Let's go."

She clamped his hands, and he pulled her to her feet. She took a step, limped, and whimpered. "My ankle is hurt."

Corbin still needed forty-five minutes to heal enough to battle. At least she didn't require clothes. He had no time to spare. "I'll carry you." He tossed her onto his left shoulder in a fireman's hold and said, "Stay quiet."

Hurrying as much as possible with pain stabbing him, he swung around and headed back the way Ares had come in. He'd like to have his gun, but he'd left it and his comm unit where he'd shifted. With every second counting, he had no time to search the area.

Even if he did, the damn tranqs had barely affected that bear.

The slumbering shifter let out a loud snarl and shook his head, clearly waking up.

Judith screeched a terrified squeal. His muscles clenched against the shrill sound.

An understandable reaction, but not helpful right now. Corbin took a quick glance to see how fast the shifter was coming around. Dark eyes in the shifter's distorted head filled with the promise of a bloody death. He ground out a sluggish roar but with energy building.

She passed out. Finally, a gift from the universe.

Corbin could feel warm liquid seeping down the side of his chest from his worst gash. Should he spend time hunting for the gun? Would the tranq slow down a disoriented shifter? Not worth the gamble.

Where were Ladrón and Adrian? Had Ladrón been in more trouble than a snagged rope? Corbin would call them if he had his comm unit, but that was with the backpack.

Corbin asked Ares, *Can you do anything to heal our wound quicker?*

I can heal any wound when I have the body.

You do realize that bear shifter will catch up with me soon, right? Corbin bit out at the annoying wolf.

Because you are not as fast as me.

Corbin fought his way through thick brush and low branches. He tried to reason with Ares again. *I'm asking for help healing so we can survive.*

Maybe I am ready to die.

Of all the things Ares could have said, that was the most ridiculous. His wolf faced any threat with only one plan. To kill and survive.

Heaving hard breaths, Corbin climbed over a fallen tree he'd usually jump, but not with Judith hanging across his battered body. Ares had stomped on his last good nerve. *If you want to die, let me know the next time I see a river, and we'll make it happen.*

A nasty snarl ripped from Ares. *You are dick.*

Tell me something new. If you aren't going to help me, why should I keep protecting you from water? Or did you forget about me being lashed eight times in human form with a leather whip because I refused to get on a boat for the Romanian one time? Corbin's head throbbed, and his vision swam. He had to find a place to hide Judith and backtrack to the bear shifter to pull him off course.

Fighting pain, he shook off the dizziness clouding his mind. He believed he headed back in the direction he'd initially traveled to reach the kidnappers. With Adrian and Ladrón tracking his scent, he had to run into them at some point, right?

With their shifter hearing, they should have heard her scream. That meant they weren't on the ground yet.

A much stronger roar bellowed behind them. Not far enough back.

Energy began to flow through Corbin's body. He wanted to scream at Ares for making him wait, but instead said, *Thank you. I'll let you know the minute I think we can safely shift.*

They both knew it would not happen before the bear caught up to Corbin. He had to use the push of energy to run instead of healing his wounds. He gripped her legs and took off running hard, which forced him to use the path of least resistance.

Unfortunately, that shoved him off course.

Wolves were fast, but natural bears could run thirty-five miles an hour over an open field. Even a bear shifter in animal form would be much faster than Corbin carrying a woman.

Running hard to stay as far ahead as he could, Corbin jarred his ribs and cursed in pain.

He jumped up on the two-foot-thick trunk of a downed tree, grunted at the effort, then raced across it to avoid slugging through dense underbrush. When he dismounted, he wove back to his right, angling toward the trail he believed Adrian and Ladrón would be taking. Energy drained away with every step.

Another loud roar blasted behind him.

Hairs on Corbin's arms stood up. That brute was closing in on him.

He caught sight of a twisted tree he recalled from earlier. His hopes lifted. If his calculation was correct, he had to move another twenty yards to his right to get back on his original path.

He ran a list of possibilities through his mind for how he could put this woman somewhere safe, but he knew nothing about this area. If he were back in Canada, where he'd escaped from Vlad, the Romanian, he could find six or seven safe hideouts on a moment's notice.

If he were still in Canada, he'd also very likely be dead by now.

The trees thinned until he saw an open area he recognized. Hallelujah. He had to be around a hundred or so yards from the tree he had climbed down at the end of rappelling. Worst case, he'd rig her up with his climbing gear and pull her far enough off the ground to—

The vicious roar of a feral monster shook the woods at the same minute a massive black body crashed through the trees fifty yards behind Corbin.

Judith dug her nails into his back, lifted up from where she'd been bouncing against his back, and screamed.

Time had run out.

Corbin had no way to save this woman. How could he fail her when he had been the only one to reach that shack?

Judith's heartbreaking cry and squirming around frantically threw him off balance. He locked his left arm tighter around her legs. "Hey. Calm down!"

"The bear … I hear him … He's …" She couldn't talk past hyperventilating.

He sure as hell had no paper bag. "Shhh. Listen to me. I've got a plan."

Her loud breathing turned into panicked panting. "Really? What is it?"

Corbin hadn't actually lied. He had no time to think anything through and had to make up the details as he ran. "I'm taking you somewhere he can't reach you." That was his only plan as he ran all out to stay ahead of that monster. "Try to stay calm to help me so I can outrun him."

Not a word followed. She drooped her body again like a noodle but clutched his sides. He bit down against a curse when her fingers dug into the still-bleeding side.

He used the sharp ache to stay focused on winning this foot race.

No roaring now, only the loud crashing of a massive bear tearing through the woods. The minute that bear reached the open space Corbin had passed through, he would close the distance between them even faster.

Ares asked, *Got a real plan?*

That's the only one I have, Corbin admitted, hating that he might end up letting his wolf down when they couldn't shift again in time for Ares to fight the bear. They had a difficult relationship, but he would never set them up to lose a battle.

Look behind, Ares warned.

Watching his steps, Corbin wrenched his neck to look back quickly. *Ah hell!*

That bear covered ground like a Kentucky Derby champion.

Panic crept into Corbin's mind. He tried to shake it off and think strategically, but he could not ignore the heavy pounding. He zigzagged into a cluster of trees.

Nothing slowed that monster that plowed a path straight for them.

Ares shouted, *Watch out!*

Corbin looked up and saw the end coming at them fast. He caught a tree with his free arm, spun around in a circle, and stumbled to keep upright.

The bear broke free from the cluster of trees, not stopping. There would be no slowing down to stand and fight. That predator would be on Corbin instantly and rip him to pieces.

Ares shouted, *What are you doing?*

Corbin couldn't answer, only act.

Judith lifted herself up and screamed. Corbin pulled her off his shoulder and down into his arms without looking at her. He slowed and turned. Walking backward, he kept the bear in view.

Six, maybe seven seconds, and it would all be over.

Pound, pound, pound of huge pads hitting the ground.

Hysterical now, Judith beat on his chest. *"Run, dammit! Run. Let me go."*

Corbin had her locked against his chest.

When he could hear the hot breath blowing out ahead of the bear's next roar, Corbin froze in place. Judith sobbed and begged for help.

The crazed black bear locked mad eyes on Corbin, bearing down hard to smash him.

Waiting for the last second, Corbin twisted to the side.

Ares howled in fury.

A deadly claw the size of a frying pan ripped a new gash in Corbin's arm, knocking him off his feet. He hit the ground, rolling to protect Judith.

Momentum carried the bear past him where he fell out of sight into the pit built as a trap that Ares had evaded earlier.

That bear sounded like a rock tower crashing to the ground. He screamed and thrashed, death throes continuing as it fought to survive. Impossible with thick, sharpened stakes jabbed into his body.

Corbin lay on the ground, not believing he and Judith were alive. She cried into his shoulder. "You, you ..." Hiccup. "Saved me, again."

Ares said, *Good move.*

Corbin blinked. Hearing that two-word compliment from Ares was like his wolf yelling that Corbin was the greatest partner in the world and a brilliant warrior. *Thank you.*

Sounds of something new running his way reached Corbin. He couldn't win a fight with anyone right now. That didn't stop him from setting Judith aside and wobbling his way up to stand. "Stay there," he told her.

She looked up at him as if she'd stand on her head and sing his favorite song if he asked her. He didn't want to see hero worship in her eyes. A traumatized woman would be glad for anyone to save her from those monsters.

He was no hero.

"Corbin!"

Relief swept through Corbin at the sound of Adrian's voice. Stepping around the hole, he yelled, "Watch out for the pit."

"Roger that." Adrian and Ladrón came running around the perimeter of the twenty-foot-square hole where the bear shifter made horrible sounds and gurgling noises.

Ladrón slowed to peek into the pit. "What have you done, amigo?"

"Survived a bear attack in human form." Then Corbin addressed Adrian, who now walked up to him while also checking the pit. "My wolf and I found the shack. We thought there was only one bear shifter at first."

I never said I thought that, Ares argued.

Corbin kept explaining. "When the bear shifter dragged the kidnapped woman out with a rope and tied her to a tree, he started shucking clothes to … make her pay for her father not delivering the money."

Ladrón cursed in Spanish.

"Exactly. I grabbed the tranq gun and shot him in the ass. I loaded the second dart and hit him in the neck. He tried to shift, then fell over unconscious. I had already shifted into my wolf once to find the shack faster."

"Amigo, we followed your scent. How did you avoid this trap?"

I am the one who found the pit, Ares pointed out, wanting the kudos he was due.

Corbin added, "My wolf located this pit, or we wouldn't have been so fortunate. We didn't find another booby trap in this direction. When we got to the shack, I shifted to this body so I could extract the woman. But when the second guy came out and shifted into a grizzly, I had to give my wolf the body again."

Adrian's eyebrows lifted. "Your wolf handled a grizzly?"

Of course I did. Tell him, Ares prompted.

"Yes. It was no easy battle, and Ares got clawed up a bit, but he ripped the side of the bear's throat and tore up his ankle. That bear bled out. I had to change again to free the woman. The minute I cut her loose, the first unconscious bear came back to life." He told Adrian, "By the way, that tranq only slowed the first bear for a short time even though I turned him into a pin cushion."

"Are you serious?" Adrian shoved his hands on his hips. "My boss will have someone's head for this. He pays for the best to keep us as safe as possible."

Corbin scoffed, "I'm glad I didn't have to find out if two shots would even slow down a grizzly."

"Madre." Ladrón rubbed his neatly trimmed black beard. "You and your wolf took on two bears. Are you saying the woman kept up?"

Corbin turned at the sound of her limping toward them. That ankle must not be broken. Terror had a way of keeping a person's mind off pain. She wiped her face with her hands and sniffled. "I couldn't walk. He carried me or I'd have died." She turned to Corbin. "Thank you for saving my life. I don't know how to repay you."

Oh no. There was that hero-worship look again.

Clearing his throat, Corbin said, "Judith, these are my two friends, Adrian and Ladrón." No point in telling her she was with more shifters.

She made a mmm-hmm sound, taking her eyes off him long enough to glance at them and look at him again.

Corbin sent an imploring look to Adrian.

Giving a nod of understanding, Adrian said, "Judith, we need to get you out of here as quickly as possible. Your father is wrecked worrying about you." He told Ladrón, "Call in Hawke."

Ladrón pulled off his backpack and dug out a satellite phone, then stepped twenty feet away to make the call.

Hawke was a bird shifter with Adrian's people who evidently piloted pretty much anything that could be flown.

"While he does that, I'd like to ask you some questions, Judith." Adrian finally drew her attention to him and guided her away from Corbin.

Corbin sighed with a heavy dose of relief. While Adrian found a place for her to sit on an old tree stump to speak with her, Corbin stepped over to join Ladrón, who was giving coordinates to Hawke. He asked Corbin, "Is there good place for helicopter to land?"

Pointing over his shoulder, Corbin said, "About thirty yards that way. Big open space, easy to find."

Ladrón relayed the message and then ended the call. He put the phone down and crossed his arms. "I would like to see this wolf of yours sometime."

Ah hell. "You will, but too many in the pack don't have good control. I'd like to wait until others in the pack are in a better place."

"I have control."

He'd insulted Ladrón. "Wasn't talking about you. Let's say I'm not ready yet."

"I hear you." Angling his head, Ladrón looked over where Adrian questioned Judith. He teased, "Pretty woman. She has eyes for you, amigo."

"I don't want any woman who looks at me that way, Ladrón, especially one that young and human."

The Spaniard frowned, creasing the spot between his eyebrows. "What do you mean the way she looks at you?"

"With forever eyes. I'm only interested in occasional bedroom eyes." To be honest, Corbin hadn't seen even that in years.

"Ha!" Ladrón grinned. "Every man says that until a special one comes along and ruins his bachelor plans."

"Not me. Biggest mistake I ever made was falling for a woman with dishonest eyes." He'd thought she was the one, his mate that would bear him pups with gorgeous eyes like hers. That was not a topic he wanted to discuss further. "What took you two so long to get here?"

Scowling, Ladrón spoke with his hands flying. "I am sorry we were late. I told Adrian to go without me, but he would not. Was a good thing. We freed the rope and rappelled fast. When we reached the base of mountain, two jackals attacked us."

Shocked, Corbin asked, "Were they with the kidnapping group?"

"No. SCIS. Adrian was much angry. He warned them to get out of our way. They were aggressive fools who are now tied up. Adrian told me he could have solved the issue with a phone call, but we had no time. He left them for his people to pick up."

Given the option, Corbin would not go near SCIS jackals.

Adrian had powerful connections, but by now the Romanians had probably cut a deal with SCIS to put a bounty on Corbin's head. He doubted Adrian and his boss could save him from that murdering group.

Chapter 2

IRENE STEPPED CAREFULLY over used syringes and a mix of nasty trash on the second floor, holding her breath against a stench that would send a human running out to barf. Being a wolf shifter meant having a sense of smell fifty times stronger than a human.

She pinched her nose and breathed through her mouth to avoid gagging. Fortunately, she couldn't get sick from the disgusting air permeating her lungs.

She loved living in Spartanburg, a wonderful city in South Carolina. For all the problems she faced daily, she at least had a decent apartment in the downtown warehouse district—the opposite of this seedy area where abandoned buildings had turned into crack houses. Human law enforcement did what they could to keep this sort of place under control, but they couldn't be everywhere all the time.

A crash sounded from down the hallway.

She paused, torn between being careful and rushing forward in case the woman she hunted had made that noise. Erring on the side of caution should be considered prudent, right? Hell, she had no idea. Untrained for this situation, she guessed as often as she had a real plan.

The trustee who sat in judgment of every move and decision in her life criticized any decision she made without his input. Screw him.

Additionally, the thieving human weasel, Jason, who she dated for a short time, would be mocking her right now. Best decision she ever made had been to boot him from her life. She'd be the first to admit she was in over her head doing this, but she was not turning back. She *would* find this woman.

Taking another tentative step forward, she wished for the magic ninja fairy to show up and wave a wand to turn her into a badass operative.

Someone with more background for this type of work who would have come dressed in cargo pants, boots, a jacket, and maybe even a Kevlar vest. She had to look like an idiot in navy capri slacks, a gray long-sleeved nylon top, and white running shoes.

Not so white anymore. Eww. She sidestepped as much refuse as possible and kept moving quietly.

Hard to be dressed properly when she'd only received the tip a half hour ago with the warning not to be late. With no time to change, she'd pulled a black knit cap over her signature strawberry-blond hair that often gave her presence away in public if her strange blue eyes didn't first.

She stifled a snort. Who in this place would recognize her? No dark glasses or wide-brimmed hat needed to avoid paparazzi here. As she reached a corner, shouting erupted ahead from behind a warped door on her left.

Standing still, she listened closely to the voices. Two men.

When the door began to open, she moved to hide behind the last corner she'd passed. Not out of fear, but to avoid hurting anyone unnecessarily. A deep inhale confirmed human scents. A guy in his twenties with thick brown hair and a lanky frame staggered out and stared at the ceiling. His hair stirred the memory of a teenage heartbreaker from many years ago. That one had been a wolf shifter with soulful brown eyes that still haunted her dreams.

Her silly heart claimed him before they ever kissed—silly teenage fantasy. The human blocking her way through the hall turned back to the room he'd exited and paused with his hand on the door.

She let out a soft breath of relief at not having to figure out how to get around him. Then he swung his eyes to the left, staring in her direction. Human eyes wouldn't see her in this dark corner. Even a human's natural instincts would sometimes warn them that a predator was nearby. She could now see that his brown eyes were too ordinary to be compared to Corbin's.

She swallowed hard and pushed down the pain every memory of him brought on. Why did her mind constantly remind her of the boy who had watched her with longing, then disappeared without a word?

He'd been hiding in a human high school, like her. A kindred soul who knew her secret and didn't think she was a monster during a time when shifters were first coming out to the public.

What had happened to that boy? If he lived, he'd become a man, for one thing.

Why did she care? He'd made her heart race from the minute she'd sensed his presence. More than race, her heart had wanted to be with him.

Why sugarcoat the past? Corbin had been just one more male among others in her life who had let her down.

His wolf was not safe. Her wolf, Pixie, had warned her back then.

But Pixie had been around no other shifters. Any alpha wolf would rattle her.

The human guy down the hall shouted through the door opening, "I'm coming in. Don't start your shit again."

Once the door slapped shut, she shoved stupid memories away and turned the corner, ready to get past the humans fast. Getting caught here would be a disaster. If she didn't want that to happen, she had to focus on the task at hand.

She rushed down the corridor on soft steps and caught sight of the last door on the right. If her information proved correct, she'd find the woman she hunted in there. Pausing outside the door, she had to pull her fingers from clamping her nose to check for scents.

An overwhelming flood of disgusting smells assaulted her. She covered her mouth and kept sniffing, sorting through the odor of human waste, rotted food, and pure desperation.

Wait. She sniffed slowly and caught a whiff. A nonhuman scent she hoped confirmed she was at the right place and the correct shifter waited on the other side of this door. Lifting her hand, she tapped then wiped the back of her knuckles on her pants.

No sound followed.

Eirene whispered, "Lauren. Your friend Nova asked me to come help you." Of course, Eirene had never met Nova and had no idea if that was even the woman's real name. What if she were here risking her life for a shifter who didn't want her interfering? It wasn't as if she had a network of people helping her flesh out these issues. She'd been doing this on the fly for the last six months since starting her quest to save vulnerable female shifters.

The human men arguing fell quiet.

Had they heard her? Doubtful.

Staying out here would draw unwanted attention. She whispered, "I'm coming in. I'm a … *friend*. Okay?"

Silence. What if she had arrived too late?

Using her shirt, she turned the handle on the door and pushed it slowly open. A heavier dose of foul smells bloomed inside. At this point, she had to deal with it. She didn't want her fingers around her face again until she could scald the grime off them.

Stepping inside, she glanced around the half-dark room piled with rusted cans, a gross mattress, a rusty five-gallon metal bucket, one broken chair lying on its side, and eight banged-up boxes of clothes that would be better off burned than washed. Across the room, a door hung half open on what could be a bathroom.

It was black as night in there and silent.

The shifter scent had grown stronger in this room and was still fresh, but the owner of that smell might have recently left.

She closed the hallway door behind her. Had Lauren struck out on her own?

That would be dangerous for her and others.

A dirty window with broken panes allowed twilight to cast gray shadows across the room. Walls had been ripped away from the upright supports exposing electrical and plumbing.

On closer inspection, the drywall destruction appeared to have happened recently. Every piece she took in had a white chalky edge with no dust or dirt accumulation. Deep claw marks raked three feet down one still-standing section.

Had Lauren …

A movement drew her around to face a crazed woman emerging from the dark room. Taller than Eirene and cadaver-thin, she walked like a zombie with dead eyes, coming at her with a broken chair leg she wielded like a stake.

Eirene held up her hands and whisper-shouted, "*Stop! I'm here to help.*"

If that was Lauren, her jaw moved with tight muscles. Her words came out raspy. "No more drugs! No more, you devil!" She swung to hit Eirene with the thick stick.

Drugs? Why hadn't she been told about drugs?

Eirene dodged the strike and kept her hands up, hoping not to harm this woman. Lauren possessed shifter strength, and drugs could amplify that even for someone skinny and sick. Backing around the room and trying to stay out of striking range, Eirene stumbled over garbage.

The bony shifter snarled and jumped up on the five-gallon can as if to get a higher advantage, but the can wobbled, throwing her off-balance.

"Please stop, Lauren. Let's talk. I'm here to help you."

Lauren waved her arms in a frantic attempt to not fall. Her eyes were two tiny black dots. She was out of her mind. Catching her balance, she pulled the broken chair leg above her head in a motion to drive the sharp end forward as she lunged.

Thanks to years of dance lessons and her shifter speed, Eirene sidestepped smoothly.

Lauren landed on the floor, hit her knee, stumbled forward to half stand, then listed sideways. She grabbed at air to stop her fall.

Eirene waited to see if that was it or if she'd gain a second wind to attack again.

Lauren stumbled around, holding the stick in a clenched fist and howling like an animal in pain until she finally fell against the damaged wall.

"*Shhhh!*" Eirene caught her as she slid to the floor. She yanked the wood out of Lauren's now loose grip and tossed it aside. "Listen to me. Please, Lauren. I'm a good person. I won't harm you."

Poor Lauren was too far gone to hear her. She grabbed her head. "Stop it. Stop. Stop. Stop killing me." Her raw voice turned into a pleading squeak.

Eirene would help any female shifter she could, but she knew nothing about drugs other than the monsters who experimented on shifters. She'd heard those stories. Bending her knees, she dropped all the way down, ignoring what she sat on to hold Lauren against her. She no longer noticed the odors, only the woman shaking hard in her arms.

Lauren suddenly gripped her arm and lifted her head to look at Eirene with shocked eyes. "You're not ... you're not *him*."

"No, I'm not." She didn't need to know the name of the man who had put this pitiful shifter through hell. Not yet. She'd find out in due time.

Lauren's lip trembled. Eyes drawn deep into the sockets, she looked much older than twenty-one. Her scrawny body tried to rock back and forth. "Save me. They'll catch me again. I can't go back."

Again. How awful.

Heart pounding at the terrified begging, Eirene used one trembling hand to smooth Lauren's ratty hair. "I won't let them get you. I'm going to put you somewhere safe and find help to deal with whatever drugs they gave you. We need to—"

The woman slumped into a boneless pile against her.

"Lauren, please try to stay with me."

Whispering in a child's voice, Lauren said, "Okay." Tears ran down her face. She cried softly as if she could barely manage the effort.

Eirene's throat tightened, hating what some bastard had done to this woman. Who was he? It would be helpful to know who might be hunting Lauren. Could it be one or two wolves using drugs to keep female shifters obedient? Or an entire pack? Were they somewhere around Spartanburg or maybe another nearby state?

More information was always better than too little.

She waited for the sobbing to slow and the woman to begin breathing evenly before asking, "Do you know who captured you?"

The room quieted for so long she assumed Lauren was out of it until she heard, "Black River wolf pack." Then her head dropped. She fell unconscious.

Eirene's lips parted. That pack produced Jugo Loco, a hallucinogenic drug for shifters.

This should have been a simple meet-up to find a lone female shifter waiting for someone to move her to a safe place. That's why Eirene had agreed to help Nova, who said she had a hotline set up for female shifters in need. Eirene welcomed any help offered in finding these women, but she had to be careful. She might as well put a target on her back by interfering with a dangerous rogue pack that lived outside of all shifter laws.

No one crossed the Black River wolf pack and lived long.

This one rescue could cost her life, right along with Lauren's if they found her.

Hesitation hit her in the gut. For a second, she wondered what to do, then dropped her gaze to Lauren's pitiful face and smoothed her hair again. She'd lost a close friend because no one had been there to help, and Eirene had been too late.

Not merely someone close, but her only female shifter friend she'd met after high school.

Eirene was in it now and would not leave Lauren to be captured by those hunting her again. The problem was going to be moving Lauren from here without being seen. She'd parked her car a half mile away, thinking the shifter she'd come to save would be mobile.

Her phone buzzed in the front pocket of her pants. She would ignore it if it hadn't been the text tone of her manager. Using the long tail of her shirt, she pulled the phone out to read the message.

Our new client has a group of six VIPs who have paid a hefty fee to meet you tonight before your show in Charlotte. Arrive an hour early. Don't bite off my head. You wanted this bonus contract. I warned you it might come with strings.

Not tonight! She gritted her teeth to keep from yelling at her phone. For the first time since walking into this building, panic took hold. How could she make it early to the auditorium over an hour away?

If only she had access to all her money. The bastard trustee controlling her money could not know what she was doing right now. If he figured out her sneaky way of financing her efforts to save destitute female shifters, he'd find a way to stop it at the cost of their freedom.

She had to have that bonus contract. Leszek had his hands on every other penny she earned.

Shifting Lauren's limp body in her arms, Eirene could not lose the funds from those charity contracts.

Tapping a simple "K" to his text was the only reply she could manage without starting an argument about how a manager should not expect her to jump through hoops on such short notice. That would eat up time she could ill afford to waste.

In fairness to him, she would normally be happy to accommodate the request.

At this moment, she still had no idea how she could leave a woman going through withdrawals from Jugo Loco, or worse, without supervision. She wasn't sure her warehouse was strong enough to prevent a shifter strung out on drugs from breaking free.

A crashing sound and yelling from the direction of the humans shook her into action.

Screaming downstairs started up. What had happened?

Sirens peeled in the distance.

Oh great. Eirene shoved the phone into the back pocket of her pants and pushed up to stand. She hoisted Lauren over her shoulder. "Umph." Lauren might be thin, but she was still a shifter.

The sound of glass breaking shoved adrenaline through her body. She had to get out before the police arrived. Even someone with her celebrity status could be arrested by shifter law enforcement and thrown in an underground cage.

Going back down the corridor she'd taken from the front entrance was not possible.

She opened the door and looked to her right. A cracked and unlit EXIT sign dangled in the dark. That had to be stairs, but would it offer a second escape point from the building?

The door she'd seen the human male step out of burst open. Three human men brawled to her left. One bled from his head. They were distracted by fighting each other. This was her best chance to make a run for it.

She slipped out to her right, glad her shifter vision adjusted as she moved into the dark corner. She yanked open the door beneath the broken sign. Rusty hinges squealed, hurting her ears. The men fighting quieted. Without a look back, she raced down the stairs, pleading silently that the rotted steps wouldn't break beneath the weight of two shifters.

The sirens howled louder now.

When she reached the bottom floor, she started out an exterior door at the opposite end of the building from where she'd entered and paused. Flashing lights zoomed past. She rushed, moving as quickly as she could with the weight she toted.

Bless poor Lauren, but she smelled terrible.

Eirene jogged through tall weeds and scattered garbage to the rental car she'd hidden, glad no one had found it, or she might have no wheels or tires. She dumped Lauren in the back seat. Legs and arms flopped loose. Good for now. If she woke up and thought Eirene was kidnapping her, this situation could turn deadly fast.

If the Black River wolf pack ever found out what she'd done today, they'd come for Lauren and take Eirene as well. Did that terrify her?

Yes, but someone had to help these women who, like her, had no one else.

Chapter 3

CORBIN DODGED A claw and spun around to stop. He flicked wet hair out of his eyes and counted another day of living free.

Badger slashed at him with claws out. Crazy Head is begging for death again by breaking the practice rules. How many times had Adrian said to fight in human form only?

Claws were not human attributes.

Corbin lifted his hands to end the mock battle. "That's it. I'm done for the day."

Badger shook his head. "Nope. No one stops while everyone's still fighting."

That was not the rule. A day ended once the six male wolf shifters in the pack had battled each other in human form. Those six included Adrian, who set up these exercises. That's how the rest of them understood the plan.

Who knew what Badger believed?

Stepping away by walking backward, Corbin clarified, "I'm getting water. You know the rule. No jumping anyone who's not actively battling you."

Would that even register with this idiot?

Their pack had issues thanks to the former sick-in-the-head alpha who had ruled a huge pack, but after Jaz killed him in self-defense, she became alpha. Some of the pack had run and been captured by shifter law enforcement. Others had to be put down. She and Adrian had treated him and the others fairly since day one.

Corbin didn't need much to be happy after what he'd endured for years.

But he could do without Badger's constant crap.

Not even that crazy was going to cost him the new level of respect he'd earned with Adrian after climbing a mountain and fighting a grizzly.

The slaps of flesh hitting flesh died down as the rest of the group ended their practice battles. Mock battles sounded harmless, right? Maybe for another wolf pack, but this one had too many who lacked control, including Corbin on some days.

Bosse had the best control. He'd recently joined the pack and was in the process of getting settled with his mate. Corbin envied the happy guy. He'd never have a mate. Any mate worth having would not have him with a crazy wolf.

"You all better after your water, pussy?" Badger stood with his arms crossed and sweat streaming down his bare chest. "See how wonderful I'm being?"

You pussy. Not me, Ares accused. *Let me out!*

His wolf hammered Corbin's insides. He tightened muscles from neck to toes, doing his best to stay in human form. Why hadn't Adrian called it a day yet?

Badger started circling him.

Corbin mentally sighed at the train wreck approaching. He stepped away from the water cooler to avoid damaging something Jaz had set up for them.

Looney bastard shook his warped head. Rust colored hair stuck out in short chunks as if he'd cut it himself with a dull axe. He mumbled angry words under his breath. Claws curled when he formed a fist.

Corbin took a quiet step back to slip away.

Badger's gaze jerked to him. He pulled back his lips, showing off incisors now lengthening.

Damn. Corbin urged, "Stop it, Badger. Don't be an idiot. Do you *want* to die?"

Ares weighed in. *Let me out. Crush stupid grin. Sick in the head. Put that one down. I need exercise. Fun, too. I fight them all.*

Shut up, Ares, he sent back so he could think. Corbin had named his wolf Ares, aka the god of war, because Toxic Chatterbox was too kind.

Welcome to his screwed-up life stuck between two wackos.

Ares pounded his insides. *Let me out. Let me out. Let me out!*

Corbin warned his wolf, *Keep talking, and I'll let Badger's wolf rip me apart before you can get out.*

Ares clammed up.

That threat had been one of Corbin's recent ways to stifle his wolf, but it wouldn't work for long.

Ares growled and clawed at Corbin's insides. Clenching his jaw, Corbin sent back, *Stop it, asshole. Got a cracked rib that's not healed. You could help with that.*

Shift and heal, Ares smarted back.

No shifting or Adrian's big red wolf will rip you into pieces.

Ares made a scoffing sound. Arrogant POS.

Corbin shut his wolf out to focus on one problem at a time. Why waste energy trying to explain that they were not the biggest predator here?

Ares had a deaf ego.

"Where ya going? Come out and play, pussy wolf," Badger whispered in a creepy sing-song voice. He hunched forward as if in some strange attack mode.

Ares howled a murderous sound.

Corbin hissed at the pain in his ribs. Ares tried to break free again. Son of a bitch! Corbin twisted and clutched at his aching body.

Patience shredded, he yelled, "You want to fight a wolf, Badger? Then go rattle Adrian's chain."

Standing upright, Badger lifted his head. He stretched his neck to look past Corbin as if he hadn't realized a shifter named Adrian was present.

Nodding, Badger headed in Adrian's direction.

Corbin cursed his mouth for spewing a stupid suggestion. He could feel the restraints on his control snapping one at a time. Stinking sweat poured down his chest, cutting lines through dirt on his skin. He mentally dangled a shower in front of his nose as a carrot. For anyone who'd spent weeks at a time without one, the feel of hot water on his skin and scrubbing with a bar of soap in the pack bunkhouse ranked as a luxury.

An image of the water running red with his blood filled his head.

Nice vision, wolf.

Ares rumbled with discontent.

Badger growled and hunched his shoulders again, this time in a bodybuilder pose. Thick forearms curved toward his stomach, ending with hands enlarging to the size of cantaloupes clenched in white-knuckle-tight fists. Muscles bulged and rippled across his upper body. Jeans that had sagged on him weeks ago now clutched his bulky thighs.

Quiet fell over the training area.

Corbin glanced around at the group. His gaze stopped on Adrian, who waited in a casual pose with his arms crossed. Nothing casual about his gaze, now focused on everything with razor-sharpness.

Bosse, with his peanut-butter brown hair and no-nonsense attitude, stood well over six feet but had no issue with controlling his wolf. He had an even temperament so long as no male looked too hard at his new mate, who was gone visiting family in another state. Ladrón usually kept to himself, but Corbin knew him better than the others after the mountain climbing. His wolf felt strange. Corbin couldn't put his finger on why. Then there was Hammer, a bruiser with thick muscles on top of huge muscles who wore his blond hair loose to his shoulders and a pair of dark sunglasses when in human form.

Hammer had threatened the pack lunatic, Badger, with his life for trying to take off his sunglasses.

Those three fanned out, anticipating entertainment.

Ares made another push to break free. Corbin's jaw muscles bulged from fighting the change. He caught a breath when his wolf backed off.

Corbin took in Adrian again. His attention had sharpened on Corbin. *Way to go, Ares, you self-centered jerk.*

The hell with this. The hell with Badger. Corbin was done being understanding. He ground out, "None of us want to pay for you screwing up *again*, Badger."

"I'm not listening to you, loser," Badger smarted back, puffed up like he owned this place. "You aren't my alpha *either*."

Claws poked through Corbin's hands again, digging holes where he clutched his sides. "*Argh!*" Stupid wolf still trying to have his way.

Stupid human trying not to be a wolf, Ares sent back.

Clearly catching scent of how close things were to going apocalyptic, Ladrón and Hammer became visibly agitated. Bosse stood still, observing.

Couldn't Adrian diffuse this?

Badger's eyes rounded and bulged.

"Back off, Badger. We're done for the day," Adrian finally called out.

Corbin relaxed enough to breathe. Fighting his wolf had been so much worse than sparring with any of the pack. He slowly unwrapped his arms, waited a second, then stood straighter.

Looked like he'd made it through another day.

Staying with this pack may not be such a good idea at times like this, but it was better than being caught as a lone wolf by the Shifter Criminal Investigation Service or SCIS. His wolf would be locked in an underground titanium-encased cage where Corbin would go mad with him. If he faced dying before he turned twenty-five, he could think of better ways.

Badger suddenly lowered his arms and wiggled his fingers until the claws receded. He stepped past Corbin and turned to Adrian. "Come on, non-alpha. I can take you."

"No." Adrian's command had been uttered in an even voice.

Badger's animosity vibrated the air. He lowered his voice

to a vicious sound. "You're denying me the right to kick your ass to be alpha? Who looks weak now, wolf?"

Adrian rolled his eyes. "How many times do I have to tell you that I am *not* the alpha? We'll train tomorrow. You can show me what you have then. No shifting until *after* dinner when anyone who feels the need can have at it."

Every day, Adrian had them waiting later to shift. He wanted to give them a chance to build control, which had been working for the group. All except Badger, who had gotten bolder as his strength returned with Jaz feeding them well.

Badger snarled, sounding more wolf than human.

Adrian's next warning came out in a low, chilling voice. "You know the rule, Badger. Shift now, and no one eats what Jaz has cooked or gets beer."

Every pack member began growling, a chorus of deep-throated warnings.

Badger frowned at the others, then told Adrian, "If you're scared, say you're scared."

Adrian's expression said his patience had run out. "Remember, I gave you fair warning. This is about all of you learning to make better decisions."

Corbin couldn't fault Adrian if he ended up having to put down Badger's wolf, but something inside of him felt sick at watching a broken shifter die from demons riding shotgun on his shoulders.

Had he not escaped the Romanian, that could have been him.

Badger teased, "Or maybe *you'll* die, and *I'll* be alpha."

Power flooded around Corbin, causing his wolf to sit up fast. If he'd been in animal form, the scruff on his neck would be standing.

Jaz walked up to the group. Tall and athletically muscular with short, scattered black hair, she moved with fluid motions. Nothing about her outward appearance warned of what she hid inside.

Corbin hadn't realized she was anywhere near them. That burst of power had been deliberate. She and Adrian had made it clear they were a different type of shifter from the rest of them.

Would her mystical power be enough to back Badger down?

When she spoke to Badger, her words were clear and firm. "You would have to challenge *me* to be alpha. You must be suffering from short-term memory loss. It wasn't that long ago when you were present when Adrian's red wolf destroyed five of the Blood King's pack with zero help. Red would break his own record in how fast he could rip out your wolf's throat. Since you're about as sharp as a bowling ball, I feel the need to put this in even simpler words. If you choose to shift into your wolf and challenge me to be alpha, I'll accommodate you. Attacking me will prove you have lost your ability to control your wolf and manage your emotions, as well as possess any sense of survival. As a healer, I prefer to offer sick wolves mercy, but in this instance, I will call up my wolf to put yours down. She will do it without hesitation. Choose wisely."

Corbin spoke telepathically to Ares. *I hope you heard every word she said and felt the rush of power she barely released.*

Ares made a grumbling sound, but for once had no comeback.

The other three shifters moved back in anticipation of the battle. Corbin cut a quick look at Adrian, who seemed content to allow the silence to force Badger into withdrawing.

A minute passed.

Badger had stilled the moment Jaz's power swept through the opening. A tiny muscle flicked in his jaw that had shrunk back to normal. Then his eyes changed from a dull gray to the unholy white silver that had to be his wolf.

Adrian and Jaz exchanged looks filled with silent dialogue. Corbin figured the others had become as accustomed to those two speaking telepathically as he had, even though no one asked about it.

This was about to turn bloody.

Badger's breathing kicked up. His heartbeat pounded loud enough for every shifter to hear. A sure sign of fight-or-flight mode. The mad shifter's gaze flicked between Jaz and Adrian. He spoke softly in a voice turning more guttural by the second. "Gonna let a woman fight your battles, non-alpha?"

Was that his wolf driving his tongue?

Shrugging, Adrian said, "This is Jaz's circus and her monkeys. As her mate, I will kill anyone who harms her, but she doesn't need my help to put down a wolf with a death wish. If you're still determined to spend the last minute of your life posturing, go right ahead. Nothing will be left of you but a fleeting memory."

Corbin angled his body slightly between Jaz and the pack dumbass. Even as he did it, he questioned what he thought he was going to do.

Ares didn't leave him confused for long. *He is not a friend. You interfere when no one wants your help.*

Jaz made a grumbling sound. "I'm cooking dinner. If you want to eat good food and drink beer, go get cleaned up. If you want a spot in our new cemetery, let's do it so the rest of us won't have to eat late."

She tended to have even less patience than Adrian when it came to dealing with stupid people. Badger's intelligence had been smothered beneath a pile of shit for brains.

He stomped around, mumbling in a low voice, "Don't want to die. No! Stay put! *No!*" Then some less discernible words. "No killing *tonight.*"

Corbin's eyebrows lifted. Was Badger arguing with his wolf and trying to keep the animal from breaking free? About time. Corbin grinned at the change until he glanced at Adrian and Jaz.

Neither one appeared convinced this was over.

Badger clamped his hands over his head as it began to change shape. "No! Stop!"

Jaz told Adrian, "He's had enough chances."

"I hear ya, babe."

She started unbuttoning her shirt.

Panic ran through Corbin cold as an icy river. Hell. This can't happen. If Badger's wolf came out now, Ares would not be stopped. Jaz and Adrian would finally know what a screwed-up wolf he harbored. The minute Ares lunged into mindless attacks on everyone, Adrian's big red wolf would rip Ares apart while Jaz handled Badger.

Ares had never been bested, but Adrian and Jaz did not brag about their wolves.

They merely warned the pack of what an out-of-control wolf would face.

Badger's jaw warped out of shape. He took a step toward Jaz.

Corbin stepped in front of him. "If any of us are forced to leave here because you trigger our wolves, we'll likely die in an SCIS cage. Think of someone else for once."

Badger growled back, "I did one time. Not making that mistake again."

Badger's eyes were wild. His head began to warp, and incisors grew longer.

"Oh, that's right," Corbin scoffed. "You can't fight in this form. Come on, coward." Calling Badger a coward might be worse than pussy. "If you can't fight like a man, I'll stay in this form and still kick your puny wolf's ass." Sweat ran down Corbin's face. He was pretty sure his wolf could rip up Badger's, but he doubted he could win a battle with Badger's wolf if he stayed in human form.

Ares shouted in his head, *Let me out or we both die.*

Corbin had only one play. To keep hammering at Badger, who flipped between snarling and shaking his head while shouting, "No! Don't!"

His wolf had to be as much of a misery as Ares.

As if something clawed the inside of Badger's skull, he grabbed his head and yelled, *"No! No! No!* My fight!" He ran at Corbin, who shoved him off to the side.

Badger spun and dove at him, swinging those clubs he called fists while shouting, "Schtay put! No. I'm winnin'. *Schop itt!"* His jaw extended even more, garbling his words.

Corbin dodged his wild swings, listened closely, and figured out that Badger argued under his breath with his wolf. Trying to end this, Corbin shouted back, "I'm not the one still fighting." He got up and feigned a limp, hobbling toward the barn in hopes that would be enough ass-kicking to make Badger take a breath.

"Watch out," Bosse called out softly.

Corbin turned in time to see the fool shifting into a rusty-brown wolf almost as big as Ares and with rough scars crisscrossed over the saddle of his coat. Anguish bled from Badger's human eyes. He mouthed the word *No!* but the only sound that followed was the loud snarling of a predator. His wolf came for Corbin.

This was it.

Faster than a thought, Jaz raced forward, ripping her clothes off as she shifted.

The stunning pale gold alpha wolf took two long strides and hit Badger's wolf on the side, sending his beast rolling eight times before his wolf's body hit the side of the barn. Wood creaked and rattled. Dirt fell off the roof in a sheet.

Silence blanketed the training ground.

Jaz called her wolf Tarski, which sounded like a name for a pleasant female wolf, not an apex predator prepared to crush any opponent.

Badger's wolf pushed up to stand, wobbling to the left and shaking his head after being knocked into next week. He snarled and growled. When the wolf finally looked up, he ceased snarling and recognized the miscalculation he'd made.

Towering over him, Tarski took a step forward. The deadly noise rumbling deep inside her raised the hair on Corbin's arms.

Badger's wolf dropped to the ground and exposed his neck, but murder still boiled in his eyes. Crazy, crazy, crazy.

Taking one precise step after the next, Tarski continued toward Badger's wolf.

Corbin thought Adrian might cut Badger some slack if

their wolves fought, but none of them knew Jaz's level of mercy when pushed too far. She had put down two shifters from the original pack. One snapped, and no one could reach the human inside. The other one got pissed when Jaz refused to feed them a home-cooked meal after he'd shifted in training. He went after her, racing past Adrian, who stepped aside and watched.

Tarski had been fast and efficient ending that one.

This Tarski was terrifying.

A self-proclaimed healer, Jaz hadn't been happy about either one of the kills, but as she'd said, she would not shy away from her duty as alpha.

Would she give her wolf a nod to be done with Badger?

When Tarski reached the growling wolf, she opened her massive jaws and placed them over the throat of Badger's wolf. His white-silver eyes widened, and a deep rumble vibrated from his chest. His body shook, but he didn't move or snap at her.

Having made her point, Tarski removed her jaws and turned to walk away, which meant she didn't consider that wolf a threat. What confidence!

Badger's wolf watched for a nanosecond and got up on all four legs. Skin pulled tight across his teeth, he exposed vicious fangs and stepped toward her.

Corbin glanced at Adrian, who stood watching it all unfold.

When Badger's wolf took a second step, Tarski paused in mid-step but did not turn around. She emitted an even deadlier growl of warning. Power rushed out from her.

Static energy raced across Corbin's skin. Ares howled. Ha. Didn't like that, huh? Corbin forced every muscle to remain still as did the rest of the pack. They had to look like a bunch of stone statues.

Tarski's snarl picked up volume.

Badger's wolf stumbled backward as if shoved. He dropped to the ground once more and exposed his throat in submission again. Whining, he begged her wolf to pull back the power.

Corbin's muscles relaxed when Tarski's power dissipated.

Tarski trotted over to Adrian, able to look him in the eyes with a slight tilt of her head due to how tall that wolf stood.

Jaz's mate gave Tarski a sympathetic smile. "Sorry about your jeans." He watched her for a moment more, then he nodded before Tarski continued to the house.

Adrian announced, "Listen up. We're still eating dinner together tonight on the back deck, and there will be beer."

The guys shouted a cheer.

Corbin asked, "Why?"

"Shut up, dickweed," Hammer snapped. "Can't you take a win and say thank you?"

"I'm asking so I understand for the future."

Lifting a hand to stifle the conflict, Adrian explained, "Fair enough. It's because you all learned a valuable lesson today, even Badger. We realize many of you have trouble with your wolves. Our goal is not to punish you or put down your wolf but to offer incentives to work on your control so we can train you. Eventually, you'll all be able to work individually or as a team as Corbin and Ladrón have recently. We'll assess your abilities when the time comes. Jaz asked me to make it clear that this is not your prison."

That confirmed Corbin's belief about those two speaking telepathically even in mixed physical forms.

Adrian continued while he had the floor. "Once we feel you can be trusted outside this property, and we believe SCIS won't grab you for acting out of control, you can have a real life. You show promise. That's enough for today."

Corbin expelled a long breath. Another day of being safe in the middle of nowhere. He craved this freedom with a yearning that only someone with his past could appreciate. As for leaving the property, let the others go out in public when they wanted. He'd do whatever work Adrian asked of him, like mountain climbing.

Still, he'd absorb everything he could from Adrian every day.

Only a fool would believe that this could last forever.

Adrian was teaching him new survival skills, unlike the ones he'd learned on his own while under Vlad's control.

Adrian walked over to Badger's wolf and calmly ordered, "Shift back."

The scarred wolf let out a pained whine and started a slow shift, which sometimes happened when a wolf fought against an order to change.

Corbin had enjoyed all he could stand of Badger and headed toward the shade trees surrounding Jaz and Adrian's front porch on his way to take a swim in the compound lake deep into the property.

Wind rushed along the ground, rearranging fallen leaves, then swirled through the ancient oak trees with limbs stretched over the front of the house. As he neared the porch, Jaz stepped out dressed in a red T-shirt and jeans. Her wild black hair, no more tamed than before, fit her free spirit. She looked out of place against the gentle country style, but she seemed content in her skin regardless of the surroundings.

She called out to Adrian, "G is waiting on the phone."

Adrian ended whatever he was saying and ran to the porch, thanking her before he leaped up the steps. He rushed inside. The screen door thwacked shut.

Jaz spent that time giving Corbin an odd look.

He told himself to keep walking and stare ahead. Don't engage.

"Corbin."

At the sound of her quiet order, he stopped and turned back to face her with his arms crossed. He could do polite and evasive but found being direct saved everyone time. "Yes, alpha?"

"Why'd you scrap with Badger?"

See? Questions he did not want to answer, and she'd hear a lie. Lifting a shoulder, he said, "Asshole pissed me off. We're all tired of dealing with him." Truth, but he hadn't answered the question she'd asked.

The longer she took to say what she thought, the more

he realized she didn't believe him. Again, he decided on as much truth as he could share. "It was all I could do to hold my wolf back after Badger's taunting. I don't need him poking at my beast."

Ares argued, *You the beast. I am best. She knows you lie. You lie, lie, lie.*

How had Corbin ended up with a magpie wolf?

Jaz admitted, "True. At least the last part."

Corbin shut his mouth to turn off the backhoe before he dug a hole to China. If Ares would give him peace for a little while, he could manage to keep them in this place. Corbin was dominant, too much for his own good, but he dropped his gaze to the ground.

She snorted. "Just don't. You're no more submissive than I am."

He hadn't intended to draw her attention. That's exactly what he'd managed to accomplish. *Thanks for no help, Ares.*

Not my fault. You the one talking.

Jaz shrugged, then said, "That's all I need for now."

Good. Corbin turned around, ready to make his getaway when Adrian called out, "Corbin. Don't leave yet. We need to talk."

Corbin sucked in a deep breath. What had happened?

Resigned, he headed back to the porch where Jaz had moved close to Adrian. Adrian and Jaz were talking softly. Whatever Adrian said pissed her off based on the flat line of her lips.

By the time he climbed the steps, the two of them turned to Corbin with a united front.

Leaning against a corner roof support, Corbin folded his arms. "What's up?"

"My boss needs me to handle something over in Spartanburg. To do this, I'll need someone with me." Adrian scratched the back of his neck. "I want to leave Bosse and Ladrón to work with the rest of the pack, so I'm taking you with me."

Stunned, Corbin enjoyed the second moment of relief

today, but he also sensed the offer might have a bearing on Jaz's mood change. "Uhm, I don't know what to say."

Jaz spoke up. "Say thank you because I would normally be going with him, but someone has to be here to keep this group from killing each other."

Corbin doubted this would be like the kidnapping job where no public cameras were around. If he hesitated now, this newfound trust on their part would shift to suspicion. Trying to sound interested, he asked, "What exactly would this entail?"

Adrian half-smiled when he explained, "We're going to insert into a security team to observe them. Their superior thinks something odd is going on and needs me to review their operation." He paused with a thoughtful expression. "Are you worried about the Romanians you said were hunting you?"

"Not exactly. I don't believe I left a trail here, so I don't think they can find me unless my face is photographed or filmed in public." He added, "But before I escaped them, I'd kept my head and face shaved as often as possible. Didn't get a lot of baths back then."

Jaz eyed him. "Is that why you won't let me cut your hair any shorter and you keep a thick beard?"

He'd shown up with the sides of his hair shaved short with the top longer. These days, his scraggly, dark brown hair stayed almost shoulder-length. "Yes." There was an honest answer for her.

Adrian explained, "You should be okay, then. The security team is primarily at a location outside metropolitan Spartanburg where an old theater is being refurbished. Not an area flooded with traffic cams. I don't see any reason you would be photographed as long as we're staying in the background."

"In that case, thank you for this chance." He looked up at Jaz and added, "Thank you, both."

"I'll fill you in on more details on the way tomorrow, but this team handles bodyguarding and security for a shifter celebrity."

"Who?" Corbin asked. The Romanian had kept him away from the civilized world for so long that Corbin doubted he would recognize the name.

Adrian smiled, drawing a narrow-eyed look from Jaz. "You might have heard of her in Romania since she's getting big in countries outside the US. She's Eirene Givenchy, the famous female shifter singer."

A fist clutched Corbin's heart, but he kept his face neutral and said nothing.

Looking at his phone that had chimed with a text, Adrian grumbled, "Not enough hours in the day." He lifted his gaze back to Corbin. "We roll at 0500. Jaz will have more clothes for you, plus a pair of tinted glasses. I want you to wear the glasses until I feel your eyes won't give away your shifter status to the humans. Plus, they'll help hide your identity. Any other questions?"

"No, sir. I'll be here ready to go in the morning."

"Great. Looking forward to getting one of you out in the field again." Adrian headed up the steps and paused next to Jaz. He dipped his head in acknowledgement and went in.

Jaz came down the steps. "This is a big opportunity. We both see promise in you."

Corbin stuck his thumbs in the front pockets of his jeans. "I'm hearing a *but* at the end of that sentence."

"You're right. I'm not crazy about you backing up Adrian while you're still hiding something from us."

His gut clenched. "What are you talking about?"

She hit him with a hard stare. "When I healed you, I sensed something foreign in your back. You never mentioned it. If it's a tracker and you're really done with the Romanians, it makes me wonder why you wouldn't have me take it out."

He could smooth this over. "You're right, and I'll explain it, but why did you wait until now to ask me about it?"

"We've been watching to see if anyone unexpected showed up."

He considered how to play this. So far, being straight had worked best with them. "Would you have handed me over?"

She snorted at that. "You should know by now that no one touches one of ours."

"Sorry, but I'm not used to anyone standing up for me."

"Understood. Now tell me what's in your body."

He let out a breath and nodded. "I have an electronic unit inserted into my back. To be honest, I never considered that it could be a tracker because I've never had an opportunity to escape before this one time." He scratched his head. "I don't think it's a tracker or they would have found me by now."

She quirked an eyebrow at his explanation but couldn't call a lie when he'd been truthful. "What is it?"

"They used electric shock treatments to train my wolf." His chest hurt just thinking about all the painful times he and Ares had suffered. The Romanians had screwed up both of them. "They starved me from the beginning. Then, when I was begging for food for my wolf, they'd use a trigger to activate that unit in my back. It shocked the hell out of me and would stun me long enough for my wolf to break free, and they'd feed the wolf. Do that enough times, and the wolf will blast out of your body just to get fed. Then they trained him to track humans on their command."

Her face didn't soften, but she no longer looked as if she wouldn't trust him to take out the garbage. "Was that all they taught your wolf?"

It was futile to dance around Jaz. He had no choice but to give her the entire truth. "For the whole time I was with them, we hunted human gangs, drug smugglers, black-market weapon dealers."

She cocked her head. "Were they some kind of Romanian law enforcement?"

"Hell, no. The Romanian ran a black ops mafia group that took on underworld contracts no one else would touch." He hated to admit this next part. "Once they had a way to unleash my wolf, they taught Ares that he mattered more than me. The next step was teaching him to attack a human target even if it was no threat to us. Every time he killed one, he got better food, and they treated him like a coveted weapon. I hated every minute of my time with that bunch. When my wolf was exhausted, I could take the body back."

She didn't say anything at first. Her face shifted with a flow of thoughts before she asked, "Can you control your wolf?"

"I will be honest. I couldn't until we escaped. It's not easy now, but we've been doing better since you and Adrian took over the pack. I've made it clear to my wolf that if he breaks free and attacks anyone and survives, I'll accept death in human form. I will have to live with the memories of the humans who died when we were captured. They were all scum of the Earth, but I will not kill anyone who does not try to kill me first. If the other pack members don't shift, I can keep my wolf inside. If one of them snaps and shifts, I might not be able to hold control."

Sighing heavily, she said, "If it were up to me, none of you would back up Adrian, but he spoke highly of how you and your wolf rescued that young girl."

That vote of confidence sent chills up his spine. Should he do this?

Screw it. He'd made a commitment and had to start building a new life. "I hear you. Is that all?" Please say she was done with him.

"No. One more thing." She stepped closer and lowered her voice. "Executing the assignment is Adrian's responsibility. Watching his back is your priority. Don't get starry-eyed over some pretty shifter celebrity and not pay attention. See you at dinner."

After that warning, she disappeared into the house.

She thought he'd get starry-eyed over Eirene-The-Queen-Givenchy?

That'd be a white-out snow day in hell.

Chapter 4

WIND BLEW INTO the open face of Corbin's helmet. Dark-tinted sunglasses protected his eyes. He normally didn't like to wear a helmet, and South Carolina didn't require one for riders twenty-one and older, but he welcomed this one.

Anything that kept his face off traffic cams.

July weather could get hot as hell, but a motorcycle made any trip enjoyable.

Listening to the peaceful sound of his motorcycle's engine, Corbin enjoyed his first real taste of freedom. One of the only pleasures he'd gotten while imprisoned by the Romanians had been riding a motorcycle. Granted, that one had been a rat bike, where this one had no more than a thousand miles on it. Even when he rode a rusted-out bucket with two wheels, it had been a welcome break from the literal noose around his neck the Romanians used to drag him around.

He could dream of being free, but he never would be. The minute they surgically installed that electronic shock device in his back, any real hope of freedom vanished.

This BMW dual sport, built for highway or off-road use, would do anything he asked of it.

Adrian's voice came in through the speaker in his helmet. *"You look like you're having fun."*

"I am. I never rode a BMW. This baby rides like a two-wheel dream."

"Glad you like it. We're close to the theater. I'm hoping for time to observe this group before I start interacting with them. If anyone questions your identity, use the card I gave you."

"I will." Corbin intended to say as little as possible and be Adrian's right-hand man, ready to fetch anything he needed. Adrian's reminder of how close they were to the theater amped up Corbin's anxiety. One minute, he wanted to see the witch of his nightmares in person and demand to know why she ruined his life. In the next minute, he fought the urge to jump off this bike and run in the other direction.

He had to get a grip on his emotions.

I told you female was dangerous, Ares piped up.

In all fairness, his wolf had argued with him about going to meet the young girl, but Corbin had suffered from what he believed was love. He'd been sure she would be his lifelong mate. In hindsight, it only proved males were female-stupid from a young age.

Ares had told Corbin that she'd get them killed. He'd almost been right.

Adrian flipped on his blinker and moved over to the farthest right lane. *"By the way, I'm going to take point on researching Beckham's security team. I want you to keep an eye on the client and report to me anything suspicious or strange that she does."*

Well, hell. Jaz had told Corbin to watch Adrian's back over everything.

When Corbin said nothing, Adrian asked, *"Problem?"*

"No, I'm good."

Adrian frowned. *"I don't have to be next to you to know that's a lie. I can't have someone on my team who is lying to me."*

At the sound of disappointment, Corbin fisted his hand. Being caught between Adrian and Jaz sucked, but he owed Adrian first. "Well, damn. I don't want to lie to anyone, and especially you or Jaz, but I'm trying to do what everyone wants me to do."

Leaning into the right turn, Adrian asked, *"Do you have*

another set of directions for this assignment?" He didn't sound angry. Yet.

Corbin leaned hard into the turn. He would not lie to Adrian again. "Yes."

"They come from Jaz?"

"Now she'll be pissed at me," Corbin grumbled. "She told me your job was to do what your boss required, and mine was to make sure I watch your back. If anything happens to you, she'll turn that giant wolf loose on me."

Adrian chuckled. *"No, she won't. Okay, let's be clear. She would never overrule my orders on a mission, so we do what I want. My mate can't stand any of her flock getting hurt, which includes you. She feels she's my best backup, which she is, meaning no insult to you. Anything else I can clear up?"*

The strain Corbin had been fighting all morning eased. "You told me Beckham wants to find out if anything strange is happening with his security team. I'm guessing he wants you to investigate the two accidents you mentioned. One for sure was murder." Beckham ran a top-notch human security outfit, based on what Adrian had said, but two people on the same team had died within the last ten days. The first had been a traffic accident when his man ran across a median into oncoming traffic. That one had been a thirty-seven-year-old man who did not drink or do drugs. He'd been in the military and had operated huge ten-ton vehicles with an excellent record. The other guard died when a gas main in his house exploded, burning him to death. That one had clearly been intentional because the man had been found with a bullet in his head.

"I believe Beckham's got a problem. I can understand his issue with a contract to protect a high-value target. He needs outside help, and we're it."

"Does Beckham suspect his client?" Corbin had to forget what he remembered about Givenchy from high school and keep an open mind to how much a person could change with enough time and motivation.

But what would the motivation be for killing her guards?

"Well, Beckham didn't say that outright, but he asked that I be careful while considering all possibilities," Adrian replied.

Corbin shook his head. Simple translation? *Don't upset the talent.* Didn't that sound like an uppity female accustomed to having anything she wanted and protected by her status?

"Beckham is trying to determine if she's innocent or is involved in something illegal she wants to keep hidden," Adrian continued. *"She complained the first day that she did not need a four-man team crowding her. Also, she refused any security that is not human."*

"Really? How can she think humans would be able to protect her better than shifter security?"

Adrian explained, *"She might have a point since some shifter security untrained to fight in human form or who can't manage their animals have caused deadly outcomes. On the other hand, humans would be easier to get rid of if she doesn't agree with having security at all."*

Would Givenchy have a man killed for the simple crime of getting in her way?

He had his own reasons for carrying a grudge against her. The infamous night he'd gone to meet Eirene after school, her guards captured him and used titanium cuffs to control him. Then they'd shown him the note he'd left in her locker at school. They said she'd handed it to them with the order for them to keep him as far away as possible.

He hadn't believed them at first.

Hours earlier, her lips had curved into the sweetest smile when she stood in front of her locker reading the note he'd left along with a wolf he'd carved from wood. She'd looked up to see him watching her from a distance and winked. His heart had done back flips.

But the next thing he knew, he was on his way to Romania.

Why did that memory still hurt so much? He was no longer a teenage boy with a broken heart.

Ares shattered his quiet moment of thought. *I want out now.*

That's not going to happen, Corbin sent back.

I am strong now. I can break free, Ares bragged.

If you screw this up, we're done, Corbin said, hoping to break through his wolf's one-track mind. *I mean it. If you didn't learn anything from what happened to Badger yesterday, then I can't save us. I'm doing my best to create a safe place for us to live, but you need to help. There are no second chances with Adrian if you break free. None. You think about that. I've got nothing to lose by letting Adrian or Jaz rip you apart except for being freed from your nonstop mental torture. I want some peace. At some point, I thought you would too.*

Corbin shoved Ares out of his mind to pay attention to the heavier traffic they were encountering on the eastern side of Spartanburg.

Adrian led them off the interstate and onto surface roads, heading toward the outer perimeter of the city. In two turns, they were in a less crowded area and rode straight into a chaotic scene of flashing lights. Several vehicles were parked in spots along the street. Four police cars, an ambulance, and a fire truck were well represented by their respective uniforms, crawling all over the grassy lawn leading up to the building. No one acted as though they had a fire to put out, but two men wheeled a gurney quickly from the ambulance and into the structure identified by a faded sign as the Libertas Theater.

What the hell was going on?

Following Adrian's lead, Corbin backed his bike into the same angled parking spot. He dropped his side stand, then stepped off with eyes still taking in the unexpected scene.

Adrian turned to him with his helmet off. He unzipped his full-body riding suit and stepped out of it. "Grab your cap. That and the sunglasses will hide your face for now."

Nodding that he understood, Corbin left his helmet hooked on the handlebars. He pulled a worn-out NASCAR cap from his tank bag and slid it over his hair that he'd pulled back into a short ponytail. His dark sunglasses made sense out here where it was bright, but he planned to keep them on inside as well.

Not much of a shield but better than showing his face.

Adrian's faded olive-green ball cap and tactical sunglasses wouldn't mark him as former military, but anyone who knew what they were looking for would see it in the way he carried himself. He led the way through throngs of people until he reached the police who blocked their path. He showed an ID to the officer who studied it with a frown, then must have read something that caused him to wave them in.

Flashing that ID again at the theater entrance to someone in a hard hat, they passed inside. The burly door guard then shoved a hand in the faces of the media trying to follow them. Corbin wanted to thank the guy for stopping people with cameras, but he'd only draw attention he didn't want.

Inside the old building, a moldy smell mingled with the scent of fresh paint. Cobwebs had yet to be cleaned from windows that needed to be scraped more than washed. Rows of wooden pews reminded him of a church by the way they were arranged with a wide row down the middle and shorter ones on each side.

Corbin stayed near Adrian who moved down the right wall before pausing halfway to the stage.

They could easily hear anyone inside with their shifter hearing, plus some people were shouting.

Speaking quietly to Corbin through the special comm unit they both wore, Adrian pointed out what he observed. "The guy lying on the floor has a Beckham Security patch on his jacket. Based on how hard the paramedics are working on him, he appears to be badly hurt, maybe with internal damage."

Corbin noted the dark blue security jacket with a white lightning rod overlaying the word Beckham stitched in red on the sleeve. The gurney from outside had been parked near the injured man and lowered closer to the floor. Three men lifted the injured guard into place along with an IV line and an oxygen mask.

The paramedics wheeled the gurney out of the building, and sirens fired up shortly after.

"I'm not going to assume anything without facts, but this doesn't look good," Adrian murmured.

Corbin asked, "Do you mean for Givenchy?"

"Yes."

Where was the queen? That thought had barely passed through Corbin's mind when out from the left stage stepped a long-legged woman in three-inch heels. Those matched her dark green skirt suit, showing off striking strawberry-blond hair that took him back years.

He couldn't drag his eyes from her. There she was after all these years. His chest ached. He couldn't explain why his heart clenched with missing her after all she'd done to him long ago.

His heart had a damn short memory when it came to the misery he and Ares had suffered. His brain needed rewiring for him to still yearn for the young girl he'd fallen for after weeks of exchanging flirtatious glances.

One thing was for sure. That was no little girl anymore.

A smudge of dirt smeared Givenchy's pink cheeks. Her shoulder-length hair had probably been styled before whatever happened to give her a disheveled look. Brushing at the sleeves of the jacket, she cocked her chin up and looked spitting mad.

His body tensed. Damn his soul. He hadn't expected to feel anything except revulsion.

Apparently, his body had no conscience or loyalty to him.

She swatted at her shoulder-length hair, knocking dust free. She still wore long bangs brushed to the left across her forehead.

He'd forgotten how unusual that shade of hair could be. He'd never seen the equivalent on anyone else, as if Givenchy owned that color.

Police stepped over to her. "Ms. Givenchy, we'd like to get a statement from you."

She kept her chin up but took her attitude down a notch to civilized anger. "What would you like to know?"

The policeman wrote notes as he questioned her. "How well do you know this man?"

With exasperation clear in her voice, she replied, "He *was* leading my security team who are tasked with my protection. Based on the issues they've had recently, including today, they should do a better job of watching out for each other. I ask very little of them."

Another security guy in the same jacket stood to the side with his arms crossed and eyes glinting with anger. "We are doing our best with what we're allowed to do."

Ignoring him, she continued speaking to the officer. "To be honest, I'd terminate them for their own safety rather than wait to see who gets hurt next, but my tour contract requires Beckham's security service."

Pausing from taking notes, the cop asked, "Were you near the guard when he was injured?"

Corbin studied her reactions. Right now, she appeared annoyed that the questions had not ended yet.

"No." Givenchy brushed at an imagined fleck of dirt on her jacket. "I was taking a call in my dressing room when I heard a crash. I ran out into the backstage to a disaster."

"What interaction have you and the injured party had today?"

She hesitated, then said, "None. I had just arrived and had not spoken to any of the team today."

The security guy standing next to his fallen teammate said, "Wait a minute. Archie followed you backstage to ask about details for the show schedule."

She ripped off her sunglasses and glared at him. "Did you see the two of us talking? If so, please share what you heard being discussed to clear up this contradiction for the police."

Fire flashed in her striking gaze. Those eyes were stormy as the Caribbean Sea in turmoil. Corbin had never seen her angry as a young girl. Back then, she'd been sweet, vulnerable, and innocent-looking.

Red flooded the guy's angry face. "No, I didn't see you talking to him, but—"

"But what?" she snapped. "This is serious. I want to know what happened as much as the police do. This isn't the time to bring up anything except *facts*."

The policeman saved him from digging a deeper hole. "Let's *all* keep to the facts." When the security guy backed down, the officer asked Eirene, "Did you have any personal history with the injured party?"

She pulled back, appalled. "What? No. He was one of my security team. Otherwise, I'd have no reason to even talk to him. You do know that I'm a wolf shifter, right?" she asked as if leading an ignorant witness on the stand.

"Yes, of course. I was only—"

"Then you should also know that the media would twist whatever I do to seem like I'm insulting the entire human race if I do or do not date a human. I'm trying to build a favorable relationship with the human population, not start a war between humans and shifters. I'm also putting on a charity event at my own cost on the day following each show on my tour." Her anger had diffused into her making a statement about life in today's world as a shifter.

Adrian whispered to Corbin, "She makes a hell of a statement, but I doubt it sways the cops. They're not overly impressed by her status or her words from what I can tell."

"That's how I'm seeing it too," Corbin agreed. He had to be careful not to expose the conflict warring inside him. She sounded innocent and maybe even the victim in this, but she might simply be good at shuffling her words to appear genuine.

Pushing his hat up on his head, the officer nodded. "Thank you, Ms. Givenchy. That will be all for now. I may contact you again with additional questions."

"What else would you need from me?" Her clipped tone indicated she hadn't expected another round of questions.

Why not? Corbin found that odd. Anyone involved in what might not be an accident could be called in at any time.

"No way to tell right now," he replied in as curt a tone as

hers this time. "We're starting to investigate. We have a lot of people to interview."

"I understand." She sounded torn between being forthcoming and unwilling to give an inch in this verbal tug-of-war. "I don't mean to rush, but I must leave soon for an appointment with my trustee, Leszek Moore."

The officer didn't react noticeably, but he did take a step back.

Adrian murmured, "Oh man, her trustee carries a lot of clout. Word is many shifters fear drawing his attention. Early this year, a wolf shifter was caught stalking Givenchy. When Leszek found out, he contacted SCIS and supposedly requested that they talk to the wolf shifter. We didn't get involved, but we have eyes and ears everywhere. It's believed SCIS jackal shifter enforcers captured him. That wolf shifter was never seen again, and SCIS claims their enforcers only had a talk with him."

Oh, sure. Corbin shivered at that thought. No one should stalk a woman or any person, but from what he knew, jackal enforcers had too much autonomy.

Glancing around where three other officers were talking to workers and searching the area, the policeman who'd been asking Givenchy questions told her, "We'll be here for a while today. One of our detectives is on his way here now."

"That's fine," she said politely. "Take your time. I only came by to confirm that we were on schedule for the show three days from now. Will that allow you and your men enough time?"

"Yes, ma'am, if nothing unexpected turns up."

After her stoic performance, she flinched at being called ma'am.

Corbin stifled a chuckle. No matter how successful or powerful some women became, the young ones still did not want to be addressed like their mothers.

She added, "I look forward to finding out how that metal walkway in the crossover fell."

"Crossover?"

"The area behind the backstage where technicians and others move from side to side without being seen during a performance."

"Got it." More note writing.

The air conditioning rumbled to life, blowing toward Corbin.

With one deep inhale, he was back in high school, staring at the girl who he'd thought was special. Someone who would want to be his friend. Maybe more one day.

After the air swirled through the building for a few seconds, Givenchy stilled and slowly turned her head in Corbin's direction.

He dropped his chin and peeked over the top of his sunglasses. She took a step in his direction where she could descend a short set of steps off the stage and walk through the seating area.

His heart thundered. Would she come down here to question them and recognize him? He hadn't counted on being exposed to her.

Hadn't he wanted to confront her? Yes, no, maybe. Hell, his head needed an overhaul.

Adrian never moved but asked, "You good?"

Damn. Corbin sucked up his courage as Givenchy turned around and headed back the way she'd come from the left.

He'd been foolish to think she could smell him from back here or even recognize his scent after all this time. The air conditioning vents had blown *toward* him, not from him to her.

Trying to sound casual, Corbin confirmed, "I'm good. I'm absorbing everything and the client." He would not screw up this chance to prove himself worthy of being chosen twice to work with Adrian.

With Givenchy leaving the stage, Corbin let out a long breath, ready to help Adrian.

The security guy she'd argued with called out, "Don't leave yet, Ms. Givenchy."

Chapter 5

IRENE STEELED HERSELF to once again face Brody, that blasted security guy. She'd almost gotten out of this mess clean. She never name-dropped, especially using Leszek's, but she'd hoped mentioning her trustee, who supported the police in many ways, would untangle her more quickly.

That had worked.

Now, the new lead on Beckham's security team, who supposedly worked for her, ruined a perfect escape.

Gritting her teeth, she turned around and gave him a snooty expression she saved for those she considered nasty media hacks. She could not tolerate a snob, but pretending to be one came in handy sometimes.

Fortunately, most of the media treated her with respect and not as a dressed-up mongrel, but a few would take advantage of her at an inopportune moment.

Striding back to him, she spoke first. "Listen, Brody, I have a tight schedule, and this situation is not helping. I assume you're taking Archie's place as the head of my team, so what do you need?"

Just as worked up as her, Brody spoke in a deep but low voice. "This was *no* accident. Someone sent a tower of metal scaffolding falling over on him."

Her heart climbed up her throat, threatening to strangle her.

If she showed any weakness right now, she'd get pinned with this accident … *if* it was an accident. She seriously doubted it given the two questionable deaths on her security team already in the past two weeks. Having humans stuck protecting her and ending up killed or harmed made her sick to her stomach.

This was not the time to appear as a weak female. She had to show quiet confidence even if it did come across as disinterested.

Keeping her arms loose at her sides, she countered, "If that is the case, why are you wasting time telling me what you should be telling the police?"

Brody countered, "I will share everything I know with them. I'm only saying you shouldn't leave until we know who did this to Archie. Don't you care?"

What a brutal question. Too many days of stress and anguish had her on edge. She snapped, "Of course, I care, which is why I was getting out of the way so law enforcement could do their job. It's a distraction when I'm here under these circumstances. I know it and so do they."

She hated to play the snotty celebrity, but she had more lives at stake than those present.

Another member of Brody's team standing twenty feet away called him over.

Her heart ached. She'd been having nightmares about these human men dying when she, a wolf shifter, had not been around to protect *them*. As soon as she heard about the one dying in a car wreck, she visited the location hours after the accident had happened and smelled a shifter scent.

That scent had never been reported or investigated.

And people wondered why she allowed only humans on her security team. Shifters couldn't be trusted, especially male shifters, plus she sometimes had to jockey around the truth.

One shifter had stalked her recently, and others had lied to her when she'd been at her lowest emotional point for six months following her father's death.

Even the first wolf shifter who had wanted to be her friend in high school vanished without a word two weeks before graduating.

Earlier in the day of that same night, he'd left a note asking her to meet him.

She sniffed deeply. Had she smelled a familiar scent in here or was that her silly heart trying to bring Corbin back again?

Why would he be here of all places?

Brody stormed back over and pushed a new button for her. "The media will be rabid once this gets out."

Giving an intentional glance to the group of officers over on the right side of the stage, she lowered her voice. "Your team has been incredibly accident-prone, which gives me no sense of safety. I think you should take some time to ensure everyone is qualified to do this." She cringed at how cold that sounded, but she'd be happy if the three men still on her team refused to guard her.

Of course, Beckham would only send more warm bodies.

Brody pulled his head back, looking appalled.

Before he could mutter another damning word, she pressed her only advantage. "What is the point of having your bunch here to supposedly protect me when you can't keep your own people safe? You accuse me of not caring, but I just told the police officer to take his time investigating despite the deadline we're all on. What else do you want me to do? Why would you insinuate otherwise? Are you trying to tank my career with your insulting comments?" She took a step forward, her anger pushing him back to maintain space. She'd done her best to keep them as far from her as possible for their safety. "All you have to do is stand around and look important until the police complete their investigation. Think you can manage that while I'm gone?"

Exasperated, he grumbled too low for human ears, "I'm asking you to *wait* until I can free up one of the guys to go with you."

She'd clearly heard him. "No. We both know I'm more than capable of protecting myself. My driver is taking me home where I have competent security. I need time to rest and work on my songs. I saw what I came to see and frankly have had enough for one day."

She'd burn in hell for her cold words, but maybe they'd save this man's life.

"Thought you said you had a meeting with your trustee."

Meeting Brody's angry gaze, she let out a slow breath. See? Sometimes she had to dance around the truth a shifter might call her on. "I do have a meeting with Leszek. I did not state the exact time. Some things are not your business."

"Beckham won't approve any of that without one of our people going with you," he argued.

Brody was dedicated. She'd give him that, but he deserved a better client.

On the other hand, what if he knew more than he had shared?

Huh. She hadn't considered that and should have. Someone close to every man on the security team would be the best person to look at hard after three unexplained incidents.

"Beckham is *your* boss, not mine," she clarified. "If *you* care about Archie, then stay here and help the police. As for Beckham, I intend to discuss this security mess with him myself." Not really.

She headed out again, determined to reach her car.

Before exiting the stage, her nose caught another whiff of the strange scent again. She shot a quick look at the two men in ball caps she'd noticed coming in during the chaos. Why were they here? Probably some media who snuck in with a phony excuse. Were they shifters? Even more reason to escape quickly.

She sniffed the air but could not catch that suspicious scent again. With the way the air conditioning blew from the stage out to the seating, she couldn't imagine having picked up any scent from down there. She hadn't slept much in days and needed some downtime.

Her phone pinged with a familiar tune. Damn. Could she not get a break? Eirene rushed out of the building to where Ivarson opened the rear door of her private sedan. She thanked the middle-aged man who had been her father's driver for over twenty years and slid in, waiting for the door to close and him to settle into the driver's seat.

This sedan had been customized with an audio-privacy window between the front and back seats much like a limousine. She'd also had a rod installed on her side of the narrow window with a short curtain that slid across for times when she had to change clothes in the car.

Young girls were in awe of her glamorous life.

If only they knew the truth.

Additionally, Eirene did all she could to protect Ivarson from getting involved in her dangerous decisions. He was human and a bit cantankerous, but she'd come to trust him with parts of her life.

Her phone played the tune again.

Lifting her phone, she schooled her expression to reveal no emotion that could be seen from his rearview mirror.

That was her life. Isolated with no friends, no love life, and no support when things got rough.

A headache pulsed behind her forehead as she read the text:

Thank you for the offer of two front row tickets. Please keep them safe for me.

She groaned. If only she could reply to this text to tell this blackmailer she was not superwoman capable of jumping through multiple hoops at once. But a reply to that number would show as non-working.

Two front row tickets.

Translation: *Two female shifters in trouble that Eirene hid in a warehouse.*

Please keep them safe for me.

Translation: *I can't take the females off your hands yet.*

She lifted the phone mounted in the console which connected her to Ivarson. "I'd like to visit my little dress shop near Raoul's restaurant. She has a few new items for me."

Ivarson answered, "Yes, Ms. Givenchy. Mr. Moore called moments ago saying he hadn't received a return call from contacting you. I explained that an emergency was happening at the theater, but I had stepped inside and confirmed you were not injured. He said to inform you that he wished to see you as soon as possible."

She rolled her eyes. She'd intentionally dodged a meeting with Leszek the last two times he called asking her to come by. She did not need anyone else hounding her about it, but she would not snap at Ivarson. "I'll return his call when I have time. I'd like you to check on someone. Archie from my security team was badly injured. A large metal scaffolding fell on him. I don't know the whole story of what happened, but I will. Please call Brody for an update on his condition."

Ivarson's face filled the review mirror with a look of concern that morphed into sad acceptance. He knew the hurdles in her life. "Yes, Ms. Givenchy."

She leaned forward and slid the little curtain across the window separating herself and Ivarson, then pulled the tote bag she'd put inside the car earlier to her lap. Out came a pair of dark green dress pants she shoved her legs into while still wearing the skirt. Unzipping the skirt, she yanked it off, then shed the jacket, putting the folded pair on the seat to her left. Kicking off the uncomfortable spiked heels, she pulled on comfortable beige walking shoes with a groan of relief.

Next, she rifled through her large designer purse to double-check that she'd have what she'd need when she left the sedan. Her fingers closed around a switchblade of high quality. She shoved it into her pants pocket.

Chapter 6

AS GIVENCHY STRODE off the stage with her heels snapping against the hardwood floor, Adrian spoke softly to Corbin. "She just lied."

"Twice," Corbin confirmed, struggling to get a feel for this woman. They never got to know each other as he'd wanted when they were teens. Maybe she was a homicidal lunatic. Or she could be as innocent as she tried to appear. Yet she'd lied about not talking to the injured security guard and about being driven home. Why?

Shaking off his suspicions, he asked Adrian, "What's the plan now?"

"Follow me outside." While striding toward the entrance door, he kept talking in a quiet tone, but one that Corbin could hear. "I didn't want to do this, but we're going to have to split up. She may eventually go home … or not. I need to be here to find out what happened to another one of Beckham's men, maybe catch someone lying to the police, and get a lead." Adrian nodded as he approached the door guard and passed through quickly. He ignored the media shouting questions at anyone who would answer—a wasted breath with Adrian.

Corbin stayed on his heels and kept his head down, letting the cap visor shield his face above the dark beard.

"You follow Givenchy and call me when she reaches her apartment building, The Adair. It's a converted warehouse in an older area of the city." Adrian hurried over to where their bikes were parked next to the highway and added,

"She mentioned her trustee, but she didn't say that she was going there first."

Corbin suffered a wave of stress when his task should have been straightforward.

Adrian must have picked up on that surge of emotion. He stopped quickly and turned around. "Question?"

This was Corbin's chance to prove he could work solo. "No, I'm good. This is the first time being on my own. It's been so long, it surprised me." The absolute truth. He added, "But I can handle this. After climbing a mountain and facing bear shifters, this should be easy."

His wolf grumbled, *You suck at mountain climbing.*

Corbin sent back, *You suck at being supportive.*

Adrian chuckled. "Good point." He turned serious again. "Keep the phone Jaz stuck in your tank bag handy. Your ID ties you to my boss's organization. If for any reason you have a conflict with someone, keep your cool and try to talk your way out of it. If you have no other way to survive, you can shift."

"Got it. I don't expect to engage with anyone." He had questions for Givenchy, but not today while he was on duty. He slammed the lid shut on that part of his brain.

"We're technically part of her security team while around her," Adrian explained. "If anyone tries to harm her, we also protect the client regardless of any suspicions we might have about her at this point." While Adrian continued dispensing advice, he shoved his cap into a saddlebag. "Should trouble arise and law enforcement gets involved, don't panic. Be respectful and calm even if they take you in. We will send someone immediately."

"Good to know. That had crossed my mind." Corbin expelled a breath he'd been half holding. All he had to do was observe and keep his nose clean.

Adrian locked his hard saddlebag and straightened. "I'll call when I have a handle on this situation so we can get back together, but ..." He glanced past Corbin. "Your assignment is leaving. We'll talk later." Then he turned and headed back to the theater.

You said this would be easy, Ares taunted. *You already lost your target.*

Jerking his head around, Corbin caught a flash of dark blue as a sedan emerged from a side street between the theater and an abandoned building also being worked on. The car pulled out and turned right. Corbin yanked his cap off and tossed it in his tank bag, then pulled his helmet on and snapped the chin strap. He climbed on his bike and kicked the stand up while starting the engine. With one rev of the engine, he wheeled out of his spot into a stream of traffic.

He stood on his highway pegs to see over a mix of vehicles. Where was the sedan?

There. Now to catch her vehicle.

Cruising in and out of opportune openings between cars and trucks, he strained to drive properly when he wanted to split lanes and catch up quickly. He had to change his thinking when on the hunt for a legitimate operation. He no longer answered to the Romanian. Vlad hadn't cared if he broke a hundred laws so long as he succeeded at capturing Vlad's prey.

Once that happened, the Romanian sent his henchmen to retrieve their trained shifter.

In the past, Corbin had been given the same assurance about someone coming for him if he landed in trouble, but with a different outcome.

Where Adrian offered security and protection, the Romanian would have beaten his human body bloody if he'd gotten caught by the authorities.

Vlad considered it a waste of money to grease palms to save an animal.

Corbin told Ares, *We have a chance at a better life with Adrian and Jaz.*

Good for you, not me, Ares pointed out. *I was more important before.*

You were treated far better than me and never realized they were only using you, Corbin groused. *I'm trying to create a better situation for both of us.* He didn't have the mental space to argue with Ares about how being fed more to kill had not made him important. The Romanian would kill Ares with a single titanium shot if Ares had ever acted like an ass to their keeper.

Corbin narrowed his eyes at the cushy private car ahead toting around the woman who had tossed him into a Romanian refuse crusher like yesterday's trash.

Now he had to protect the Givenchy Queen.

No one had to explain irony to him.

"Whatever." Corbin would not allow his anger to overrule his common sense. He'd treat her like any other stranger for now. Once he and Adrian completed this task, Corbin intended to reveal his identity to Givenchy and get an answer to the one question he'd lived with for seven years.

Why did you destroy my life?

He'd get his chance even if it meant standing in line for an autograph.

Corbin wormed his way between cars, drawing a few honks, and made a questionable move with success. No time to celebrate as traffic flowed toward a street where the sedan began forcing its way from the middle lane to the left lane with a blinker flashing.

That had been a quick move.

Had the driver made Corbin?

Holding his breath, he executed a hairy move, drawing a few honks, but he reached the next left turn without causing a traffic issue.

With two cars between them, the sedan turned left, offering Corbin a brief glance at Givenchy riding alone in the back seat. He had to keep reminding himself that the quiet young girl he'd fallen hard for was gone. She'd grown into a stunning woman who carried herself with brutal confidence and cold arrogance.

Maybe she'd been like that all along, and his attraction to her had blinded him to reality. He mourned never having had the chance to get to know the young girl, but that time had passed. Now he had a front row seat to observe her in real time.

Still two cars ahead of Corbin, the blue sedan angled to the right, taking an entrance ramp to the interstate.

Rolling on the throttle as he entered the fast-moving traffic, Corbin shoved everything from his mind to narrow his focus on finding out all he could on Givenchy for Adrian. His stomach soured at the thought she could be involved in the security guards' deaths, but he shook that off.

He had a responsibility to Adrian, not the memory of a girl from high school.

After following his target heading west, Givenchy's sedan exited the interstate before downtown, where he'd expect a powerful trustee's office to be located. Next time, he'd ask Adrian the trustee's location. After multiple turns, the car drove along an eclectic retail area that appeared to have been revitalized from a past era. The sedan suddenly pulled over to the curb on the right.

When Givenchy jumped out of the car, she no longer wore a skirt. Striding quickly toward a boutique dress shop, she'd changed into deep green pants but still had the same beige blouse. Her pretty hair had been tucked under a floppy hat, and she carried a large purse the size of a tote bag on her shoulder.

The most notable change on her way into the store had been from spiked heels to casual walking shoes.

None of that appeared suspicious at all, right?

Corbin pulled into a parking spot from where he could watch the shop entrance. He tapped his fingers, trying to decide if he should follow her into the store. He'd stand out like a blazing beacon. She had to be up to something.

Should he call Adrian?

No, that sounded like he needed handholding. He gave it a minute, then recalled how he'd been trained to hunt by a deadly group who never lost a target—the Romanians.

Though productive, that had often required questionable methods.

He considered his options. Leaving this spot was risky if

she came back out, but his gut shouted that she would not come back out the front door.

If he guessed wrong, he'd have to explain to Adrian why he lost track of Givenchy. The one thing he didn't want to do was fail on his first day of this operation.

Screw it. When in doubt, go with instinct.

He found an opening in traffic, flipped his bike around, and took off. He had one goal—to discover if she was only Eirene-the-Queen Givenchy or Eirene-the-Killer Givenchy.

Chapter 7

EIRENE FIDGETED, WORRIED about the motorcycle Ivarson had mentioned possibly following them. She had almost not exited the car at this dress shop until he announced the bike had disappeared in traffic.

For some reason, her stomach refused to see that as good news.

She walked around the shop that smelled of lemon-floral potpourri. She touched the back of her head for any loose hairs falling from the floppy brown hat concealing her hair. Nope, her hair remained intact where she'd pinned it up high. She removed the dark glasses that she'd worn in case the paparazzi showed up.

Some days, she felt like a cartoon character in disguise.

Had the motorcyclist following them been one of the two she'd seen standing by their bikes outside the theater? Or a coincidence?

She didn't have the energy to become paranoid over motorcycles with so many on the roads. Moving around a rack of skirts near the display window, she started to worry. Where was her friend who managed this shop? Eirene remained across the room from a thirtyish woman she did not recognize who carried an armful of clothes, clearly helping a middle-aged lady. They headed toward the dressing room.

Eirene kept glancing out the display window.

No motorcycle had passed by in the last three minutes, and she could see none parked nearby.

Good, but where was Lilly?

The front door opened, and in came a trim, energetic twenty-three-year-old Gen Zer carrying a white paper bag emitting a delightful aroma. Lilly had picked up something from the Persian restaurant two blocks over.

Her head swiveled in Eirene's direction. "Hi!"

Eirene flinched at the loud sound in the too-quiet shop.

Lilly scrunched her shoulders and whispered, "Sorry. Didn't mean to blow your ears."

Smiling, Eirene shook her head. "I'm fine. Your lunch smells divine. Wish I had time to visit Raoul's place."

"You should. He's got a new item on the menu." Lilly rushed over to the shop's checkout desk, depositing her meal bag and purse. She hooked her thumb toward the back of the store without saying a word.

Eirene nodded and headed that way, passing into an area where clothes hung in clear bags and cardboard cartons sat unopened on a long table.

Lilly waited until Eirene was close enough to whisper, "I'll go back to give you a couple of minutes to exit."

Eirene grabbed the young woman's cool hand and shoved a hundred dollars in it. "Thank you for giving me some free time alone, Lilly."

Grinning, Lilly stuffed it down her cleavage. "Anytime. I can't imagine being followed by rabid photographers."

Eirene smiled. "Be sure to grab the four tickets I'll have for you at will call." Whenever she performed in Spartanburg or relatively close, she arranged for Lilly to have tickets. It was rare to meet anyone who could keep their mouth shut about knowing Eirene this well, but Lilly could. She came from a poor family of eight and had grown up with no privacy, so she protected her own. She'd been surprised when Eirene had first sat next to her at the Persian restaurant where they both ate at the bar. Eirene had spent many visits observing Lilly before deciding she could be trusted.

Another friend, Raoul, had never fawned over Eirene

either, treating her with the respect of a cherished patron. He would also slip her out the back door when necessary.

The moment Lilly returned to the front of the shop and closed the door softly behind her, Eirene got busy. She hurried to a set of stairs that would take her upstairs to a hallway which led to the owner's second-floor apartment when the woman was in town.

Currently, the elderly lady had another four days left on her trip to Italy, thanks to her trust in Lilly running the shop.

Rushing past the front door to the woman's home, Eirene reached a locked door. She used the key to open it, thanks to Lilly, who kept one for when maintenance needed access. Hanging it on the nail they both used, Eirene crossed through a small storage area to take the stairway to the roof.

Once up there, Eirene scampered across the roof, bent over to keep her head below the three-foot-tall parapet wall running across the front and back of each two-story brick building. Thanks to wearing pants now, she was able to climb over the short fire-break wall erected between connected buildings.

When she reached the back corner of the next building, she peeked over the rear wall to check the permanent fire escape ladder that had been attached to the building many years ago. Eirene paused to listen.

No unusual traffic sounds like a motorcycle motor.

Her primary mobile phone in her pants pocket rang with the annoying sound of Leszek's jingle. Slipping her hand inside, she clicked the silence button.

She'd use the excuse that she had been in the middle of the fiasco at the theater for missing his call.

Heart beating hard at the chance of being caught, she paused and took a good look up and down the rear access road to the shops. Over an hour after conventional lunchtime, all seemed quiet. Convinced she could get down without being spotted, she swung a leg over the short wall and descended the ladder.

She'd have to travel on foot to her secret warehouse, then the same way on to her apartment. Ivarson had not been happy when she told him she wished to walk home for some fresh air. He'd expect her to be home before dark.

If nothing slowed her up, it would still be a tight timeline.

She took in the wooded natural area on the other side of the road and jumped the last four feet to the ground. She'd barely entered the tree line when she sensed being watched. Pausing to take in the quiet back street, she saw no one near the dress shop delivery door.

She asked Pixie, *Am I jumping at shadows, or do you sense anyone else out here?*

Yes, you are tired, but I am not at ease with you being here alone.

Her wolf was never at ease about a lot of Eirene's actions, but she was always ready to help. Stepping into the woods ten feet, she swung around to peer at the back street.

A delivery van drove by and continued past the restaurant.

That was it. Nothing else stirred.

Pixie said, *If we are going to do this, sooner would be better than later.*

Agreed, Eirene sent back, but she couldn't risk anyone following her on this run.

Chapter 8

PARKED NEXT TO a dumpster behind an empty shop space he'd noted had a For Lease sign, Corbin watched to his left where two cars sat at the back of the dress shop. He wanted to stay ready to roll and seriously doubted anyone would notice the front edge of his tire poking out.

Much farther down than he expected, Givenchy descended an old fire escape ladder attached to a building next to the shop she'd entered.

Givenchy looked around and raced across the road, stopping at the edge of a wooded area.

What had caused her to pause? He heard the engine sound of a sport bike rolling down the main road. Had she spotted him following her on a motorcycle?

She disappeared into the foliage.

Damn. He cranked his bike and raced close to where she'd entered the trees and parked quickly, shoving his stand down. Having strapped his helmet to the rear seat moments ago, he already had his hat and dark sunglasses on.

He entered the woods ten yards back this side of where she had gone in, then ran what he hoped was parallel to her path. Could she be meeting someone involved in eliminating her security?

Was that why she'd requested human guards only?

A sickening thought. He couldn't align that image with the reserved girl he'd known in high school. Had she turned into an adult who was willing to harm—or kill—another person?

Then again, he'd never gotten the chance to learn much about her, had he?

He slowed, listening.

There. He caught the sound of her moving quickly, not seeming to worry about the noise she made, and smiled. He'd guessed correctly and was now in his area of expertise. Moving with purpose, he began tracking her, moving closer as he determined her direction. Small trees and thick undergrowth might slow her down, but this was easy terrain compared to places in which he'd had to hunt a target.

The moment he realized she'd turned in his direction, adrenaline gave him a surge of energy. So did the satisfaction of catching her. He raced ahead of her and made a move he hoped would intersect with her path.

Steps pounded closer and closer to the tree he hid behind.

He stepped out. She was closer than he'd anticipated.

They collided.

Her body went flying backward. He lunged to catch her arms to keep her from hitting the ground. Her feet slid out from under her—now beneath his legs spread apart.

Worried he'd knocked her for a loop, he asked, "Are you okay? I didn't expect you to run into me."

She blinked then sharpened her gaze. Her full lips went from surprised to flat-lined. She walked her feet back until they were under her where she could stand.

Yanking her arms from his hold, she shoved the strap of that big purse back up on her shoulder and ordered, "Keep your hands off me."

He held his hands in the air. "I have no intention of hurting you. I kept you from falling back onto those rocks."

Rubbing her arms, she looked around to see where a small pile had been stacked up on one side of the path in an intentional arrangement. Probably kids from the area who had been playing in the woods. A refreshing thought when many stayed indoors with technology.

Shoving hair off her face, she panicked and looked around.

He spotted her hat hanging on a branch and stepped over to retrieve it. Then he found her sunglasses under a bush. Turning back to her, he offered them. "Looking for these?"

Her expression changed to embarrassment. She took the hat and shoved it on her head but held onto the sunglasses.

That's when he lost all sense of time and purpose while staring into gorgeous aqua-blue eyes. How could a pair of eyes take him back years to being a shy and gangly boy of seventeen? His heart rate had remained steady while racing to catch her, but that organ now banged in his chest like a honey badger trying to escape.

With one deep inhale, her sweet scent struck a blow to any thought of his initial goal. How was he going to do his job for Adrian when he still felt a deep attachment to her?

"You're …" She seemed to catch herself. "Why are you stalking me?"

He thought for a moment she recognized him, but her question slapped that idea away. Facing a pissed-off woman was one thing. Facing a furious female shifter put him on his heels while he scrambled to reply. "I'm not, uh, stalking you. I'm with your security team. My partner and I were called in this morning. I was sent to protect you."

No surprise crossed her face, only irritation when she asked, "Who are you?"

She knew. She had to know.

That she wouldn't acknowledge him cut deep. Corbin gave her a roundabout answer. "I work for my partner who said a man named Beckham had contracted us."

Looking up at the sky, she shook her head, muttering, "He broke our contract. Humans only." Drawing a quick breath, she stopped suddenly. After two slow breaths, she narrowed her eyes. "Are you who I think you are?"

Ah, she did recognize his scent after all but not his face. The beard, long hair, and glasses were working, plus being older than a teenager. He snorted out a chuckle in no hurry to make this easy for her. "Who do you think I am?"

She hadn't found that amusing based on her scowl. Drawing herself up in a regal way that contradicted her disheveled look and cockeyed hat, she said. "You were with that other guy standing at the back of the theater earlier. That means you must have heard me tell Brody, the head of my security, that I wanted no one to accompany me when I left."

"I heard you."

"Then what the hell did you think you were doing chasing me through the woods?" Her fisted hands were more about frustration than aggression.

He felt a smidgeon of sympathy for her. She likely lived under a microscope of humans and shifters judging her every movement.

Ares said, *You lied to Adrian. You like this one.*

Guilt flooded him when his wolf pointed out what he'd tried to ignore. He had to get back into character, but he refused to give Ares an inch. *As usual, you offer no help at all. Just be quiet.*

You hate when I am right. Ares, getting the last word again.

Corbin shrugged. "You could have been running from a threat." He folded his arms over his chest. That was possible, so not technically a lie. "Why would you be sneaking out the back of a retail store if you weren't escaping someone?" He waited to see if she'd lie.

Leaning forward and proving she was not intimidated by him, she said, "I am not under threat. In case you forgot, I'm a shifter. I don't run from the everyday threats. I merely wanted a chance to stroll through the woods *in private*. Thanks for screwing that up."

He swept a slow gaze down to her feet and back up to her face. "You aren't exactly dressed for hiking. You were moving so quickly when we collided that you lost your hat and sunglasses. Aren't there some safe parks you could jog through without getting your clothes ripped and your skin scratched?"

She ran a hand up her left arm where several surface scratches were in the process of healing.

Sliding both hands into the pockets of her pants, she took on an unperturbed stance. "You're not going to leave, are you?"

"Afraid not. I have orders to ensure your safety."

"Fine. Why don't you walk me out of here and give me a ride back to the theater?"

What had caused the change of heart to be more accommodating?

Did she know he had a motorcycle and not a sedan? He doubted she'd ride on the back of his bike, but decided to let her think he had other wheels.

"Sure." He waved his hand in the direction of the retail shops. "Ladies first."

She cocked an eyebrow. "A gentleman? What pack has taught their males manners?"

Catching her sarcasm, he stopped before snarling a reply. He'd been thrown to worse than wolves by her father's men. Memories of that time flooded him, and he had no trouble treating her like a suspect.

He leaned in and warned, "Don't assume I'm a gentleman."

That shut her up. She headed back in the opposite direction.

Just when he thought he had everything under control, his gaze locked on the swing of her hips. Damn, that woman was hot. She might be psychopathic, too, but his body didn't care what his brain thought. He searched the woods to keep from tracking the sway of her sweet bottom. This job sucked.

They trudged along without speaking until they exited the woods.

He walked over to his bike in a surly mood and lifted his helmet, offering it to her. "Why don't you put this on?"

She looked around in both directions, mumbling, "Adults don't have to wear helmets here."

Was she expecting someone? "I have to ensure your safety no matter what."

She snapped back at him, "Yet again, I must remind you I'm a shifter capable of protecting myself. If I fall off, my bones will heal."

"You're being obstinate for no reason. I have orders to follow. Have you ever considered being nice to us little people?"

She drew back at his words. Then she leaned to look past him.

He heard a vehicle coming their way from behind him and turned.

Ah, shit.

A police cruiser rolled up near his bike and parked.

He swung back to her and recognized the sedan approaching from the opposite direction. "How would your driver know where you are?"

Her lips parted when she looked over her shoulder.

While she was ignoring him, Corbin turned to the cops.

Car doors slammed on the police cruiser. He stared at the two officers headed his way. She never used a mobile phone while he had eyes on her. How could this be happening? He asked her, "Where'd the cops come from?"

For all her bravado, she had the guilty look of someone caught. "I, uh, well …"

She shoved her hands into her pockets, and her shoulders drooped.

He recalled when she'd put a hand in her pocket right before her attitude had changed from confrontational. Fury burned off any sympathy he'd had for her. "Ah, shit. What have you got? Some kind of save-me button that pulls in law enforcement?"

"That's not what—"

Her driver walked up to them. "Eirene? Is he creating trouble for you?"

Corbin answered, "No, I was the sap stuck with protecting her."

Not acknowledging his words, the driver said, "Come on, Eirene."

The first officer addressed Corbin. "Step away from Ms. Givenchy, sir. Is that your motorcycle?"

"Yes. I did not harm her. I'm on her security detail, assigned by Beckham Security." He hoped that could be confirmed. Corbin lifted his hands to prove he was no threat. He ground his teeth in anger and moved to the side. She'd put all this in motion and now strolled away with the casualness of someone with no worries. If nothing else reminded him of when he'd known her as a teen, being tossed aside for others to deal with did.

Still talking to Corbin, the shorter officer with a thick neck and skin the color of strong coffee, said, "Please pull out your license."

"I'm going to reach into my back pocket for ID, okay?"

"Yes. Use one hand and leave the other up."

Once Corbin withdrew his wallet, the second officer with freckled skin cuffed him.

Givenchy and her driver headed for the car. She stopped before reaching the sedan and called out, "He didn't harm me."

Corbin twisted his neck to toss her a look of *you're-not-helping*.

She frowned at him.

Really? He rolled his eyes and ignored her.

The first officer nodded. "Thank you, Ms. Givenchy. We'll handle this."

Corbin crushed the urge to blast her for all the trouble she'd caused him. This already had the earmarks of a disaster.

Two doors had yet to slam on the sedan, and the car made no sound of driving away. Corbin heard her driver urging, "We should go."

"Just a minute," she said, then walked briskly back to Corbin and the officers. "I'd like to ask this man something."

The officers looked at each other. The short one said, "As long as you don't get too close."

With him cuffed, she evidently felt safe walking up to him, but the officers didn't move far enough away for her. She used her charming voice. "I'm fine. Would you give me a little privacy?"

Once they stepped to the rear of their squad car, she turned on Corbin. "You're Corbin, aren't you?"

She did know. His brain disconnected from his mouth when he realized she'd finally acknowledged him.

Possibly irritated at receiving no reply, she snapped, "Just tell me the truth about why you're here and I'll consider dropping charges."

She'd consider dropping charges for what?

He had not harmed or threatened her. He was now on law enforcement radar. He wanted to be fully cleared and not allow her to throw out a token of dropping charges.

He took a quiet breath to keep his tone polite with witnesses nearby. "There is no reason to drop charges because I committed no crime. I was doing my job, *Givenchy*." He'd said her last name like a curse since he couldn't spew a curse when Adrian had asked him to behave in a situation like this.

But damn, he was pissed. They see each other for the first time in years, and that's all she had to say? No sorry or asking how he'd survived what she'd done to him?

"Unbelievable," she muttered. "I try to give you a break after all you did, and you still want to act like an ass."

"After all *I* did? That's priceless. Let's keep this professional. You go ahead and behave like an overindulged celebrity, and I'll stick to doing my duty as a security guard trying to follow orders. That is if I get out of jail before next year. At least the police might be more objective than goons." Yes, he was pissed.

Maybe she'd had so many men he was nothing more than a fleeting memory from her past.

That ground on his nerves. He couldn't say why.

Movement near the building caught his eye. He squinted to see men who weren't around before now squatting behind garbage cans.

She followed his gaze. As she did, two photographers stood up and pointed their cameras with huge lenses their way.

Once they realized she knew they were there, three of them jumped out and hurried forward, snapping shots as they came.

"Damn. Look what you've done to me this time." She wheeled around to glare at him. "The blasted paparazzi." With that, she abandoned any further conversation and raced to the sedan where her driver held the door open. She dove inside, and he slammed the door, then got in and peeled out of there with paparazzi racing behind.

This felt like a time warp. Corbin could not believe he'd finally spoken to her, and she acted as if he'd wronged her in the past. As for the paparazzi showing up, how was that his fault? Didn't those vultures listen to police scanners and have snoops everywhere?

The freckled officer who had driven returned. "Please follow me to our cruiser, Mr. Torrante."

Corbin asked, "Am I being arrested? What are you charging me with?"

"We'd like you to answer some questions. If your answers are satisfactory, you won't be charged."

Call him suspicious, but he doubted this was a routine action had he been a human detained. That could mean the people wanting to question him might end up being SCIS.

Talk about going from bad to worse—this day sucked.

Adrian had said to comply and not cause a conflict.

While he trusted Adrian, Corbin could end up gone forever before Adrian's people came to the rescue.

How had this happened?

Chapter 9

EIRENE WATCHED THROUGH the sedan's rear window as Ivarson drove away.

That was Corbin. He never admitted it, but she knew his scent. She asked Pixie, *Did you recognize his scent?*

Yes. He was the boy you knew in school. Where do you think he went after the night he didn't show up?

I don't know. I'm more concerned right now with why he was at the theater and following me. Eirene had realized by the time she jumped into her sedan that something was off. Why would someone from her past, the only shifter she'd known in high school, be here now?

What do you mean by him following you? Pixie asked.

I'm worried someone is going to find a way to blame me for the deaths of those two security guards and Archie's injuries. Why would Beckham send shifters when I said only humans? I think he's being pressured to prove the accidents have nothing to do with his human people. That could be why he called in shifter investigators, which points at me.

There is no evidence of you harming anyone, Pixie argued.

That's true, but shifters are treated differently than humans. Eirene swallowed hard. Why would the boy who had been so kind to her in school return after all this time to work with people trying to hang these deaths on her? Her damaged heart couldn't take many more hits without giving up completely on people.

Maybe she was misreading everything.

Corbin had surprised her in the woods, but … he had not tried to manhandle her or act inappropriately.

Why had he kept his eyes hidden behind sunglasses?

Not that hiding his eyes mattered. She could be blind and recognize his scent. Wherever the shy young boy had gone, he'd returned grown up with a muscular build and overflowing with confidence. His tanned arms had bulged against the snug short sleeves of his gray button-down shirt.

When he'd kept her from falling and pulled her up to him, she'd leaned against a powerful man, no question about it.

Pixie often sat back until she had something to say. *That man's wolf is strange and powerful.*

Eirene sent back, *When we were in school, you told me you feared his wolf. Do you think they are dangerous?*

Not the man. He was angry, but he did not act aggressively. I would be careful around his wolf.

Eirene considered her wolf's observation. She hadn't sensed any danger from Corbin, but she had never met his wolf. She trusted Pixie's observations, especially when it came to a shifter's animal.

Corbin had scared her in that instant when he'd caught her and stopped her fall.

Oh, not in the conventional way of being frightened. She'd felt a pull toward him as strong as she had in high school. Her body came awake with the first contact with him when other men had come and gone, their presence barely registering. Even during her dark days after her father had been killed, she'd taken off with a human male to get away from a difficult life that no longer had an anchor.

The only man she'd ever truly trusted had been killed in a vicious attack.

Then she found out even her father had betrayed her.

She shook her head, thinking of the worst decision she'd made at that point when she ran away. The human male lover she'd taken had been sexy and fun for a week, then she woke up one day and realized no one outran their emotions.

Lost and with no idea what to do, she'd hung out with him for a few more weeks until he asked her to marry him.

She'd laughed. Marry a human or anyone else for that matter?

She'd believed she had met her mate for life in high school. That had turned out to be a foolish girl's dream. One that still punched her in the solar plexus when she thought back to the last day that she'd seen him.

Just before her human lover stormed off, she discovered he'd wanted to marry her for fame and fortune.

If he had stayed any longer, he would have been appalled to find out she intended to live frugally and save every penny she could to help desperate female shifters. Not the life of luxury he'd been expecting.

That had been her reality check.

She'd blamed men for her problems for too long. The time had come to face what she'd lost and the fallout from her foolish actions. She accepted that she had to buck up and become an adult if she wanted to be treated like one.

Losing her sole female friend gave her a purpose in life greater than being fawned over as an entertainer.

She'd had her emotions under control since then.

Then why had meeting Corbin again left her … struggling to sort out emotions she'd tucked away in a corner of her heart? How could he still affect her after all this time?

Maybe because he was no longer a young boy.

She couldn't get over how sexy he'd looked with that filled-out body, his dark brown hair pulled back in a ponytail, and his beard. Hot motorcyclist for a fantasy dream.

Flipping back around, she slumped next to the door. Guilt dug a hole in her chest. She had good reason to be angry with Corbin, but what were the police going to do with him once they discovered he was a shifter?

Would they call in the Shifter Criminal Investigation Service?

Please tell her that would not happen.

"Are you alright, Eirene?" Ivarson asked, his face filling the rearview mirror again. As usual, he had already slid the curtain to the side after she left the car.

"I'm fine." She had a question for him too. "Why did you call the police?"

"Because I had no idea where you had gone after I dropped you at the dress shop. I have never invaded your privacy, but I swore to your father I would do all in my power to keep you safe. You did not hit the button that indicated you only required a ride. You sent the message to come get you quickly."

She closed her eyes and leaned her head back. She'd screwed up. Pushing the wrong button had made Corbin appear to be stalking the local wolf shifter celebrity. She had never wanted to be a celebrity, which meant having to constantly question everyone's motives around her.

Look what a mess she'd left him in.

She'd been angry so long she didn't know how to function otherwise. Mistreating a person, human or shifter, had never been her. She had to get out from under Leszek's thumb so she could rule her own life and think straight.

If Corbin was one of Beckham's people, which he must be since he hadn't lied, she owed him an apology. She felt lower than the sole of her shoes for overreacting.

Could things be any worse?

Ivarson cleared his throat. "I've had two conversations. One with Brody on the way to pick you up. He said they've taken Archie in for surgery, and his chance at recovery is not encouraging. Also, Mr. Moore called and was anxious over not hearing from you. He wants me to bring you to his office right away."

Yes, the universe replied. *It can get worse.*

By the time Ivarson drew near Leszek's building, Eirene had swiped the curtain in place again, removed her hat, fixed her hair into an upswept do, and freshened her makeup. Her pants had a bit of dirt which couldn't be brushed away and her blouse sported a tear.

She might be able to hide that from Leszek if she were lucky.

Ivarson maneuvered the sedan gradually through dense traffic in the financial district of Spartanburg as he neared the building for Leszek's office. She hated coming here and humbling herself to appease the man pulling all the strings in her life.

Even worse, to bow down to the man she believed had her father killed.

The day she controlled her own money and life, she'd find the evidence she needed to put him in prison forever, but that would not be today.

She reached for her black Louis Vuitton tote, glad she had not scratched it today. She'd purchased the bag new six days ago and made a mental note to auction it off online this week under her secret account. That trick was one of the sneaky ways she generated money for her vulnerable women.

Leszek hated for her to spend so much on accessories. She smiled at being able to flaunt this bag in front of him before she sold it.

The mobile phone she used only for business played a depressing jingle.

Leaning back against the seat, she answered, "I have a bone to pick with you, Beckham."

"Hello to you, too, Eirene." The man in charge of her security sounded tired.

"Sorry for the lack of manners, but this day has sucked. Now, I'm headed in to meet with Leszek to plead for money once again." She would not hide the disgust in her tone since Ivarson could hear nothing.

"Huh. I've had no trouble getting paid by the label."

Of course, Leszek paid any other bill presented to her record label, especially Beckham's. His men sent a daily report of every move she made. To many people, Leszek Moore personified a dignified businessman who managed her record label and finances with the same deft ability he'd used to build his medical empire.

Leszek had plenty of accolades. None of them impressed Eirene these days the way they had when she'd been a naïve child, one he still believed her to be.

When her trustee's building came into view, she hurried the conversation along. "If you're calling about the new men you added to my security team, you're late. You also broke our deal of humans only."

He made a grumbling sound but ignored her jab. They were both tired of arguing over how she hated having anyone dog her every step. "I'll keep this short, Eirene, so you won't be late for your meeting. I need these two men to—"

"*No!*" She stopped herself from ranting and lowered her voice to a more civil tone. "I do not want any more people getting in my way all day."

"You agreed to this, but the humans-only part is not working," he replied in a flat, stop-giving-me-a-hard-time tone.

Yes, she had, but she'd been willing to do anything to add a bonus charity event to each of the six venues on her tour. "I don't want another man injured or killed. At this point, your people are endangering my tour." She cringed at how cold that sounded, but she had a role to play and needed to give him a reason to wait before adding anyone else.

"I am *very* concerned about the welfare of my men." He rarely let his emotions show. Reminding him of the deaths on top of a third one injured had set him off. "If you want to know the truth, if I could, I would pull every one of them out of the field this minute, but I can't. I find it appalling that you're more worried about your tour than the men we've lost."

"I did *not* say that!" she bit out, feeling a new vein of guilt slide through her. "I told you I don't want anyone else harmed."

Ivarson eased his way toward the covered entrance where vehicles dropped off and picked up passengers.

"I have to go, Beckham. We'll discuss replacements later."

"No, we won't because I've put two new ones in place that I must have."

"I'm out of time." She ended the call rather than hear a rundown of their qualifications. At least he had not heard about the motorcyclist being arrested. She wanted to help her vulnerable female shifters, but she'd never wanted to hurt other people. Now she questioned how effective she'd be with a shifter watching her movements. Even if that motorcyclist got cut from the team, the other guy had to be a shifter too. Her heart sank. It had been difficult enough to carve out time to slip away from everyone to take care of her ladies with so many security guards watching her. She'd managed early on because the original security team had been bored and easy to evade.

Ivarson parked and opened her door facing the building.

We will help the women, Pixie said, having likely picked up on her anguish.

Her wolf had been with her through so much. Eirene would be lost without her.

Eirene hooked the designer tote bag on her shoulder and stepped out. Leszek would wrinkle his nose at her dirty shoes, but she'd had the last pair of expensive heels for almost three weeks. Keeping shoes pristine for resale was tough. They wouldn't be as valuable with a scuff. If her feet weren't killing her, she'd wear them one more time to confirm what her trustee believed—that she squandered an insane amount of money on high-priced designer clothes, shoes, and purses.

Before her dad died, he had included a generous budget for her business and performance clothes. She smiled over one thing her trustee couldn't alter.

On the other hand, her father had kept her monthly income moderate because she had never needed anything while living in his house. She struggled with blaming him for her situation. He never planned on being murdered and their home getting sold, but he was the one who structured her trust fund.

She had a feeling Leszek had stood over his shoulder while her father made the edits.

Damn Leszek.

When she reached the top floor of the six-floor, stone-and-brick building, the elevator doors opened to an elegant reception area. A lovely woman in her fifties sat facing visitors as they stepped out.

"Hello, Alexandria." Eirene had always appreciated the woman she'd known since long before the lady's hair turned gray.

"Good to see you, Ms. Givenchy. I'll let him know you're on the way."

Eirene thanked her and walked the long corridor decorated with photos of Leszek at celebrity events and in the company of notable business leaders. Among all that, he'd placed her first three platinum albums between glass-walled personal offices and two large conference rooms. Her trustee hired the best in their fields. He wanted no visitor to doubt his success.

At the end of the hall, she passed through an open door where she encountered the second person who shielded Leszek. "Hello, Timothy."

"Ms. Givenchy." He stood and held tight to his expression of polite disapproval when his eyes landed on yet another Louis Vuitton purchase.

He found her undeserving of his boss.

She found him amusing.

Ready to get this done, she started toward the door to her trustee's office.

Timothy hurried to open it only to remind her he was the gatekeeper.

Unamused to find the office empty, she took a seat facing his desk. She would wait, but she refused to show a weakness by fidgeting. He could be watching.

She'd loved the smell of Leszek Moore's wall of books behind his desk, which included some of his favorite fiction, memoirs by people he admired, and a ton of medical journals he'd read along the way to becoming a celebrated psychiatrist. She'd spent hours playing on the sixteenth-century Persian rug he purchased at auction when he had no important meetings scheduled.

One memory after another assaulted her.

It had all been a lie.

The polished wood door to his private bathroom whispered open and closed behind him as he entered his office. He carried his five-foot-ten height as if he were over six feet tall. No longer wearing a white coat in his office these days, he wore a dark suit and polished loafers. His hairstylist likely spent hours placing each medium-length black hair in a perfect photo-worthy style. Looking closer to forty than sixty, he had invested well with plastic surgeons.

Nothing would ever make him decent in her eyes.

He'd been her father's best friend and partner in their medical business. She shoved away memories she no longer cherished.

That allowed her more time to envision ways to bring him to his knees.

Another wolf shifter in her position might plot his death, but neither she nor her wolf possessed the ability to kill someone.

"So wonderful to see you in person again, Eirene." He sent that sarcastic shot across the bow, then walked past his desk to place a chaste kiss on her cheek.

Pixie said, *Yuck.*

Eirene angled her head and smiled, but it was for Pixie's reaction, not Leszek. He'd take it as her acting obedient. She'd never dreamed her father would leave her under this man's thumb, but he had probably seen it as protecting her from vultures.

She regretted the months she had gone off the deep end, trying any way she could not to think about losing her dad. Sadly, she'd only accomplished handing the courts proof that even though she was an adult by human laws, she still needed an overseer.

They confirmed Leszek as her trustee.

Keeping her hands relaxed on the arms of her chair, she schooled her voice to sound sincere. "What is so important?"

"I'll get right to the point. I've discussed this with your agent before informing the tour company. You may do the planned event in Spartanburg, and then you can perform one more event. After that, I feel you need to take a badly needed rest."

"What?" She stood. With all pretenses of calm gone, she asked, "Two weeks? We have a six-week extension. You can't cancel a commitment with my name on it at the last minute."

"The label controls your tours. I'm giving you the option of owning this respite."

She seethed but managed to stay calm. "No. I'm fine. I want to do the tour."

"Just the other day, you threatened not to sing at all if the contract was not signed. I took that as a cry for help."

She would not stand here and listen to psychobabble. "I'm not even going to address that ridiculous comment."

His eyes flared with anger at her insult. "Be very careful. My diagnosis is considered unquestioned in the psychiatric field."

She fought a moment of panic. What was he trying to do? What had brought this on?

"I see you understand the gravity of this situation," he went on.

"Actually, I don't understand *what* the situation is."

"I've discovered your little secret."

Her heart dropped like an anvil in thin air. How had he found out about the women she rescued?

"Oh, don't be so surprised." He smiled and sat back in his leather chair. "Did you really think you could agree to partner in a run-down theater for sweat equity, and I would not find out?"

Air filled her lungs again. Her chicks were safe.

Trying for his confidence, she walked over to look out the ten-foot-tall floor-to-ceiling windows where traffic moved along the street. She drew a deep breath and replied on the exhale. "It's not that big of a secret. Just something I wanted to do to give back to my fans. Why is this a problem?"

"Had you simply spoken to me first, I would have researched funding for this venture rather than using your time for sweat equity. That would have allowed you to stay on schedule to finish your current album and focus on the tour."

Now she understood.

Turning around, she leaned against the corner of the window with her arms crossed. She didn't want his hands in the theater or for him to find out what she really had planned for a charity. "I want to have a part of something that grows from the ground up. My sweat equity is singing for charity events. It's my time."

He sat back and studied her long enough to make most people uncomfortable. She knew how he operated and didn't flinch.

"Are you refusing to include me in this project, Eirene?"

She tried for diplomacy. "If I needed your help, I would have asked."

"In that case, we're back to the two weeks and then a break."

Evidently, diplomacy was wasted on a madman.

"No! I committed to six events. To back out would damage my reputation." She lifted her chin. "My father never intended for you to rule every piece of my life. I have tried to be a model person since coming back home. I have worked very hard to develop my music and my following. Why would you do this now? You don't care about this little theater or whether I sing for charities. What is it you *actually* want?"

A tiny smile teased his lips. "I want that album finished and an international tour to support the release. I want another album completed a year later."

She should be relieved to get a straight answer, but his olive branch would tie up the majority of her days for a year. She needed more time than he was allowing after this six-week tour to finish the album she'd been dragging her feet on intentionally.

However, if that would get him off her back for a few months, she'd give him the album.

Slumping her shoulders as if she'd lost a battle, she nodded. "You're right. It's time to clean up the album and plan a release."

Here came the full vulture smile. "That's more like it."

"As soon as I return from this six-week run, I'll go into the studio and iron out the bumps in the songs. I have a new one in mind, too," she added that last part to offer something special.

But she would not give him her best material, barely enough to kick him off her back.

He leaned forward with his elbows on the table and his hands folded together. "I want the album finished in two weeks."

Her mouth opened, but she shut it quickly. "I can't do my best work on the road. I'd have to fly back once every four days, cram for a full day, and then go back out."

"Then you should consider two events and staying here to finish the album."

Could she hate anyone more than she did him? Not possible.

He continued, "In case you're wondering what will happen if you fail to finish the album in two weeks, I shall break every contract, which means paying damages to each company."

He'd ruin her label.

She would have nothing once she freed herself of him. Her heart banged her ribs. It wasn't as if he weren't wealthy, but he expected every facet of his business life to perform exceptionally.

She'd give him what he wanted. "I'll finish the album in two weeks." Without another word, she snatched up her tote bag and walked out of his office. He didn't deserve a proper goodbye.

He would be the trustee of her estate until she turned twenty-four in a year unless he convinced her to extend the contract or … died before that day.

Chapter 10

VLAD CUT HIS eyes at the two broad-shouldered Romanians he'd brought in for this hunt. They stood near him with their backs to the wall in a small Mediterranean restaurant a short distance from Chicago O'Hare International Airport. He needed more than someone from his country. He required powerful humans who had dealt with keeping shifters in line.

They carried wicked tools of the trade that some shifters had never encountered.

Corbin should recall how Vlad punished dogs that misbehaved. This time, that wolf shifter would curse the day he had been born.

Once his food arrived, he waited for privacy to insert his earpiece and called Mitch, who answered with an abrupt, "*What?*"

"Vlad here." He placed his temporary mobile phone on the table and cut into his lamb chops. Not Romanian food, but very tasty.

"*Oh.*" The jackal shifter's dark tone immediately smoothed. "*I have some news to report. I would have called you, but I do not have my hands on the wolf shifter yet.*"

Vlad took his time before replying. "I do not pay money for a jackal to do nothing." He chewed slowly.

"*I've been busy. Your money is not wasted.*" That came out terse, worried. Mitch calmed his voice and continued, "*I received an unexpected break today, which may end with finding him.*"

Sometimes no response was best for motivating an underling to step up his efforts. Though officially employed by the American SCIS organization, this jackal shifter freelanced for black money. Vlad's favorite kind, but Mitch had an addiction in the form of two dice. He owed bone breakers.

Once the silence had stretched too far, Mitch started talking faster. *"I will give you what you want. I could not find the wolf shifter until he was caught with that famous female shifter celebrity. The one that sings. The paparazzi photographed the two of them as local police detained your wolf shifter."*

That stilled Vlad's hand. He carefully placed his fork and knife in their appropriate location on the linen-covered table. Servers moved silently through whispered conversations in the modestly sized restaurant.

After months of hunting, Corbin had made a mistake.

Vlad said, "Tell me all you have discovered."

Mitch launched into how he'd had inquiries across the Eastern states for a dangerous wolf shifter of Corbin's description. *"I have a very select group of investigative snitches who only share information with the person paying them. There had been no traffic cam videos or sightings of a male even close to his description ... until today, when I saw the online photo with my own eyes."*

Mitch sounded excited. Very proud of himself.

Wasting no more time on the call, Vlad gave Mitch an opportunity to receive return business. "I want the wolf shifter found yesterday."

"I understand. I'm ready to do whatever you want, even kill that wolf bastard."

"No!" Vlad had lifted his hand to slam down on the table but stopped. He did not want to draw attention to himself. These Americans tended to be ridiculously upset about someone shouting around them.

"Sir?" Mitch sounded concerned Vlad might have terminated the call.

Vlad ordered, "You will find him and contact me. I want him alive, or you will not be."

Chapter 11

CORBIN STARED OUT the grimy window of the cruiser where the soiled back seat assaulted his shifter senses with every disgusting body odor a person could imagine. That didn't piss him off anywhere close to having let his guard down around Givenchy. She was *not* the sweet young girl his confused brain kept recalling.

He had been played. *I'm such an idiot.*

You are big idiot, Ares agreed. *Woman much smarter than you.*

Not up for his mouthy wolf's criticism, Corbin sent back, *Once again, your opinion holds as much value to me as a bottomless water cup.*

If you listened to me sometime we would not be locked up.

Officer Thick Neck, who rode shotgun and might have played football at one time, took a mobile call. "Yes, sir." He paused a moment, then another, "Yes, sir." He hung up and told the driver something in cop language involving acronyms and numbers.

The driver frowned at him but nodded.

Only one day on the job and Corbin had lost the client plus gotten picked up by the police.

Not arrested, according to the officer driving, who had advised him to remain calm. Corbin was being taken in until his superior could confirm his employment with Beckham Security. He further explained the reason for being questioned was due to all local law enforcement had been instructed that only humans were allowed to protect Givenchy.

Then he'd closed the car door on any hope of this turning out okay.

Corbin's identification had exposed him as a wolf shifter. Yes, he'd caught Givenchy sneaking out the rear of the buildings, but he should have followed her. Instead, he'd decided to confront her. Deep down, he had to admit he wanted that confrontation, but with that one wrong move, he managed to wipe out the trust he'd earned with Adrian and Jaz.

All because he couldn't get his head turned in the right direction with this woman.

Seven years and nothing had changed.

Still the Givenchy Queen, she had only to snap her fingers to flip his life upside down. Again.

The officer riding shotgun received another phone call. "Yes, we have him in the squad car and—"

Corbin could hear noises coming from the phone receiver, but the guy talking had a thick Latin accent, which he had trouble understanding. The only thing that came through crisply was anger.

Lots of anger.

Hell. Less than twenty-four hours in public, and his life was headed down the proverbial drain.

"Yes, sir." The officer's grip tightened on the phone, but his tone remained respectful. "Yes, sir. Immediately."

Then nothing. The caller had hung up on him. Thick Neck told the officer driving, "Chief wants him handed over to someone waiting at the theater, then we return to the station."

"Why the change?" The officer driving kept splitting his attention between the road and his partner.

"Don't ask. Hit the siren and let's get this done."

Corbin understood how to read between the lines, but the words he heard made no sense. Why were they taking him back to the theater?

That made no sense after going through all of this to all

but arrest him. Maybe Adrian was still there. That gave him hope, which disintegrated as he recalled that these two believed he'd been stalking Givenchy.

What other law enforcement could be involved?

Oh, hell. Could it be at SCIS?

His heart rate surged.

He would not go quietly. Adrian had said not to fight law enforcement if an issue arose, and his people would come for Corbin. SCIS was entirely different in Corbin's mind. They could shove him in an underground cell where Ares would blast out and go bat-shit crazy in a matter of hours.

Corbin would rather take a bullet to the head over a slow, maddening death.

Sweat pebbled on his neck. He looked around, searching for the best way to escape. He wouldn't kill the human officers, but they might be banged up and unconscious by the time he broke out. That would bring Adrian's people down on his head, but this had turned into a crisis of survival.

The driver whipped in and out of traffic at a crazy speed, and the siren cranked up. Corbin tried to cover his ears. The cuffs stopped him.

Ares howled incessantly and clawed to get out.

The noise suddenly died as quickly as it had started. The driver slowed to pull into a spot near the curb along the front of the Libertas Theater.

Corbin's hope shot through the roof, then fizzled.

In the next parking spot, Adrian sat against the seat of his motorcycle with arms crossed and a dark expression clouding his face. He stood up as the cruiser parked. Corbin would give Adrian the truth, including the fact that he could not complain the officers had treated him badly. They'd seemed uncomfortable with him inside the car, but they'd been polite.

The driver stepped out and turned to open the rear door for Corbin. He hooked a hand under Corbin's arm to aid him in stepping out, then uncuffed him.

Rubbing the feeling back into his wrists, Corbin drew a

deep breath of free air as the driver climbed back in and stared straight ahead.

Stepping around the car to where Adrian waited, the thick-necked officer said, "Our captain received confirmation of this man being on the Beckham Security team."

Adrian had always appeared even-tempered particularly in the worst of times, but his ears should be smoking from the fury blazing in his eyes. He said nothing.

The officer backed up, looking very uncomfortable. "We, uh, apologize for any misunderstanding."

Corbin strolled over to Adrian and stopped near him. "They treated me fairly." His words had come out tight, but that had been the best he could do under the circumstances.

Adrian nodded without taking his gaze off the policeman.

Thick Neck added, "One of our officers is delivering your motorcycle here. Should arrive in the next five minutes."

Corbin gave a short nod, but this was Adrian's show. He had no speaking role.

Heaving out a deep breath, Adrian said, "Next time, read everything on the identification to avoid making an unnecessary mistake."

"I will pass that wisdom on to the Chief who gives us our marching orders."

"Understood."

There was Adrian, the peacemaker.

Thick Neck returned to the passenger seat, and the cruiser sped away.

Time to suck it up and face Adrian. Corbin's first word had to be said before any explanation. "Sorry."

Adrian cocked an eyebrow at Corbin and turned to face him. "I had a call from Beckham telling me the police said someone called you in as a stalker who had frightened Ms. Givenchy."

"Wait a minute," Corbin started, unwilling to accept blame for what he *hadn't* done. "I never made any threatening move around her, and I informed her I was part of her security team."

"Yep, I know." Adrian ran fingers through his thick hair.

"I told Beckham I'd sent you to follow Ms. Givenchy to protect her since she'd refused her human guards." He dropped his arm. "I explained that based on what I'd observed of her manner here at the theater earlier, I had no doubt she'd overreacted and caused a problem."

Corbin swallowed hard. Being with Jaz and Adrian had been the first decent place in his life. They'd treated him better than he could ever expect.

But no one, absolutely no one, had ever given him a gift like Adrian's belief in him just now. That was damn humbling. "Thank you, Adrian."

"You're welcome." He angled back around. "Here comes your bike."

Another officer rode it into the spot the cruiser had vacated and parked the bike, setting it on the stand. He dismounted, then looked at Adrian and Corbin before addressing Adrian. "Everything appears to be functioning properly. Let us know if you have any issues."

"Thank you." Adrian gave the bike a quick perusal.

"I appreciate the delivery." This time, Corbin meant the words.

A second cruiser drove up, and the officer slid into the passenger side before they drove off.

Corbin gave Adrian a confused look. "Why are they treating us so nicely?"

Grinning, Adrian slapped him on the back. "Treating *you* nicely. Givenchy might be local royalty, but my boss is far more powerful than any of these people. I called him to report what was happening, and he said he'd handle any repercussions."

"Damn. Don't wake me up." Corbin laughed with sudden relief. "I don't want to live in the real world."

"You're finally with good people, Corbin. Now tell me what all happened."

After briefing Adrian on everything, Corbin finished with, "To sneak out of that dress shop, she accessed the roof and crossed the buildings to reach a fixed fire escape. I had parked around back next to a dumpster for the retail location, one building before the one I'd seen her enter. That put me close enough to keep an eye on the rear exit of the dress shop she'd entered. I almost missed her climbing down that old ladder farther down until she shot across the street and entered the woods."

Adrian scratched his neck and looked up as dark clouds began packing in. He said, "I want to stay close to Brody and the other two of Beckham's people while Archie is in the hospital. If any of them think to finish him off, I don't want it on my watch."

Cool air warning of rain brushed over Corbin's face. He couldn't care less about getting wet. "What do you need me to do?"

"I need you to stick to Givenchy. See if she tries to slip away again. If she's got someone doing her dirty work, she may avoid calling them. I know it sucks to send you back to watch her, but you're doing great."

"Hey, I'm here to do whatever you need." Corbin should thank Adrian for the chance to nail Givenchy in the act.

Chapter 12

A HALF MILE FROM her apartment, Eirene asked Ivarson, "Please stop along here."

His alarmed face filled the rearview mirror. With the privacy window slid open, he was able to ask, "Why?"

Sighing mentally at having to constantly explain herself, she said, "I want some time to clear my mind. Leszek has crammed my schedule. To give him what he wants, I've got to think through a few things."

Sounding slightly annoyed, which surprised her, he replied, "I will do as you ask, but I request that you allow me to follow you."

That was the last thing she wanted. "No. I'm fine. I'm in a safe area for humans. Let's call it a night. I won't need you before seven tomorrow morning." She hit the button to close the window and slid the curtain into place, ending all conversation.

Ivarson conceded defeat by pulling to the curb a quarter mile from her apartment building. He had never been a fan of her disguises, but he kept the cloth bag she'd filled with an assortment of everything from clothing and multiple pairs of glasses to hats and wigs in the vehicle.

This time she donned a short-cropped blond wig, black-rimmed glasses with clear lenses of no optical strength, and an embroidered blue vest over a faded red T-shirt she now wore in place of the blouse. She changed from pants to casual khaki shorts and a pair of black sneakers, both showing heavy wear from plenty of repeated use.

Once she stepped out onto the sidewalk, her sedan drove off with an unhappy Ivarson. He seemed grumpier these days. Maybe he needed a vacation. She'd told him to let her know whenever he wanted a break.

Doing her best to care for female shifters in need left her little energy for those in better situations. Ivarson was a grown man, and the label paid well. He merely had to ask for time off, but she doubted that was the problem.

He wanted to know where she was every minute. Keeping secrets from him was more likely the cause of his foul mood.

She would not tell him about her exploits. He'd be safer kept out of that loop.

A warm breeze teased loose hairs around her face as she walked along the sidewalk pretending to be any other young woman out for a stroll. Those women also had problems of all kinds, but they didn't have to hide an animal from the world or battle to move around without hundreds of eyes on their every step. Or try to keep that loony blackmailer, Nova, in line while also needing her to save the females Eirene found in deep shifter trouble.

A grumble built in her throat.

Wah, wah, wah. Enough whining. Someone out there always had it much harder.

She forced herself to focus on one problem at a time. The first one? How to get away from everyone to check on the two shifter sisters she'd hidden? She had to slip out of her apartment tonight without Ivarson finding out, because she'd caught Mr. Overprotective keeping an eye on her from afar in recent weeks.

If she didn't leave too late, she could take the bus. Nope. She tossed that thought aside. The older warehouse district was not that far away on foot for a shifter. The fewer people she ran into, the better luck she'd have not being caught.

Also, she'd once climbed on a bus with a shifter who tensed the moment he'd scented her. She didn't need some rogue to cause her trouble.

At the third corner, she took a right onto Pearl Street.

An older brick warehouse, once used for manufacturing and now converted into her apartment building two blocks away, came into view. She still had problem number two, Leszek, but the short walk had released some of her tension.

She smiled, enjoying the late-day cool air on her face, and kept working out her escape plan as darkness closed in on the city.

Someone peeled away from the building and stepped into her path.

She slowed and stopped, not believing who stood there.

The tall, brooding male figure stepped toward her. This day refused to get any better.

She dismissed apologizing to him and demanded, "What are you doing here?"

"I could be here to thank you for introducing me to Spartanburg's finest." Corbin crossed his powerful forearms on display with the black T-shirt he'd changed into. "I could be here to ask why you did that to me. I could be here to—"

Holding up a hand, she said, "Stop. I *only* called for my driver. I did not set you up to be arrested."

Below the dark sunglasses, his lips almost curved up. Was he laughing at her? He said, "I see. The police who thought I had been stalking you showed up as magically as the sedan. Sure, I'll believe that."

Heat climbed her throat. It *had* been her fault, but the law enforcement part had not been her doing. "I thought I hit the button alerting my driver to come pick me up. I didn't. I accidentally pushed the button that asked him to come get me immediately. He thought maybe someone was threatening me."

Tapping his cheek, he said, "Ah, now I see. All that occurred because you pushed a panic button. Good thing someone with the nuclear codes doesn't have your twitchy finger. I've never known a shifter to have a panic button of any sort."

Why did he have to pile on top of her embarrassment?

She had no strong comeback. She might have inadvertently

put him in a bad spot earlier, but he started this, not her. "I don't owe you any explanation. You showed up out of the blue and chased me while I was minding my own business. You should apologize to me."

"What?"

"You know what? Never mind. I don't care about your apology. In fact … "

Reaching out so fast she hadn't seen his hands move, he cupped her arms and lifted her off the sidewalk, placing her to his right next to a tall bank building. He called out, "Hey, slow down, buddy."

She heard the grinding sound against cement heading their way.

A kid with curly red hair on a skateboard whizzed by over the spot where she'd been standing. "Sorry, man."

She should have been yanking away to free her arm, but her thoughts stalled at the gentle strength he'd exuded simply to protect her. In fairness to her brain, she might have shaken off his hold, but one thumb slowly brushed across her arm, sending tiny shockwaves along her skin.

Added to that was his intoxicating scent. Every breath confused her hormones as much as her brain.

She leaned in for a deeper inhale.

His thumb stopped moving… the moment shattered.

He slowly released her arms, leaving her standing like an idiot.

She took a step back, embarrassed at having lost her composure, and snapped, "You could have simply warned me the child was headed our way."

"If I'd known which way would be his final swerve, I would have, but he was looking down at something. Not at who he was about to knock over."

A reasonable explanation.

She wanted to be gracious, not chiding him for taking a protective action. "Okay … thank you."

He started laughing. "That sounded painful."

Screw being polite. "So now you're laughing at me? Not so much a gentleman after all."

Hooking a hand around the back of his neck, his words came out with strained patience. "I was only teasing you earlier to see what your smile might look like, but you got more pissed at me for trying to keep you safe. You must be tough to date."

Date? She couldn't define that word.

The only young man she'd spent intimate time with had been her awful attempt at self-medicating against the anguish of her father's murder. That guy turned out to be a human gold digger. She'd been isolated from regular contact with others for so long that she'd come to realize what she'd always suspected.

Her soul had been damaged beyond repair, and her father's death had broken her.

She did not possess the ability to recognize when a man was poking at her to get a smile. Her life didn't give her much reason to smile.

Had he been … flirting with her?

"Hey, don't take that to heart." His soothing words tugged her out from under the dark cloud hovering over her thoughts.

Completely flummoxed by this man, she searched for the fury from earlier but could not find it. An apology might fix this, but she still had an issue with him. "I'm sorry for my part in how things went down between us today. With that being said, I want to know your real reason for following me around. Don't waste my time with the bodyguard explanation."

All signs of teasing and humor fled. He lifted his shoulders. "I don't know what you want to hear. I'm doing my job. Nothing more, nothing less."

"No. You appear in the middle of my life like it's normal and on Beckham's team to boot. Are you here to snoop around in my life, or do you think I had anything to do with those guard deaths?" She wouldn't give up.

He shoved a narrow-eyed look her way. "I would never falsely accuse anyone of anything."

She mentally reeled from him taking a dig at how she'd gotten him in trouble with the cops, but she held back from retaliating. She'd let him get it all out.

"I'm working for a group who have shown me more decency than anyone else in my life. My pack leader runs security and rescue operations sometimes. I was asked to help him. If I learn anything about those deaths, I will report it to him. Is that clear enough?"

She snapped her mouth shut. Damn him.

Why was he still so angry? She apologized. What else could she possibly have done to cause this man to go from teasing to furious in a blink?

She would be justified in shouting at him. Right?

That would not be helpful right now.

Above all, she wanted to know why he had crushed her heart. Why had he gotten her hopes up and then left without a word? She deserved the truth.

That would likely be a waste of time. He'd probably dismiss her as a whiny celebrity.

She dropped her head back to stare up at the tall bank building next to them. Evening had shown up sooner than expected because of storm clouds gathering overhead, turning everything dark. She had to get moving, but oddly, this had been more casual conversation than she'd shared with anyone in a while, even if he did irritate her.

Pulling her chin back down, she said, "I'm tired. Let's call it a night." She made a move to step around him, and he blocked her path.

Her wolf growled inside her. Pixie rarely growled unless they were in danger.

His scent locked up her brain when he leaned close to say, "I now realize you meant me no ill will today. Thanks for clearing that up."

"You're welcome," came out breathless. Oh, great. She hated to embarrass herself, but she clearly lacked the ability to channel her inner control freak around him.

Chiseled lips moved slightly, enough to make her wonder what caused that action. She'd been so busy staring at his mouth, she'd lost track of the conversation until Pixie told her, *He should not come up with us.*

"What?" Eirene mumbled, leaning back from him.

"I said I need to follow you up to your unit and ensure your apartment is clear of any threat."

Thank goodness Pixie had been paying attention. Eirene shut that down with a firm, "No. I've been clearing it myself since I moved in. You can watch out down here."

She stepped past him this time only to hear, "I can find my own way in."

Part of her wanted to throw down a bet.

Her apartment building had some of the best security in the city, thanks to a man living there who also worked in upper management at the high-end security company contracted to protected the residents and building. She continued walking until she reached the entrance and greeted the silver-haired gentleman with impeccable manners who opened the door for her.

She never looked back.

With rain coming, she couldn't see Corbin standing out here all night.

The longer she spent away from his mesmerizing scent, the more her head settled back into a functioning unit. Everyone in the know understood that she'd agreed to humans only on her security team.

Had Beckham brought in two shifters to sniff out who could be attacking his men? Could that be the only reason?

Or did Beckham think she was behind the deaths because she wanted no bodyguards?

That possibility sent her blood pressure shooting up again.

No shifter was safe from SCIS if found guilty of a crime against a human.

Not even her. She had done nothing to harm anyone. Innocent people still went to prison.

SCIS for a shifter was far worse than ending up in prison for a human.

As the elevator stopped on the top floor and the door

opened, she pulled out her business mobile phone and called Beckham.

She closed the phone before the call connected because a new thought hit her.

Could Corbin possibly work for Leszek on the side? That man paid off everyone to get what he wanted.

She refused to believe that of the wonderful boy she remembered.

A niggle of worry climbed her neck.

That boy had grown into a man she didn't know.

Chapter 13

LESZEK WAITED FOR Alexandria's call to let him know she was leaving her desk to go home. He gave her ten minutes to gather her things and lock the glass double doors to the entrance before taking the private elevator down.

Once she left the building, guards in the lobby would call his private line to clear any visitor before keying the elevator to stop on his floor. Even so, Leszek took no chances. No one could be trusted.

Certainly not that bitch, Eirene.

He called someone he also did not trust, but who knew better than to cross him.

"Brody here."

"What's the status of the injured guard? Has he finally died?" Leszek drummed his fingers on the polished surface of his marble desk.

Lowering his voice, Brody said, "Not yet, but Archie is not doing well. They took him for a second surgery this evening."

"You say that as if I should be pleased with the results. That is *not* what I want to hear!"

"I … I understand, but law enforcement has a guard on his room."

Leszek sat forward at that news. "A uniformed officer?"

"No. He's in street clothes, but … he's either law enforcement or military. I've gone by to see Archie and explained that my teammate has no family. I told the guard I was his best friend."

If Archie had seen Brody trying to kill him at the theater, that boast of friendship would never hold up unless Archie had amnesia from the accident. "Did you get into his room?" Hopefully, Brody could inject Archie's feeding tube with the heart attack drug that couldn't be traced. He'd given Brody every tool necessary to produce results.

"No. The nurses told me no one can see him until he regains consciousness, which might not be for a day or two."

"Find a way in there sooner," Leszek ordered in a voice that warned against arguing. He expected everyone to do as told, including Eirene.

She'd come home from running around like a bitch in heat with her tail tucked. He'd thought running her world would be simple until she started questioning every decision he made for her label and her finances. He'd lost his temper once and warned her the courts would be observing her every move and contacting him for updates on her progress in the human world.

That they cared little about her singing. He'd kept her few months of acting out quiet, but he could have as easily given the courts proof she needed his skills as a trustee longer than initially expected.

She'd become more docile since then … until today, when he learned of her ridiculous deal for partial ownership in the Libertas Theater. That's all it would take to give her a boost of confidence. He had to pull her back under his thumb … permanently.

If Brody could kill the third security member on his team without a suspect being found, many would begin to question the common denominator.

That would be Eirene, who refused anyone except human guards.

Fingers would point at the person most capable of killing them because too many people had heard her complain about wanting no guards to get in her way.

She'd set her own trap by opening the door to being

brought in for questioning over the deaths and possibly charged.

That would be the day she needed Leszek to save her.

He'd do it too, but not until she signed an agreement extending her trustee position indefinitely. The papers sat in his wall safe where he could pull them out at any second.

Chapter 14

WIPING WET HAIR off her forehead from a run in the misting rain after dark, Eirene slowed to walk through knee-high weeds as she watched for trouble. She'd left the land between the building and the highway entrance, forty yards away, overgrown on purpose. With no For Lease sign in view, most people dismissed it as a forgotten property in decline, which was true.

The young man in Wisconsin who had inherited it had no interest in spending his valuable career time traveling to South Carolina to clean up an old building to sell it. He'd been happy to receive the rent she'd offered with the understanding she might purchase it at the end of a year.

A simple deal executed online and out of Leszek's sight.

The path she'd taken from her apartment building had been two miles as the crow flew, so to speak, but three when she wove through areas with sparse trees. Not a strenuous run for a shifter and one she'd normally enjoy, but she'd had little sleep in the past five days.

One good night and she'd be in top shape again.

She listened for any unusual noise even though the light rain sometimes dulled telltale signs. Time to find out how her two female shifters were doing.

At the four-inch-thick steel rear entrance door, Eirene keyed in her code and entered, pulling the door shut behind her. She'd hidden her females upstairs on the only other floor. Lowering her backpack to the floor, she pulled out a towel to dry off.

She pulled off the wig and hat to toss aside, then had just wiped off her legs and hooked the towel over a nail in the wall when the mobile phone in her backpack buzzed.

Snatching it out of a pocket, she swiped to the video feed from the outdoor cameras visible to only this phone.

Her jaw dropped open. This can't be happening.

She had snuck out of her apartment building dressed in camo running shorts, a black bra, and a dark gray short-sleeved shirt. A ragged ball cap covered a brown ponytail wig.

No one should have recognized her leaving the building after the many times she'd dressed this way to get out in the past. No one.

Even so, she stared at a man on her camera who had the determination of a dog chasing his own tail.

He'd obviously tracked her here.

She had no idea how and no time to find out. He had to go. Right now.

Leaving her backpack filled with supplies for her ladies inside, she stepped out and remained under the rusty canopy where water leaked, but it was better than nothing. He'd been working his way around this side of the building. If he stayed on course, he'd appear in front of her in five, four, three, two. There he was.

She stepped out of the dark corner. A human wouldn't see her. A shifter would catch her scent before any noise.

His tall figure stopped moving. "Why are you hiding out here?" He'd spoken quietly, and she did as well.

"What is it with you following me after I told you not to, Corbin?"

"I'm trying to keep you safe. What are you doing running around this time of night and in this area?"

She grabbed her head. "What does it take for me to have one freaking private moment?"

He got quiet.

Losing her grip would not help, but she desperately wanted to run around in the rain screaming at the top of her lungs. Instead, she said, "I do not need security. I am within my rights to be here and have no interest in explaining why. Is that simple enough?"

"Why don't you tell me what's going on so I can help you?" He flipped on a flashlight with a red filter, which he pointed at the ground.

She stepped out from under the canopy to draw his attention away from the door hidden in the dark. "You're starting to act suspiciously like a stalker after all. For someone who doesn't like being detained by the police, you should go before I call for help."

Chapter 15

CORBIN HAD TO quit lying to himself. He'd initially followed Givenchy to this building to figure out if she was involved in anything illegal, struggling to see her as a murderer.

Now that he'd found her destination, he had to admit her scent had driven him harder than catching her in a crime. Having found her again, he needed his questions answered before he tumbled off a steep ledge.

What did she do when he offered her help?

Immediately started threatening to call in someone to deal with him.

That sounded familiar as hell.

All his good intentions just got stomped on.

He'd tried to keep his emotions locked down, but they'd been incarcerated for too long. "That's your default, isn't it? Call in the cops or some goons to drag away anyone who doesn't bow down to you." He was on a roll and couldn't hold back the bitterness of years he'd paid for attempting to make friends with this woman. For a moment earlier on the sidewalk, his weary heart had sputtered to life when she looked at him like he might be her savior.

What a fool he'd been. How could his damned heart still hold out hope for this female?

"Bow down to me?" She sounded as if he'd insulted her. "You're acting suspicious and trying to sound like you're a friend. What do you expect me to do?"

"I'm not the one acting suspicious, princess. I'm *supposed* to follow clients. You're the one out in the middle of nowhere at night on foot. What the hell are you up to out here?"

Hands on her hips, she bit out her words. "I don't have to explain myself to anyone! You act like I-I'm guilty of having my own plans and not publishing them in the news."

He heard panic. Why? Who was she here to meet?

Quieting her voice, she said, "Look, go back to the apartment building and wait for me. I'll talk to you once I get there *if* you're willing to answer my questions."

His deep voice had a gritty sound when he was riled. "*You* have questions? Well, you bet I do, too, princess."

"Stop calling me that. You're angry for no reason, and you create things out of thin air about me. You don't know me."

Water ran off the brim of his ball cap when he tipped his face down closer to hers. He vibrated with the need to shake her for making him crazy again. But he'd never harmed or threatened a female.

With his jaw tight from holding his tongue after years of punishment by the Romanian mafia, he struggled to figure out how to make her understand his disappointment and hurt. "I'm not making things up. I do know you, or at least I thought I knew a sweet girl in high school. A girl who lived with no friends like me. I thought that girl was the only one for me. Someone special."

Her lips parted as she took in every word. Her eyes lit up at his admission of how much she'd meant to him.

Now for the whole truth.

"But that young woman existed only in my dreams because the one I thought I knew screwed me over badly for many long years. I'm only now recovering."

Water drizzled down her stunned face. "What? I have no … idea what you're referencing."

She couldn't be serious. He scoffed, "Oh, I guess you've screwed over so many males you can't keep us straight." Sure, that was rough sounding, but being captured that night and handed to a monster as a teen had destroyed a chunk of his humanity.

His words must have finally struck a chord with Givenchy.

"That's bullshit," she shouted in his face then backed up. "I have *never* screwed over anyone, male or female. Ever."

Huffing a cold laugh, he said, "You really have changed. You can't even admit your actions when faced with the truth."

"You're confused or off your meds." She shoved her hands up in the air in a frustrated move. "I am *not* whoever you had a falling out with in your past."

He shook his head. "I trusted you with my life. I trusted you with all my being and—"

A muffled scream interrupted his tirade.

She swung her head left. He mirrored her action, now looking at a door of the warehouse he hadn't seen before.

Corbin stepped back into his original role today of investigating security guard deaths. "What's going on in there?"

"None of your business. I have to get inside. Get out of here." She started for the door.

He rushed ahead, blocking her. Even now, he couldn't convince himself she was a killer, but he did believe she had gotten involved in something bad. "Better to tell me the truth now before the cops show up."

Long fingers grabbed his shoulders, digging in, then she shoved him aside.

Hell, that never happened. For a female shifter to push him anywhere, adrenaline must have flooded her body.

She tore inside the building.

The door had been left unlocked the whole time.

He lunged forward, pulling the door open before she could lock him out. The hard yank knocked her back, but he caught an arm and kept her on her feet. She snatched her arm free and came at him.

Another scream pierced the air. It sounded worse than the first one.

He put a hand up and snarled at her, "If someone is being

tortured or dying, tell me now. I might be able to save him and help you."

"Tortured? Dying? I can't deal with you." She turned and raced down the dark hall then up the metal stairs that had low-voltage lighting.

Yet another horrific scream followed.

He pounded up right behind her.

At the top of the stairs, she turned and ran down a long corridor that divided the building on this level.

He stayed on her heels. If she stopped, he'd run her over.

Holding up a hand in his direction, she hissed, "Stop or you'll terrify her."

Her? That word exploded in his head. He didn't move.

She banged on the metal door, every motion more fearful than deadly. "It's me, Eirene. Let me in."

The door swung into the room hard and slammed against the wall.

A frantic thirtyish female with black hair askew cried out, "Hurry. She's been in labor for hours. I don't want to lose her and the baby."

Chapter 16

EIRENE HUGGED SULLY. "I got here as soon as I could. When did her water break?"

"Almost five hours ago. I didn't want to call until she was closer to delivery. She's been having spasms more than labor pains. For the last half hour, she's been in so much agony I don't think she can tell when a labor pain comes and goes."

"What's wrong then?" Eirene fought the chill of facing a crisis beyond her ability range. Helping Sully and her pregnant sister, Kesa, had sounded doable when Eirene thought that bitch Nova would pick them up by now.

It sure didn't seem doable at this moment.

"The baby is not right." Tears streamed down Sully's face. "I tried to help turn it with my one good hand." Sully's right arm had been broken by their abusive alpha who tied her to a tree, so the arm never healed correctly. She could hardly use it.

Why had Eirene thought she could manage the care of a woman with a badly damaged arm and another ready to give birth? She'd been excited to bring the women a change of freshly washed clothes, diapers, food supplies, and other baby products, including a blanket. All this time, she'd been telling herself she could make a difference, but she had no experience with a breech birth.

She had no experience with *any* birth.

Had she damned Kesa and her baby to death by failing to

provide the medical aid they needed? Her heart jumped up and down, driving a stake of guilt into her chest.

Kesa howled in pain.

Eirene ran to her and knelt at her side. Her pale face showed the strain she'd been under for too long. Sweat poured off her. The sheet-covered mattress beneath her dipped with the weight of her huge bulge. The baby moved, pushing and kicking.

Kesa's head rolled from side to side. She uttered heartbreaking sounds.

Eirene said, "I'm here, Kesa. We're going to take care of you." Would that sound like a lie to a shifter?

"My baby … is dying."

Blood drained from Eirene's head. She felt dizzy. She had no idea how to fix this.

A deep voice said, "She's got to get the baby turned or … this won't work."

Hearing Corbin reminded her she'd brought a stranger into the room.

Sully had been so shaken that even she hadn't noticed a man standing at Eirene's back, but she did now. "Who is he?"

Eirene tried for an answer that would give her comfort. "He's on my security team."

"The longer you wait to help your friend, the worse this will get."

His critique snapped the last thread of Eirene's patience. She stood up and turned to him. How could he look so calm?

Easy. He was not faced with losing a baby and possibly the mother.

Stepping close, she warned, "I don't need a running commentary. If that's all you can offer, get out."

"No." He shook his head as if surprised at her words. "I've got this."

"You've got what?" she demanded.

Angling his head like a confused wolf would, he calmly replied, "I can handle this if you'll gain her permission."

Pissed at his arrogance, she snapped back, "I realize male shifters all think they are gods with unlimited knowledge, but unless you've done this before—"

"I have."

His quiet reply silenced her next words. He hadn't bragged. He sounded as if he meant those words. In fact, he'd told the truth.

She still didn't believe him, but Kesa's painful noises forced Eirene to open her mind to the possibility of real help. "When?"

He snorted a chuckle. "Twice in the past few years while I was … working for someone who had females in his group, and we were in remote locations. I'd be happy to tell you more once the baby is here, but—"

Another scream iced Eirene's blood.

He pointed out, "That baby is coming soon. The mother is in dire straits. She hasn't even noticed a male shifter in the room. You can either do this yourself or ask her if she'll let me take over since she trusts you."

Sully had been watching them both, especially the male. She asked, "Can you handle the birth, Eirene?"

Everyone would hear a lie. "No, I don't have training for this situation."

Without doubt, Sully had heard the truth in his claim as well. "In that case, I agree with him. Kesa is out of her mind, but she knows *your* scent, Eirene. If you trust him to deliver the baby, then I will trust him too. Kesa will do better with you holding her from behind and me gripping her hand."

Eirene could not in good faith risk the mother and child by refusing his help. She asked Pixie, *Do you think we can trust Corbin with delivering a baby?*

Pixie said, *He is your only option. He does not feel dangerous at this moment, and he tells the truth, but I do not trust his wolf.*

Eirene took him in from head to toe, only now realizing he had no sunglasses on. She could see his beautiful, deep-brown eyes, so familiar, but something was different. These eyes were much older. They had soul and integrity.

Time to make a decision. She couldn't believe she was going to do this on the fly, but he *had* spoken the truth. She stepped over to the man she was entrusting two lives with and gripped his arm firmly.

He didn't bark at her. He waited patiently without pressuring her.

It came down to either him or her playing midwife. Pixie had nailed it. Eirene had no choice. "If you deliver this baby breathing and the mother alive, I'll listen to everything you have to say and answer all your questions. I swear to you I do not know of any time I mistreated you, but we'll talk. I need your help. My wolf and I have never turned our backs on any child, but I don't have the expertise for this."

He put his hand over hers and squeezed. "My wolf and I have never turned our backs on a female or child either. I'll do all within my power to save them."

She gave him a short nod of acceptance, hugged Sully, and said, "I'd let him birth my baby right now, given no other person with experience."

Kesa started shouting, "Someone help me. Help my baby! *Pleeeease!*"

Corbin began giving gentle but firm orders, sending Eirene for a bucket of hot water, towels, and to bring her backpack up. When Eirene returned, Sully had directed him to a basin for washing his hands.

He finished and knelt beside Kesa, brushing his hand over her forehead and talking to her gently but quickly. "Hi, Kesa. I know you're scared, but I've done this before. I'm going to turn your baby, and then we'll be able to time your labor pains."

She stopped flopping her head back and forth. Her wild eyes focused on him. "A healer. She brought me a healer. Thank you." Tears ran freely.

Eirene would not correct Kesa because she had no idea where he'd gained experience in helping a woman give birth, but he never said he was a healer. Please don't let the first time she'd trusted a man in many years be misplaced.

The man they all pinned their hopes on was drenched in sweat by the first half hour, but he continued talking to Kesa in a soothing voice even when she wailed out of her mind. He told her when he'd turned the baby and began counting her labor pains.

The following two hours felt like a lifetime, but the moment Eirene heard Kesa's baby cry, it seemed as if those hours had flown by.

With the intuitive ability of a person who had done this many times, he handled everything, never flinching at any of it. He turned to Eirene with the bloody newborn in his hands and said, "You should clean up the baby. Sully can't manage."

Stunned, she couldn't move.

"Eirene?" he nudged. "You okay?"

That had been the first time he'd said her name, but it sounded familiar coming off his tongue. Enough that it shook her out of shock.

She took the baby to the second bucket she'd brought, recently filled with slightly warm water. Using a soft cloth from her backpack, she cleaned the baby, and then she started crying. Kesa had lived, and this baby girl had made it into the world.

Sully kneeled beside her with an arm hooked around Eirene's shoulder. "Thank you for saving my family."

Eirene cried harder.

Sully hugged her. Somehow, Eirene managed to finish cleaning up the tiny infant. Kesa's first pup. Eirene diapered and wrapped the child in the pretty baby blanket she'd brought, then took her to Kesa, who had both pillows propped up beneath her shoulders. Once Sully got behind her sister and helped Kesa sit up more until she could lean back against Sully, Eirene handed the baby to her mother.

A masculine hand offered Eirene two bottles of water. "Thanks." She opened one for each of the sisters, placing the water on the floor. She tried to stand.

The same powerful hand cupped her elbow, bringing her to her feet.

Kesa had cried for hours. She looked up at Eirene with a red face and swollen eyes. "Bless you for being our lifeline." Then she looked past Eirene and said, "You are a wonderful healer. I don't think this miracle would have happened without you. I wish I had a way to pay you back."

"Just stay safe and healthy," he said.

Eirene was determined to find out what injustice he believed she had done to him. The mere thought of that was breaking her heart after what she'd witnessed. She would never have hurt the young boy who had been the only person to make her happy by seeing him in two classes at school and from afar at the lockers.

She remembered every moment of every day around him.

How could he say he'd screwed her over?

Mentally and emotionally spent after not sleeping enough, her body felt like an abused stress ball.

Now that the baby was alive and breathing, her brain came back online. Corbin suspected her of something shady going on here, then threatened to call in law enforcement.

Then he jumped in to save a baby and a mother. None of that added up.

Thoughts raced around in her head, hitting walls, then backed up like a panicked rabbit lost in a maze.

She could make sense of only one thing. Every time she drew a deep breath while struggling to remain calm amidst all the pungent smells of the delivery, she could always find his scent.

The more she smelled him, the more she felt a wave of peacefulness associated with her memories of him.

"Hey, you okay?" Corbin asked in a soft voice.

She blinked and looked to her left where she found his concerned face. "What?"

"I was saying, how about we find a quiet place to sit down and drink water so the sisters can have a moment together?"

"Oh. Sorry, I didn't hear you."

A half grin curved his mouth. "I know. Everyone's drained." He wrapped his fingers lightly around her arm and tugged. "This way."

Corbin carried two bottles of water as he led her to the bottom steps of the stairs. Using a rag that he pulled from his back pocket that she'd seen him wipe his brow with earlier, he cleaned a spot where she could sit.

Her clothes were filthy from running through the woods. Her face and hair couldn't be much better. She could only imagine her tangled mess of hair that hadn't seen a brush since she'd pulled off the wig.

In fact, only her hands were clean.

For him to treat her with such respect after she'd berated him earlier left her feeling lower than a slug. She had never been so twisted up emotionally around anyone else.

This man, whose eyes and voice brought up long-buried memories, had turned her inside out. She sat on the metal step, glad to only have inches between them when he settled his big body next to her before passing her a water bottle.

Silence wrapped them as they both guzzled water that cooled her throat and had a calming effect.

She'd promised to talk to him.

She'd never volunteered to answer questions from others but saving that baby and mother would have been worth any conversation. Truthfully, she wanted to know why he thought she'd screwed him over at some point. That accusation stabbed her chest every time she thought about it.

He'd been telling the truth again.

If she'd treated Corbin poorly in the past, she would make it right and convince him she was sincerely sorry. She kept waiting for him to start asking a barrage of questions, but he seemed content to take a few drinks and lean back with his elbows on the stairs behind him.

First, she had something important to say. "Thank you for saving Kesa and her baby."

"You're welcome. I'm happy everything went well."

She waited for him to ask his questions. The more he dragged this out, the more anxious she became. She finally said, "I made a deal to address your belief that I screwed you over. Please tell me what I did."

When he said nothing, she turned to him, ready to unload her frustration, and mentally stumbled.

He stared at her with the sweetest expression.

She hadn't been this self-conscious since high school when every look held judgment.

"Why aren't you asking questions?" she put to him in a more polite tone.

He sat up, the wistful expression on his face gone. Moving his elbows to his knees, he dangled the empty bottle from one hand. "I would not hold you to your offer in that frantic situation. I'll let you ask questions first and then see if you're still willing to hear mine." He glanced her way. "Okay?"

For the first time since allowing him to step in and save the baby, she realized she had been right to trust him.

Offered the chance to clear up her confusion first brought on a bout of self-conscious nerves. "Have we seen each other since high school?"

He looked down at his boots and drew a long breath, then lifted sad eyes to hers. "Not until now."

He'd stolen her heart with a tiny wolf he'd carved from wood and wrapped inside the sweetest note saying how much he wanted to spend time with her. He had said he'd be at the cemetery that night. His wolf had tracked her scent there and believed that's where her wolf ran at times.

That young boy would never have walked away from her. She'd believed that for a long time. She'd gone by his home and asked his father where Corbin had gone and when he would be back.

The mean man had said, "No idea. I hope he never returns. He didn't like living here, and I didn't like him being around."

She'd wondered if those two had gotten in a fight and

Corbin had run away from home. Even so, she believed he would come back to her one day—that they'd have a chance to be together.

With nowhere else to go for answers, she finally gave up waiting for him to respond.

Her heart pounded wildly at a possibility she had never considered. Had something bad happened to him? "Corbin?"

He nodded.

Tears threatened at the corners of her eyes. "What happened to you?"

He cocked his head and asked, "Do you really not know why I disappeared?"

"No."

"Truth." He sounded shocked and then sad. "I was on my way to meet you in the cemetery. I'd smelled your scent there more than once, which is why I suggested we meet there."

Her head would explode any minute now. "I still have your note with those words and the little wooden wolf you'd wrapped up in the paper. I went to the cemetery to let my wolf run that night. We stayed as long as possible, but then we had to go home."

Corbin sat right next to her.

How many years had she dreamed of finding him and demanding why he vanished without a word? How many times had she wanted to see his warm brown eyes and heart-warming face?

The boyish face of her memories had morphed into a strong-jawed man. Those eyes had seen far more life since that fateful night.

How many times had she wanted his arms around her when life yanked the ground out from beneath her feet time and again? Where had he gone?

He inhaled slowly and said, "I was grabbed by your dad's two security goons who followed you constantly."

She blinked. Had she heard him correctly? "I don't understand. I told no one about the note or the meeting. My father would never have approved. I was careful leaving for my standard run and made sure no one followed me."

A hint of disbelief tinged his words. "Your bodyguards didn't have to follow you. They were too busy at that moment delivering me to a Romanian gang leader who needed a shifter slave. He gave the bodyguards cash, enough to pay off my dad to stay quiet. He would never miss me anyhow."

She covered her mouth with a hand to keep the wail from escaping. Why had her dad's men done this to him?

Now she understood why Corbin had accused her of treating him badly in the past. Pulling her hand down, she asked, "Why did you say *I* screwed you over?"

His chest moved with a deep breath. Every word seemed to be pulled from deep inside. "For years, I believed you'd played me that night. The tall goon handed me the note I'd written you as proof that you'd sent them. He said you had ordered them to send me far enough away that I'd never make the mistake of talking to you again."

Her emotions were stumbling through a mine field, hitting one at a time. She gasped, "That's not possible. I told you I still have the note."

Taking a moment to reply, he asked, "Did it stay in your possession the whole time?"

She gripped her forehead, thinking back to that night. "I found it in my locker and took it home. Then I put it in my jewelry box where I keep my mother's necklace and the few things I cherish." She raised her gaze to his with a sick feeling in her stomach. "I went to the library to do my homework at record speed. When I told my father I was done and going for a run, he said his usual 'have a good time' but be sure to take one of my bodyguards. Time was running out, so I rushed to put on clothes easy to remove for shifting and took off."

He sat silently as she replayed that night.

She could see how it all happened now and whispered, "I didn't think to pull the note out again until I hadn't seen you for days. I smelled no other scent, which means they must have worn gloves. After that, I left your note hidden away for years."

Corbin filled in the missing parts. "They must have seen me put the note in your locker and figured out something was up."

Her chest hurt from learning the truth. How would she have felt if someone had done that to her? She'd have been out for blood. "I don't think my father knew, which makes me wonder if someone else had paid his guards to do that."

"Who?" Corbin asked with genuine surprise.

"My trustee has been around since my birth. He was my father's best friend and business partner, but he is now fully in charge of my life. I can see him paying those two to keep an eye on me and removing anyone he believed would be a threat to his power down the line."

"That's awful."

How could Corbin have any sympathy for her after she'd been the reason that he'd lost his freedom? "I am so sorry they did that to you, Corbin." She wanted to hug him more than anything, but she understood why he had been what had at first seemed like unreasonably angry with her.

He lifted a hand and gently stroked her cheek. "You didn't do it. I'm happy and relieved to know that now. I've been blaming you all this time. I wanted to know why you would do that to me instead of simply ignoring me."

A tear broke free despite how hard she'd tried to hold onto her composure. In high school, humans had called her the ice queen. They judged her every action and played mean jokes on her.

None of those kids ever saw the lonely girl who suffered in silence and tiptoed around to keep from being exposed as a shifter.

Corbin had seen her. He'd been the only person. He'd offered her the one thing all her father's money couldn't buy, and that was friendship with someone of her own kind.

No judgment. Genuine kindness.

The minute she'd read the note about meeting him, her heart had told her this one belonged to her.

In return, Corbin had lost his freedom and his future.

"I could never ignore you, Corbin. I never noticed another boy except you."

He lifted a hand to her face and wiped away her tears with his thumb. "Even in my angriest moments, I still missed you."

She gripped his hand and held it against her face, wanting to keep him close. "You have no idea how much I hoped you'd show up one day." She held on to his hand and lowered it to her knee.

"You weren't happy to see me today," he reminded her.

She sighed heavily. "I have so much going on and thought you had been sent by someone trying to pin the security guard deaths on me as well as Archie, the badly injured one. I've tried to do what I can to figure out what is going on."

His tone perked up. "Do you know who is behind the attacks?"

"Not yet. I keep expecting SCIS to show up any day," she admitted.

"Oh, hell no. We will figure out what's going on."

We. She had never been part of a *we*. It felt so good to have someone willing to step into her dangerous world and offer his help. She put her other hand on top of the one holding his and marveled again over the only important thing at this minute.

A happiness she hadn't felt since the last time she'd seen him surged through her, filling her body and heart with fresh hope for a real future. She'd battled alone so long to save her female shifters, to stand against Leszek, to build a theater for her vision of charity events, and to … make it through every day to start another one.

Life should be about more than surviving.

Corbin had undoubtedly faced worse obstacles to survive. She would be there for him now too.

He seemed content to just be with her.

She was still awed over what he'd done for Kesa and her pup. "You said upstairs you'd delivered babies twice in the past while working in a remote area. Were you talking about your time with that Romanian creep?"

"Yes. I spent the first year in Romania. It was a bad situation for many of us, especially women they brought in to be trafficked or who lived in villages he entered and demanded they feed his people. The first time had been after he'd captured a female shifter to sell who turned up pregnant. None of the human men wanted anything to do with her. She'd been moaning and moving slowly for hours before being ordered to feed us. Her water broke, and they started yelling. They were going to beat her."

"Oh, no. What kind of monster would do that?"

Corbin gave her a sad smile. "The worst kind you never want to meet." He continued, "I got up and asked Vlad, the leader, if he wanted her to live. No other question would have gotten a yes answer. He nodded. I told him if he'd let me, I would help her with the baby. That was the longest night of my life, but she gave birth and survived. The next time, it was another shifter female, and Vlad ordered me to deliver her baby. While working with her, she told me that right before Vlad captured her, a healer had said her baby would have to be turned. She did her best to explain what I needed to do, but I was terrified of killing her and the baby with my lack of experience."

He took a couple of deep breaths and blew them out, then washed a hand over his face and shook his head as if clearing it. "It did not look like the baby and mother would make it at all. If she had died, then Vlad would've beaten me senseless, but once I started, I couldn't have stopped if Vlad had been kicking me. I could feel the baby and closed my eyes to shut out all distractions. I turned it." He smiled at her a bit sheepishly. "Hearing that baby cry was the greatest sound of my life."

"I am so glad you followed me tonight." She reached over and brushed a loose lock of hair off his forehead, admiring the man he'd become. "I was terrified I had condemned Kesa and her baby to death by my lack of resources. Thank you for all you did even after I had sounded more like a shrew than a friend."

His smile remained but softened into one that lit hope in her chest.

They sat that way for a while, then he glanced around and asked, "How did you get involved in all this?"

See? No one else wanted to know what she cared about. "My father had allowed me to shift and let my wolf run in a national park while we were on a road trip out west. The bodyguards stayed with him. My wolf, Pixie, was deep in the woods when she heard a child cry out and changed directions. I was sixteen and had never seen Pixie rush toward danger. She's not dominant, but she ran straight to where a woman was beating a small boy with a stick. He acted like he was trying to get away, screaming for his mama."

Corbin guessed, "It sounds like she was capturing him."

"Exactly." Eirene nodded. "No human would have heard the boy unless they were that deep in the woods at that moment. Pixie jumped at the middle-aged woman who had been in good shape, knocking her to the ground. The woman went crazy yelling at Pixie that she would kill her. When the woman got back on her feet, Pixie stood in front of the little boy who was curled up and bawling his eyes out. Pixie snarled and started stalking the woman who took off running. We stayed there until my father sent the bodyguards to find us. They followed Pixie's howling to locate us. They called in law enforcement while Pixie ran back to where my father waited. The bodyguards said the police had been hunting a missing child, thinking he had wandered off."

Corbin turned an impressed look her way. "Wow. How can you say your wolf is not dominant? That was strong."

Eirene's lips curved into a sweet smile. "Pixie is very bright and the best friend I've had all these years, but she goes along to get along. Well, with one exception. She has a protective streak a mile wide for a child."

Talking about her journey brought up a thousand questions

she had for him. "What happened with the Romanian, and how did you end up here? Do you live here? Are you staying?" The last question held more importance than the first ones.

He started laughing. "Whoa. One at a time."

"I love hearing you laugh," she blurted out like a schoolgirl with a crush again. In all fairness to her, she'd never been free to say anything like that to him in school like other girls her age could.

He stopped laughing and studied her face as if needing to see every detail. "I love the sweet smell of your scent, the sound of your voice, and your vibrant eyes."

Her lips parted. He'd stolen her ability to form a reply. Even during her time with that miserable human guy, she'd never heard any declaration that sent warmth flowing through her soul like Corbin's words.

Without thinking, she leaned toward him. He didn't hesitate to meet her halfway and gently kiss her lips. It was as if that want had been left suspended in time until now, when it felt perfectly natural to succumb together.

She lifted her hand to his shoulder, holding him in place, fearful of losing him again.

The kiss bloomed from sweet to searing heat. He lifted her to his lap, where she had better access to his mouth and took advantage of those sexy lips.

He paused, smiling at her. "You're a demanding princess."

She quirked an eyebrow at him. "Yes, I'm demanding, but I'm no princess. There's nothing special about me."

"I would argue, but I refuse to waste a precious second with you when I've dreamed of this for so long." He leaned in and kissed her again as her secret phone chirped.

Groaning at the world for not allowing her a little time to herself, she pulled back reluctantly. "I have to read this text and make the woman sending it talk to me. I can't stand her, but she has resources for the sisters. I want her to move them somewhere safer with real medical care."

His eyes lit up. "Do whatever you need to do, babe. My life is finally making sense. I can wait for us to talk."

"Or we could kiss some more," she quipped, drawing another laugh from him. "I need to stand. I tend to pace when I talk to her." It helped with the nervous energy already rising inside her. She was not a negotiator, but she intended to sound like one tonight.

He lifted her to her feet. The phone chirped again with the bitch's text.

Wiping happiness from her mind, she focused on being furious and out of patience. Instead of replying to the text with a thumbs-up to let Nova know Eirene had received the message, she kept her fingers still. If she replied as usual, Nova would expect her to do as told.

Eirene killed the noise and watched her phone as she paced.

A duplicate text message came through thirty seconds later.

She did not move a finger.

Her phone rang. She answered and heard, *"What's wrong with you? Answer the damn text, or you can forget—"*

Eirene had reached her limit and was far enough away from the sisters not to disturb them. She snarled, "Shut. Up. Now."

"Who do you think you are talk—"

Undeterred, Eirene kept her tone firm. "Shut up or forget me doing another thing for you."

"You don't want me to expose what you're doing, Givenchy."

The threat pushed Eirene's final button with this woman. She did not want this bitch to expose her connection with these female shifters on the run for many reasons, one being that SCIS would come after her for harboring rogue shifters and the sisters for being rogue. Leszek would have all the ammunition that he'd need to tie up her future forever in court.

Her frightened chicks would have no one to help them then.

But she would not back down now. Not after being left with no help for Kesa.

Forcing ice into her tone as she'd learned to do with the paparazzi, Eirene warned, "If you try to hurt me or any of the women I'm helping, I'll expose *you*."

Silence.

"Are you wondering how I might do that?" Eirene taunted. She wanted to get her hands around this cryptic shifter's throat, but for all this woman's faults, she had resources that could help Kesa and her pup. "I still have the original slip of paper you left for me at my Charlotte performance. You tried to hide your scent, but it's still there. It might take a while, but you will be found if I hand it to the right people."

Had she threatened another person's freedom right in front of Corbin? He was catching every word of this conversation with his shifter hearing. What could he be thinking?

She glanced down at him, and he appeared content to wait on her conversation. Her worry eased a little.

The bitch's voice blasted through her phone, cursing her into next year.

"I feel the same way about you," Eirene replied, her fingers gripping the phone so hard that the plastic squealed. She eased her fingers loose. "I went into that crack house to find Lauren, who was half out of her mind going through withdrawals from whatever drug the Black River wolf pack shot her up with. I almost didn't get out before the police showed up. You took that female shifter immediately, and you keep asking about each one I find on my own if they escaped the Black River wolf pack."

She paused to see if Nova would argue. Not a word yet. She continued, "I didn't think much about it at first, but I've waited almost three weeks to get some help with these two sisters, one of whom was pregnant, and I had no way to get medical aid for her. I can't even visit this location easily while trying to ensure no one follows me." She glanced at Corbin, who had not taken his gaze off her. "These women now have a new pup to protect. We delivered her baby in this warehouse when you could have had her under medical care. You aren't doing your part, so don't ask me to rescue and harbor anyone else until you tell me what the hell is going on."

A beleaguered sigh rushed through the phone. "I thought Lauren might have known … my daughter. She was kidnapped four months ago, and I have a sick feeling the Black River wolf pack has her because she'd have found a way to escape any other shifters. I'm desperate to get her back even if they've fucked her up."

Eirene turned and leaned against a wall. She dropped her head back then whispered, "You should have told me that from the start."

"I couldn't risk trusting you and that sick pack finding out. They'd probably kill her, then come for me and the ones I'm protecting."

Standing away from the wall, Eirene drew herself up, but wanted to be sure this woman understood what she was saying. "Hunting your daughter will put all of us at risk, including those we protect. I hate that they have her, but keep in mind that she may be so far gone she won't know you."

"I'd rather she be anywhere except with those monsters," Nova ranted. "She's mine, and I want her back regardless of any condition she's found in."

What would Eirene do in her shoes? She murmured, "I understand. I'd wreck the world to save a child of my own." The line remained silent while she thought everything over. "Okay, let's make a new deal, Nova. We need to be straight with each other and no threats. You may think my life is a joy ride, but I've got some big problems of my own. I don't want any female shifter ever handed over to SCIS or anyone else, and that includes you."

After a long pause, the woman said, "Agreed. You could have given that piece of paper to SCIS by now. I'm going to trust you."

"Great. Let's get these two women and the pup safe, then give me whatever you're comfortable sharing about when your daughter was taken. I'll do anything I can to help you find her. Fair enough?"

"Yes. I'll keep up my end so long as you make good on your offer."

"Absolutely," Eirene confirmed. "I'm building a base of resources, but I'm careful about sharing information unless I trust someone with my own life. Please pick up my group as soon as you can. Get them medical aid. The older sister is healing a badly damaged arm. Since being here, she has only shifted once late at night while I watched her back. The new mother may want to shift and let her wolf run after so many months of being unable to, but it's too dangerous here."

"Where are they?"

Eirene gave her the address and directions on how to access the least visible door around back, where to find the sisters inside, and a temporary alarm code.

Nova said, "I can be there in a little over an hour."

"Wonderful. I'll make sure they have what they need and that they understand the plan. I'll tell them to only answer the door when they hear the code words. *My favorite song is You've Got A Friend.*"

"Okay. Good thinking to be sure it's me before opening the door."

Eirene cocked an eyebrow at the compliment from this woman. Maybe Nova's abrupt attitude had been nothing more than a scared mother herself during their brief interactions. Time would tell.

Feeling much lighter with a real plan in place, Eirene replied, "Thanks. Once I know the building is safe, I'll leave and be long gone so you can slip inside unnoticed—"

A low buzzing sound interrupted her. She unhooked the phone-like device clipped to her waistband and pressed a button. That activated a small screen connected to one of the outdoor cameras. A car approached, driving slowly from the highway toward the warehouse.

Nova asked, "What's going on? I hear a weird sound."

Corbin was up and at Eirene's side. "Problem?"

His quick reaction and concerned tone surprised her after she'd spent so many years struggling to do this alone. Eirene told Nova, "A car is coming down the drive to the building. I need to go, but I'll make sure whoever it is does not get near the sisters."

"What are you going to do?"

Were they chatty best friends now? Eirene snapped, "The longer we talk, the less time I have to ensure their safety as well as yours. Be on time."

"I will." The line went dead.

Eirene looked hard at Corbin. She'd been so happy to be together again and have him by her side, but now she battled the urge to ask for his help. She could not put him in danger again because of her. "A vehicle is driving up to the building. I'm going to tell the sisters the plan, which I'm sure you heard, and have them lock the door from the inside. Then I'll run from the building and let the intruders see me, so they chase me. You should go now. I'll find you when it's safe."

"No." Corbin's face morphed into stony determination. "*We* are doing this. Not you."

Shocked at his announcement, she shook her head. "I don't have time to argue, but this is my problem. That could be SCIS driving up. I don't know how they found out about this building, but I'm not taking any chances of you getting captured a second time."

He cupped her face and kissed her lips gently. "I understand, but you need my help. I'm tougher to kill or capture at this point in my life. Get your ladies set. Tell them to stay quiet no matter what they hear until that woman shows up with the code words. Then we'll go."

Chapter 17

CORBIN GRABBED EIRENE'S hand and hurried back to the birthing suite. "If you'll give me that camera monitor, I'll watch for when someone gets out of the car while you tell the women what is going on."

She hesitated.

He understood how trust was still fragile with others at risk, but then she shoved her mobile monitor into his hand and murmured, "Thanks," and rushed into the room.

While she told the sisters what was happening, Corbin studied the video feed. The vehicle slowed down as if the driver tried to decide how far forward to go.

Ares told him, *Let me out. I kill them and get some exercise.*

No. Corbin didn't want to think what releasing his crazy wolf would end up like. Ares would rip humans apart in seconds if the car didn't hold shifters.

You scare her wolf, Ares said abruptly.

Corbin went perfectly still. *What did you say?*

You heard me.

Maybe she fears you, Ares. When Corbin received no reply, he asked a different question. *How can you know if Eirene's wolf is frightened?*

I know.

He would have pursued that conversation, but Eirene came running up to him.

She ran past him, leading the way back downstairs to the steel door and lifted her fingers to a control panel on the wall. "Get ready for a warning alarm to sound as we step out. Then the door will lock behind us." He held the door open for her. When the warning beeps started, he pushed the door closed.

On the last beep, the lock clicked into place.

Cool air swirled the drizzle still falling outside. Not enough rain to shield their scent.

Corbin whispered, "Stay close to the building until we reach the front."

As she followed him, she held the camera monitor up to her face. "Two men are exiting what looks like a dark SUV."

Near the front corner, Corbin inhaled deeply.

Ares told him, *Shifter. Stinking jackals.*

Corbin spoke right next to Eirene's ear. "Shifters. Smells like jackals."

Eirene nodded. "My wolf agrees."

"I'll try to use more hand signals starting now." He pointed at himself and made the running motion with his fingers, then pointed out to his right to show he'd circle wide and run close enough to get their attention.

Whispering right into her ear, he told her, "Count to ten, then head for me as if catching up. When we're together, we'll run in that direction." He pointed again.

She hesitated but gave him a sharp nod.

He gave her the hand signal to wait, then moved quietly at first. When he was far enough out from the building, he intentionally rustled the weeds. Any shifter would catch that sound. Looking to his left, he saw silhouettes of both men turn his way from where they stood in front of the headlights. They had likely left the vehicle's motor running for a fast getaway.

He and Eirene would throw a wrench in that plan by turning this into a chase on foot.

He slowed his pace as he neared the jackals and listened for Eirene to catch up to him.

No special hearing needed.

She ran through the weeds like a wild buffalo pounding the ground. Five steps away from Corbin, she slowed.

Both jackal shifters started in Corbin's direction. He took off at a steady pace, sure that she could see him in the ambient light. By the time she fell into step with him, he had upped the pace until they were running fast, but not yet at full speed.

The noisy sounds of being followed confirmed that both shifters were on their trail.

Corbin asked her, "Ready?"

"Yes."

"Let's kick it up a gear." He took the lead with her a step behind him. He'd rather have her in front, but he had a feeling she did not have his experience of racing through an unknown area while being chased by someone determined to kill her. Sadly, Corbin and Ares had plenty of experience running for their lives.

Those jackal shifters might stop short of killing them, but Corbin did not want to risk them getting near Eirene. He'd had no chance to celebrate finally talking to her and finding out she had honorable reasons for sneaking around. That time would come.

He was not leaving her again or letting her go for as long as she wanted to be with him.

Ares informed Corbin, *They will catch us.*

Well, hell.

Pressing his point, Ares said, *You will not win in human form.*

Corbin argued, *You don't know that.*

These shifters have strange scent, Ares sent back.

What do you mean? Now his wolf had him worried.

Smell like the shifters we fought in Yukon.

Corbin's heart dropped to his knees. He'd thought these might be run-of-the-mill SCIS jackal shifters, but if Ares was correct, these jackals were involved with the Black River wolf pack in some way.

Drugged-up killers.

He slowed enough to run in stride with Eirene, asking her, "Can your wolf fight?"

She frowned. "If she has to, but I told you she's not dominant."

"My wolf and I have encountered drugged-up jackals raised by the Black River wolf pack, which were used as assassins. My wolf said these two smell like those. If so, they won't fight in human form. I can take down a non-juiced wolf or jackal shifter in human form, but we almost died the last time before my wolf escaped a battle with the ones amped up on Jugo Loco."

She kept pumping her arms and breathing hard but turned to him with a confused look.

He assured her, "I'll explain it all when we have time, but we have to survive first."

"Okay. What do you want to do?"

Corbin slapped a branch off a small pine tree out of her way. "We race ahead in a burst of speed. They'll get cocky because they know we can't hold that speed for a long time. Once we're far enough ahead, we'll shift. When my wolf tells me, we stop and rip our clothes off, then roll up only the clothes we need for shifting again later. Then we immediately shift. All of that has to happen in less than a minute."

She slanted him a worried look.

Corbin said, "My wolf is called Ares, by the way, and is very hard to kill."

Ares said, *I keep telling you that.*

Ignoring the mouthy beast, Corbin continued giving Eirene instructions. "Our wolves will carry the clothes and shoes. Please ask Pixie to follow my wolf's lead. Ares is a vicious and deadly fighter. Hopefully, your wolf won't have to draw any blood, but Ares might need backup or a lookout against two juiced-up shifters."

Ares said, *Hurry.*

Corbin ordered, "Time to power run. Follow me as closely as you can."

She told him, *"Go!"*

He ran faster than he'd ever moved before because being too slow meant Eirene getting hurt.

Behind him, Eirene dodged to the left around skinny trees. Speaking between choppy breaths, she said, "Pixie does not trust Ares."

Ares sent Corbin instructions. *Tell her wolf to stay out of my way so she doesn't get me killed.*

Assuring Eirene stayed with him, Corbin tried to calm her concern. "My wolf will not harm yours. He wants her to stay back from the battle, so she doesn't get hurt."

Ares growled. *Lie. Not my words.*

Corbin had to nip Ares in the bud right now to save his energy for running then shifting. *You said you wanted her wolf back out of the way. You could have meant what I said, so I did not lie. Also, my translation is the only reason her wolf might trust you.*

Eirene asked, "Then why have Pixie shift if she can't help?"

Corbin gave her his reason. "She'll be able to run faster than you if Ares loses and we can't run."

Eirene sputtered, "I won't—"

Ares shouted in Corbin's head. *Stop and shift now!*

Corbin passed that along to Eirene as he skidded to a stop. He had his shoes and shirt off in seconds, then shucked his underwear and jeans, rolling his shoes up in the pants. Eirene moved as quickly, but her fingers shook as she unbuttoned her shirt.

He grabbed the front of her shirt and murmured, "Sorry. I won't look." Then he yanked it over her head, spun her around, and unclipped her bra. She squeaked a noise, but pulled the bra free, then stepped out of her casual canvas shoes as she unzipped and shed her shorts.

Her underwear too.

He knew this because she tossed them away.

The snippet of white lace landed at his feet. Damn.

The jerk deep inside him wanted to look, but he wouldn't do that to her. As soon as he heard the noises of her shifting, he checked to see that she had shorts, a shirt, and shoes ready for her wolf to carry, then called up his own shift.

Ares burst free, shook off the change, then turned to find Eirene's reddish-golden wolf standing still. Pixie's eyes bulged with fear.

Corbin told Ares, *Go over and give Pixie a gentle nudge so she knows you won't kill her.*

Ares growled at being told what to do.

If you don't, she may run. Do you want her caught by the Black River wolf pack? Corbin had no idea if that would motivate Ares, but his wolf hated the Black River group after they'd been stuck doing degrading jobs for that pack.

Without a comment, Ares turned around, startling Pixie with his quick movement.

Way to go, Romeo, Corbin complained.

Shut up, human. Ares stepped over and rubbed his much larger snout against her muzzle. She had a sleek build. Next to Ares, who bulged with muscles, she appeared smaller and feminine. Vulnerable.

Not a great attribute for a wolf.

She'd been breathing hard but seemed to calm down after Ares touched his snout to hers.

Ares jerked back around and scented the air. He lowered his head and began stalking in the direction of the noisy jackal shifters who raced in on top of them. Ares ground out a deeper snarl, warning death would follow.

Caught unprepared, the jackals started shifting without pulling off their clothes. They made high screeching noises and cackles.

Ares ran at the closest one, ripping into the half-human, half-jackal's throat in mid-shift. Blood flew everywhere. Ares dropped the jackal's neck and focused on the next one that had shifted all the way.

This one had bright yellow eyes and stood almost as tall as Ares. That was unusual for a jackal. He would not be so easy.

Opening a mouth filled with razor-sharp fangs, the jackal

cackled with delight. His animal body had muscular legs and a chest warped out of shape.

This would be bloody and fast.

Corbin hoped Ares could hold his own long enough to find a vulnerable spot on that monstrosity.

Ares and the jackal dove at each other, jaws snapping and claws ripping. The jackal twisted unexpectedly and snapped at one of Ares' legs, barely missing.

No, the jackal managed to rip open the side of that leg.

Corbin steeled himself against the pain, which felt worse than a standard cut. Could it be from Jugo Loco poison in the jackal's body? Ares had been right. This was like the drugged-up shifters they'd fought in the Yukon.

When the jackal had his jaws on Ares' snout, he could have killed Corbin's wolf. That the jackal hadn't gone for a kill meant he intended to take them prisoner.

Pixie chose that moment to step forward, distracting Ares, who snarled at her.

She backed up.

The jackal released Ares, but Corbin's wolf got a claw across his shoulder. Ares swung around and went headfirst into the battle again. He had a way of jacking up his attack to a whole new level, which he did now. Acting oblivious to the pain, Ares used bigger claws to rip the jackal's neck open. With the jackal in retreat, Ares kept up his buzz saw impersonation until the jackal fell to the ground.

As fights went, this one had been quicker than Corbin expected by the time Ares broke free and stumbled sideways. Not good. He could feel warm blood running down his wolf's damaged leg and shoulder.

They had to heal or risk losing consciousness due to loss of blood.

Ares waited as the jackal lay on its side panting for air. Some shifters might play possum at this point, but blood spewed from the jackal's neck. He'd been the more arrogant one this time, which was unusual given how Ares usually held that title.

When the jackal gave his last breath and stilled, Ares

lifted his head and howled a victor's call. He stood on shaky legs. Energy boiled through his body. Corbin grunted at the blast of power, but agreed with his wolf's decision to heal the worst now so they could move ahead.

Eirene's beautiful wolf stepped tentatively over to Ares when Corbin had worried that she'd run away. Ares still shook from blood loss but didn't turn on her.

Ares seemed confused, of all things, which Corbin found almost funny.

Pixie continued until she paused, lifting her nose to reach Ares' snout. She licked at the cut on his muzzle. Ares stopped shaking and had no comment.

The female wolf had shocked him.

Corbin had a feeling Pixie had acted on her own with no encouragement from Eirene.

He hadn't seen Ares be this calm since before Corbin's mother had tried to drown him as a pup. He would love to ask Eirene what was happening with her wolf.

The wind kicked up with the storm gaining strength. Rain came down hard, knocking Ares out of his shock. He gave Pixie a quick lick and then drew a deep breath into his wrecked body.

Ares asked Corbin, *Where do we go?*

Back to Eirene's apartment. My motorcycle is there, and we need to get cleaned up. You need time to heal.

Give directions. Not much time.

His wolf never admitted to any weakness, but the more abrupt Ares spoke after a battle signaled concern over blood loss. Corbin knew firsthand how badly Ares had been injured and worried about his wolf feeling lightheaded soon.

Corbin explained, *Based on a map I studied with Adrian, I have a pretty good idea of this area. Grab my jeans and take off to the right of the direction you're facing. I'll feed you more information as you need it.*

Amazingly, without a mouthy reply, Ares bit the jeans rolled up around Corbin's sneakers. He trotted forward six steps, then stopped to look back.

Pixie stared at the carnage.

Ares let out a muffled growl.

Lifting her head at the sound, she took in Ares then picked up Eirene's rolled-up clothes and shoes. She trotted over to Ares, following when he took off again.

Corbin had no idea how long this truce would last between his and Eirene's wolves, but the sooner they found a place to hide and heal, the better.

Chapter 18

IRENE GROANED AT shifting again so soon, but now in human form, Corbin stood in front of her, watching their surroundings. He wore his jeans and shoes, but that beautiful male body was naked from the waist up. Why did he get to look badass while she'd end up looking like a wet rag?

Her clothes were on the ground next to her knees. She stood then pulled on her damp shirt and stepped into her crinkled shorts. Thankfully, the warehouse security monitoring unit remained in one pocket of her shorts, and the phone she used for her shifter ladies made it through that run in the other pocket.

How was she going to enter her snooty apartment building looking like a wild-haired homeless woman with filthy shoes?

She quietly said, "I'm dressed."

He glanced around at her. "We have a problem."

Of course they did.

She walked up to where he stood in the shadowed alley across from her apartment building. Everything appeared fine to her. "What's wrong?"

Speaking out of the side of his mouth, he said, "Looks like a male on the roof of your building. He's surveilling the area and may not be alone."

She squinted up at the roof line, waiting until a head moved behind the parapet wall. "Crap."

"I can get to my motorcycle if there's a parking garage we could enter unseen."

"There's no underground parking." What could they do? She considered everywhere she could go and said, "I have somewhere else to go if we aren't followed."

Swinging a smile her way, he said, "Give me a few minutes to meet you at that covered bus stop on this side of the street. Wait until you hear my motorcycle approaching, then step up next to the shelter."

"Okay." She had come a long way since the start of the day for her to agree without knowing all the details.

On the other hand, so had he because Corbin had not questioned where they were going. She had a place owned by the group remodeling the theater. Because of her partnership in the theater, they'd offered it to her as a quiet location where she could practice without anyone bothering her.

She'd used it twice when she managed to slip her security detail. While Corbin was gone, she pulled out her phone to check quickly for a message from Nova. A text waited for her that confirmed she had the sisters and pup. One thing had gone correctly. They were safe with her.

How could it only be a little after ten at night? Her body felt as if the last hours had been stretched into days.

At the sound of a motorcycle that she hoped was Corbin's, she hurried to the bus shelter, standing tucked up close. Would the guy on her apartment building see her?

Corbin flew up to the bus stop, hit his brakes, and she climbed onto the rear seat and hugged his body.

A bullet ripped the edge of the plastic panel on the shelter.

He accelerated so fast from a stop the front end lifted and dropped back down.

Had someone tried to kill her?

A mile away, Corbin pulled over and unhooked the helmet from where it had banged around on the handlebars. "Put this on."

"Stop ordering me around," she groused and yanked the helmet on.

He added, "Please."

She smiled at his effort to sound reasonable, snapped the helmet strap, and then wrapped her arms around him again. "Let's go."

He patted her arm and took off, riding through light traffic with a steady rain this evening. She hoped they did not skid out of control. He handled the bike like a professional racer while still managing not to draw the attention of traffic police.

Corbin wove in and out of the sparse traffic, hurrying ahead when he could. She'd told him the address and how to reach the building, but he took turns that were not part of the route.

Was someone following them?

Her stomach still clenched at the gunshot that struck the bus shelter.

Why would Leszek send someone to kill his golden goose?

That bullet could have struck Corbin. Her throat tightened at the thought. She'd just found him, and she would not let anyone take him from her again.

Corbin had missed her too. That he still cared for her was a gift after all he'd been through. What she felt for him went beyond simple emotions. In school, she'd thought they were fated to be together and then later criticized her foolish thinking when he disappeared. She had never allowed herself to believe she'd find him again, but now that she had, she wanted … everything they could have together.

That sounded good, but she first had to share the dumpster fire her life had become. She would not sugar-coat anything. Treachery and lies had separated them. She still had to find a way to put Leszek in jail and free herself of him.

She had the sense that Corbin had carved out a decent life for himself after escaping the Romanian. She would not allow anything on her part to jeopardize that.

Tightening her arms around his hard body, she held on to

the only person she'd chosen to be in her life. Strong and confident, he took being protective to a whole new level.

She'd watch his back too.

By the time he slowly cruised down the road to the destination she'd directed him to, they were drowned shifters. She shivered with so few clothes on. He pulled up in front of the overhead door to Eirene's street-level parking garage for her secret getaway place.

Taking the bike out of gear, he reached around and helped her off the back, holding on as her legs steadied. She ran over to a security panel and punched in the code they'd given her.

The garage door groaned its way up, and Corbin rode his bike into a cement floor space forty feet wide and thirty feet deep with a twelve-foot ceiling.

She removed her helmet as she followed him, punching the inside panel to lower the door.

Off to one side were metal cabinets and shelves filled with tools, which she assumed someone used to work on vehicles or maybe props for the theater. Above that area hung two long fluorescent light structures currently not lit, but the single security light above the garage door stayed on.

He found a secluded spot to park his motorcycle, turned off the engine, and set the helmet on the seat.

She paused at the silence after traveling in the loud rain.

The same old van and trailer parked in the deep corner to her left had not moved since her last visit. Dust had settled across both vehicles. She had no idea who drove them but hoped they did not visit tonight.

For the first time in many hours, she believed they were safe. At least for the night, and she needed to rest.

Corbin came striding over to her.

She smiled. "That was some impressive riding ..." Her words trailed off at the hungry look in his eyes.

She suddenly lost any interest in sleeping.

He never stopped, lifting her off the floor when he got to her and kissing her senseless by the time she had her legs wrapped around his middle. She gripped his head and tugged him closer. When he broke the kiss, they were both breathless.

"I've wanted that forever. I never could fully convince myself that you had set me up to be captured."

"I'm glad. It broke my heart to hear what happened to you, but it would have been worse to find out you never wanted to see me again."

He chuckled. "I convinced myself I would find you and get answers. The truth is I was going to find you." He brushed a hand over her wet hair. "I want you so bad I'm in pain, but I won't ask for anything you aren't ready for."

"You're in luck. I've been ready to be with you for a long time." She leaned in and kissed him with a loud smack and laughed. Was worth it to see him grinning.

"Tell me where to go. We're not doing this on a cement floor."

A zing of heat ripped through her at his declaration. They'd been kids the first time they met, but they were two adults who knew exactly what they wanted. She was entirely on board with what he had in mind. "Elevator off to my right to the second floor then the first door you find when we get there."

She hadn't felt this free or happy in all the years she'd been alone, waiting for a miracle to bring him back to her. She bit his lip.

He growled and cupped her bottom, carrying her to the elevator.

By the time the elevator stopped, and Corbin carried her out, her top was half off. She wanted the shorts gone even faster.

"Any chance this place has a shower?" he ground out.

"Yes!" Great idea. She should have thought of it first. "Let me down."

"No."

She laughed at his disgruntled answer. "Let me down and we'll get to the shower faster."

He grinned at her and kissed her again, but in a slow,

thorough way. Breathing heavily, he admitted, "I've missed you for so long without knowing what all I was missing. You are everything to me, but are you sure about this?" Genuine concern came through his words.

Her heart did a crazy happy dance. "I dreamed of our first kiss. I wanted to hear you say you want to be with me as much as I want to be with you. Yes, I am sure. You mean the world to me." She ran her hand over his cheek, studying every sharp angle. "Let's go shower."

Lowering her down the front of his body, he held her close and hugged her. She could feel his hard length against her stomach and shuddered with her own need. "Now. I need you now."

She grabbed his hand and hauled him through the open space where she often sang alone and then through a door to a small apartment she'd used to catch naps after long days. It came complete with a shower. Nothing spectacular, but when she'd been dirty, cold, and wet for hours, she didn't need extravagant.

Just hot water, soap, and towels.

This shower could accommodate two people at the same time.

Spectacular.

He had her shirt completely off and flipped away, then knelt to pull her shorts slowly down her legs. He was killing her. "Faster."

"No."

She laughed again. "Are you always going to be this difficult?"

"Yes." Then he gave her a wicked smile and added, "When it comes to making love to you." He reached up and touched a breast, moving his palm slowly over her hard nipple. She gripped his shoulders, hanging on when her legs shook.

With her shorts around her ankles, he freed his other hand to run a finger through her folds, back and forth at too slow a pace. She groaned, "Faster."

"No."

Damn! He played with her other breast and changed the speed of stroking her. She clenched her legs and held on to him, pleading, "Don't … stop."

He answered by upping the speed of his fingers between her legs.

She cried out. Her knees buckled, but he caught her and pulled her to him, continuing his assault until she fell limp in his arms. He was kissing her face and eyes.

Never had an orgasm been that fast or that explosive. This was going to be amazing because she wasn't done.

He whispered, "We're not done."

Had she said that out loud?

Standing, he lifted her with him until her feet hit the floor. When she stepped out of her shorts and turned to him, he'd shed his jeans.

Yay for commando.

Giving him a long, hard look because one part of him deserved it, she said, "You're right. We're not done."

He chuckled and turned her to face the shower. Like a happy sex zombie, she let him, sure they were going to focus on his needs now. He held the door open while he reached in and spun the knobs. Then he wrapped an arm around her to keep her from walking into a blast of cold water.

His hand smoothed down across her abdomen to delve between her legs again.

She gripped each side of the glass structure, shocked that her body could be ready again. When he pulled his hand away, she whined, "No."

He laughed. "That's my word."

"Starting now, we share everything."

Laughing harder, he nudged her forward until hot water blasted over her tingling skin. She hadn't thought much about having sex with him when they first met, but she had a feeling it had been on his mind. Even so, she knew in her heart he would not have rushed them to this point even back then.

With Corbin gone, she had resigned herself to never having a one and only.

She'd been right. No one else could have filled his shoes.

She wanted to stay together, but she would not rush him either. He deserved all the time he needed to make a step as big as she had in mind.

Corbin found the soap and lathered his large hands then began washing her hips and stomach with languid circles.

Every touch of his fingers brought her back to the edge again, but slower than that first time. She wanted to hold out for as long as her body could take it.

He leaned around to kiss her cheek.

She reached up to wrap her hands around the back of his neck, trembling at the way he drove her need higher.

"I like that. Hold on tight," he ordered.

Then his hands moved to her breasts, making both his personal playground at the same time. She trembled and lost her grip.

He stopped. "Hold on."

Could she really do that while he teased her into insanity? She wanted him to keep going, so back her hands went.

His thumbs massaged under her breasts, relaxing her. Then his hands wrapped around her breasts until he held her nipples between thumb and finger. What he did next shot heat from her womb to her folds. She cried out as one hand moved down to tease her folds into a frenzy. Holding back was impossible. She let go and arched, raising up on her toes, reaching, reaching, then … breaking into shards of happiness. Her mind went places she'd never experienced.

What a mistake that human man had been.

Sex was only a physical release with someone she had no investment in. He'd known it from day one, too.

But lovemaking with Corbin reached a completely different level, one that couldn't be achieved with a stranger.

"I can't take more," she muttered when she realized he held her off the ground with one arm.

His voice had a rough edge. "You never know what you can do until you have the opportunity to find out."

That sounded like a sexy threat.

She reveled in the feel of his arms holding her for long enough to regain her equilibrium then dragged herself upright. "Really? Let's find out your breaking point."

He spun her around and ran his hands into her hair, holding her close as he kissed her as if he'd never tasted anything so fine. His chiseled mouth toyed with her lips, her cheeks, and onto her neck.

Smiling had never come easily to her after losing Corbin, but she couldn't wipe the silly grin off her face now. She looped her arms around his neck and began rubbing herself on his dick.

He let out a throaty groan and hoisted her up to his waist again. She accommodated him by wrapping her legs around his waist.

Finally, she'd managed to give him a taste of what he'd been doing to her.

He looked down at her with water splashing off his face and upper chest like a Titan in a storm. When she moved up against him, he grabbed her hips. "Careful. It's been a long time."

Her mind jumped to who he'd been with, but years had passed, and she'd been with someone. As shifters, their bodies burned away any germs or disease. She would not hold anything over him that happened while he was captured and mistreated.

"Are you angry at what I said?" he asked with a sick look on his face. "They brought females in during my first year. I was half out of my mind and wanted to feel the touch of a female more than sex. After two times, I couldn't stomach being around those women. I kept seeing your face and wanting you."

Just the fact that he said it had been a long time reminded her that his life had not been easy, not filled with dating and laughter. No love.

She had plenty to give him. She laid her head on his chest. "I had a dark period after my father died. I tried to outrun the pain with a human male, but it was short-lived. I regretted my lack of control, which was before I found out he was more interested in the life of a celebrity than anything." Lifting her gaze to Corbin, she smiled. "If he'd known what a nightmare my life has become, he'd have run screaming before I kicked him out. You angry with me?"

Shaking his head, he said, "I care too much about you to be angry over something I wasn't here to help you with."

Tears ran down her face. "I'm so glad you're with me right now."

Lifting her up to him, he kissed her tears, then made love to her mouth. She held his face in her hands.

He held her heart in his.

The more his lips demanded of hers, the more her body wanted to claim his.

Moving up and down, she moaned at the heat stirring between her legs.

His hand reached between them and stroked a finger inside her.

She tightened her muscles and held on. "I want you inside me this time."

His eyes darkened with a hungry need that matched hers. This close, she could see streaks of gold through his sultry brown gaze. When he slid his finger from her, she lifted her hips and rubbed the head of his length, then eased herself down one inch at a time.

He stilled. His big body shook. Dropping his forehead to hers, he dragged in one hard breath after another. "You feel incredible. I am so damned lucky to have you in my arms."

This morning, she wanted nothing to do with another man.

Right now, she could not imagine being without this one.

Moving in and out at a snail's pace at first had her ready to beg again.

Her leg muscles were strong from years in dance classes.

She used them to grip him harder. His fingers tightened on her bottom then he relaxed them as if worried he'd bruise her.

Shifter here. She could take anything he dished out. "Don't hold back," she said before sliding up and down faster.

A growling sound rumbled up his throat. He gripped her hips and took over setting the pace, pushing hard, pulling out slowly, then back in deep again.

Pleasure grew from a hot spot to a burning surge in her belly.

His hand found her breasts and tormented the tips of her nipples with his rough thumbs. She bit down hard to keep from crying out.

He hammered into her faster and slipped a finger down to stroke her. She clutched his arms, her fingernails digging in, and arched up, calling his name on a long wail. He exploded right behind her, filling her with warmth.

She rode him until he slowed down and pulled her safely against him. He rubbed a gentle hand up and down her wet back. She finally noticed the water streaming off her skin. Her arms fell limp at her sides.

He throbbed once more inside her, and then he was done.

Another big old smile curved her lips.

Life with him would be amazing. She had to tamp down on her feelings. They were safe and happy in this moment, but she had problems that could bury them both. To be fair, she had to fix her mess before thinking about a future with anyone, especially a future with him.

Tomorrow would show up with plenty of headaches.

She would shove all that away so they could have tonight for themselves.

They stayed wrapped up together under the shower until she could lift her arms to his shoulders and bring her face up to his. She kissed his chin and cheeks then his mouth. His tongue darted in to play with hers.

His hands massaged her bottom and moved too close to the hot zone.

"I vote we grab some rest and … who knows what might happen." She gave him a cheeky grin.

His eyes glistened with happiness. "I'm going to enjoy keeping that smile on your face."

This man held the power over her happiness. The young boy who offered her friendship so long ago had grown into an exceptional man.

Finding him again was a gift she could not squander because she'd never want another man as her mate.

Hopefully, one day, Corbin would want that too. In the meantime, she'd do her best to keep that contented look on his face.

She could easily love Corbin, but trust meant everything to her. She had never discovered it with any other man, but she trusted Corbin with her entire being.

It dawned on her that as a shifter she didn't have to worry about diseases, but she did have a responsibility as a female shifter to let a man know if she was in heat.

"I should have let you know first, but I'm not in heat," she said, getting that off her chest. She had to be honest with him for Corbin to gain trust in her.

"I stayed away from female shifters in heat, but to be honest … I never gave it a thought." His throat moved as he swallowed, then finished, "We've had a tough time getting together, but now that I know everything that happened, I trust you. You're even prettier than you were as a young girl, which kept me tongue-tied. That's why I wrote a note." He laughed. "I spent time learning to whittle. I'm not good at it, but I wanted to give you something that was mine alone."

Her womb voted him the greatest man on earth. "I have that wolf in a safe to ensure nothing ever happens to it. I'd like to give you a gift, but I'm not good at making things." She laid her head on his shoulder.

"In that case, I'd love to hear you sing sometime."

She raised her head. Her lips parted. "You've never heard me sing?"

"No. I heard about it in school, but I was never in the

right place at the right time. Once the Romanian got me, I had no access to televisions or radios. We stayed off the grid."

Her heart tapped at a jubilant pace. "Let's get some rest and warm up my vocal cords in the morning. Then I'll give you a private concert."

"I can't wait." He turned off the shower and stepped out to snag a thick towel for her and another for him.

She dried off and toweled her hair. It wouldn't be event-ready when she woke up, but she didn't care. Putting on a look was for fans, not Corbin.

When they made it to the bedroom, he yanked the cover back and pulled her down with him, then rolled onto his side. She snuggled back against him, eliciting an exaggerated painful sound that had her laughing until he eased her back to spoon against his body.

He whipped the covers over them. "Is an alarm set?"

"Yes. If anyone opens a door or tries to get in a window, it will activate a shrieking alarm even if it's the building owner. They meant it when they said I would be safe here."

"Good. I normally sleep light, but … woman, you wore me out."

"Don't worry. I'll protect you."

He pinched her butt, and she laughed louder.

Outside this building, she had a world of problems, but tonight she would not care. Together, they'd figure out their lives going forward. She soaked up the heat of his body and fell deep asleep.

Chapter 19

TOWEL DRYING HIS hair after an early morning shower, Corbin strolled over to where he'd deposited a small duffel bag filled with the few belongings he'd brought up from his bike after waking. Eirene said she had stored casual clothes and shoes here to prevent having to visit her apartment first when she needed a couple hours of downtime.

Last night, Eirene had teased that she'd keep him safe. Sixteen seconds later, she'd fallen sound asleep. He chuckled over his thoroughly loved woman, then kept her next to him for the best night of sleep he'd had in years.

She whispered words to a song in her sleep. He'd never heard anything so charming.

He could hear her warming up her voice in the shower. He was learning so many things about her like the fact that she wanted to be loved at all hours. She'd awakened early this morning and poked him.

He'd jumped up thinking a threat was nearby until she leaned over and sucked him into her mouth.

He got hard again just thinking about it and muttered, "Down, boy. I can't walk like this." Dropping onto a low back sofa too stylish to be comfortable, he put on the boots he'd left in his saddle bag last night when he opted for running shoes. Glad to have a clean gray T-shirt, he had to figure out what to do today.

Propping his boots on a low glass coffee table supported by four large rocks, he picked up the mobile phone he'd left stashed in his tank bag when he followed Eirene to the warehouse last night.

Six in the morning should be a good time to call Adrian. He punched the button.

Adrian answered, "Where have you been?"

Corbin pulled the phone away. He hadn't had a mobile phone before now and realized he'd missed calls from Adrian. "Sorry. Last night was enlightening and almost deadly. I didn't have my phone with me until this morning."

"Hmm. Sounds like you need to fill me in."

Corbin went over everything and cringed but admitted, "We came to a place Eirene said the theater let her use sometimes that fans didn't know about. She hadn't even told her trustee about this place. She wanted somewhere she could have some privacy."

Adrian didn't say anything, which had Corbin ready to squirm. How was he going to explain what a good job he'd done watching over Eirene? All night.

"Any idea who sent the jackal shifters?" Adrian asked.

"No. My guess would be SCIS, but those two had unnatural muscles and smelled like shifters my wolf and I have fought in the past that had been doing Jugo Loco. I had no choice but to shift and release Ares. He killed them but not without paying a price."

"What about Eirene? Did her wolf help Ares?"

"No. Her wolf is not dominant. Eirene said her wolf can't kill anyone, and neither can she."

Ares hadn't spoken all night, but piped up, *Her wolf needs protecting.*

Corbin couldn't decide if Ares considered Pixie useless or if he meant … that he would protect her. Interesting.

"You think that's true, Corbin?"

"I know it is." The minute those words left his lips, Corbin regretted the way he'd answered.

"Why are you so sure?" Adrian asked.

"She told me so, and I heard truth."

"You don't believe she's involved in killing Beckham's men?"

Corbin knew when he was being maneuvered into a corner. In too deep at this point, he refused to play games or lie to Adrian. "I knew Eirene when I was in high school. We were the only two shifters hiding among humans. Her father was very wealthy and had two human bodyguards who protected her. I wanted to be her friend. I left a message in her locker to meet me at a place where I'd located her scent. She had planned to meet me that night, but her bodyguards saw me put the note in the locker and captured me. They handed me over to the Romanian."

Adrian was nothing if not patient and fair, but his words came out loaded with disappointment. "You should have told me before coming on this operation."

For all the joy Corbin felt at finding Eirene and having last night with her, he hated having broken Adrian's trust. "I agree. I originally planned to keep my feelings to myself and finish this job. If she ended up guilty, I would have handed you the evidence you needed. If she had been innocent, I wanted to ask her why she'd ruined my life. Neither happened. I'm sorry I broke your trust. I didn't start out to do that."

"We'll have to discuss this back at the compound. I'm neck deep with digging into the security team, and you have to stick with her because it sounds like someone's trying to kill her."

"I will not allow anyone to harm her," Corbin declared. "What's happening with her team?" Would Adrian let him push them off the topic of Eirene?

"Brody is a roaring pain in the ass."

"That's not new information," Corbin pointed out.

"No. What I did learn was that the other two on his team don't like him. They didn't say anything specific. It's more about what they didn't say. Brody knows I'm a shifter, but he isn't intimidated. I've let him think I'm Beckham's yes man."

Corbin snorted at that. "First rule in any conflict is to never underestimate those around you."

"Very true, but I've kept my power locked down. The

minute I started asking questions, Brody got huffy and told me he ran security on site. He wanted to know why he had not been informed of my coming in. I told him my schedule was none of his business. He carried on that Ms. Givenchy was his responsibility and that everything about her was his business. I found that amusing since not one of those three had tried to follow Givenchy when she left the theater."

Anger climbed up Corbin's neck at whoever had been protecting her before him. "No shit. All three are worthless."

"Archie is still in a deep coma," Adrian continued. "The hospital staff told Beckham that Brody keeps trying to get in to visit Archie. They won't allow anyone in while he's in a coma. The police are first in line to talk to him. I wonder if he was behind the deaths of the first two team members. If so, was it ego-driven to reach the top, or does he have some other ulterior motive?"

"I don't know, but too many details are starting to point at him."

"Hold on." Adrian spoke to someone who let him know two men were at the theater to repair the damage, and it would take three hours. Adrian gave him the okay and got back on the phone. "Well, damn. I spent last night on the roof watching in case someone showed up to go inside. No one came by. I haven't seen Brody and his two people since they realized they couldn't find Eirene yesterday. He stormed over to me this morning, demanding to know your name and where you were."

Corbin thought about the overbearing guard. "I wondered if Brody had anything to do with the shot fired last night from the top of Eirene's apartment building, but I don't see the reason anyone would try to kill Eirene."

"Was it meant for you?"

"I'm considering that. I'm causing a kink in someone's dirty machinery. I wonder if the same person who ordered that shot sent the jackal shifters after me, but I haven't figured out how they found us at her warehouse. From all I've learned, she's been doing a good job keeping it secret. If I had not been tasked with keeping up with her, I wouldn't have taken off on foot to follow her. I know I wasn't tracked. Those jackals arrived in a car. They didn't track us."

"Shit fire!" Adrian grumbled. "If you've got a target on your back, we need to take you out of the field."

Corbin sighed. Guess he had to disappoint Adrian again. "Please don't ask me to leave her side. I can't do it."

Adrian cursed under his breath. "You do realize how unprofessional that sounds, don't you?"

"Yes."

"What's really going on with you two?"

Time to come clean. "She's the woman I want as my mate."

Adrian started saying, "Are you, uhm ..." Noises came through that sounded as if he banged the phone on something. Then he came back. "Are you sure or are you only saying she's special?"

"I'm sure. She's special, and she *is* the one for me. I believe she feels the same way, but we haven't had a chance to discuss the future, plus with everything going on in each of our lives. I never expected to have a mate once I ended up with the Romanian, but now that I've found Eirene again, she's all I want."

Sighing loudly into the phone, Adrian said, "I'm starting to understand how much grief my Gallize brothers gave our boss. Okay, we'll table that discussion for right now, but I understand your position. Can you follow orders that don't conflict with Eirene being your potential mate?"

"Without question. What do you want me to do?"

"Stay put until I get back to you."

He could do that. "I appreciate all you and Jaz have done for me, Adrian. I made it my mission to impress you on this job. Sorry I failed you."

"Listen, Corbin. You've done a great job so far, but ..." Adrian paused for a few seconds. Was he going to admit he'd made a mistake with Corbin? Sounding bone tired, Adrian said, "I had no plans to separate us and leave you to watch our client alone, but I knew I could trust you to keep her safe even while she was a suspect in this operation."

Corbin felt that compliment deep in his chest. "I intended to even when I thought she'd thrown me to the Romanian."

"Jaz and I watched what you did for Badger. He's a crazy loon and a misery to deal with most days, but he is salvageable. You stepped in and kept him from shifting and attacking me or Jaz. That might have ended in his death. We want to give everyone in the pack a chance at a real life. I'm good at sizing people up quickly. I knew when I brought you with me that you would have my back and follow orders. You have. We'll take that into consideration when I debrief this operation with my boss. He'll have the ultimate say on your future."

Corbin had only wanted somewhere to hide until he came up with a new plan for how to evade the Romanian. That changed when Adrian showed faith in Corbin. At that point, he'd wanted a place in this world and that loony pack.

To have a home and others he could count on.

The eagle shifter boss was not Adrian.

All Corbin's plans for him and Eirene had no more support right now than a house built with tissue.

"They're calling me over for something to do with the repairs," Adrian complained. "If Brody doesn't show soon, I'm going out to hunt for him. Don't leave where you are without letting me know."

"Yes, sir."

"If you can't reach me, call the second number in your phone. That's Cole."

"No worries, Adrian. I've got this." He did his best to build back a little faith with Adrian.

Corbin ended the call and listened for singing. It had stopped. Was she dressed yet?

Footsteps pounding toward him brought his attention all the way around to where he found her wearing a long-sleeved green T-shirt, jeans, and running across the room in clean white sneakers, barreling toward him.

She shouted, "*We have to get out now!*"
What the hell?

Chapter 20

IRENE HAD A denim bag slung over her shoulder. Did Corbin not hear her? She repeated her words with more urgency as she neared him. "*We. Have. To. Go!*"

Corbin moved faster than lightning and jumped up, grabbing her shoulders so they didn't collide. "What's wrong?"

Seeing fury in his face worried her until she realized it was out of concern for her. "Police and SCIS are on the way here. I got a text from my trustee, the bastard. He learned that I had been seen leaving my apartment on your motorcycle. He sent the police and SCIS for you!"

"How would he even know we're here or who I am?"

"I don't know. We don't have time to talk."

Corbin offered, "I could call my people and get help with this."

"No, you can't. If they're shifters too, Leszek will not hesitate to send a horde of monsters after them. He's willing to do anything to keep full control of his golden goose. I think Leszek likely cut a deal with SCIS to leave me alone as long as I'm his responsibility. I also think he has the police in his pockets."

A siren shrilled in the distance.

He gave her a look stuffed with incredulity. He grabbed the bag from her shoulder, tossed his phone into it, and hooked the strap over his shoulder. "Is there another way into the garage from the outside besides the overhead door at the street?"

Standing still, she stared at nothing, then snapped her fingers. "There's a refuse elevator rarely used with no one permanently living in the building. The access is a smaller garage door on the rear of the building. There's a little road out there for any tenant to use."

"Perfect." He vibrated with the need to move. "Ready to go?"

"Yes." She did not add that she was terrified after being shot at last night, but she *had* asked the universe for ninja skills.

Her request had been answered in an on-the-job training sort of way.

"Stay with me." He gripped her hand and towed her to the stairs he'd noted this morning.

Watching his every move, she hurried down behind on the pads of her feet, mimicking his low-noise descent.

He opened the door to the basement floor, looked around, and pulled her out behind him.

Sirens wailed, getting closer.

Calm and confident, he strode across the floor to where a sign above a door warned not to enter the trash collection area. It was locked.

He asked, "Do you have anything like a hairpin?"

"No, but I have a universal key to this building." She dug it out and handed the key to him.

"Love it." He kissed her quickly and opened the door to look inside, then handed the key back to her. "Stand here while I get the bike."

He ran over to his bike, kicked the stand up, then leaned it into him and wheeled it over to where she held the door open.

Once in the trash area with the access door locked behind them, she heard the streetside garage door roll up and voices coming into the building. She ran to catch up with Corbin, who now had his bike in front of the smaller garage door. He released the manual locks at the bottom on each side and slowly rolled the door up.

When it was far enough for them to get out with the motorcycle, he said, "Sounds like people went upstairs first to search and are now coming back down. Put on the helmet. The minute I start the bike, jump on and hold tight. Which way should we go?"

"I don't know. Left?" she guessed since she'd never exited from the back of the building. She had the helmet on and strapped when he started the bike. She hopped on and wrapped her arms around him, hoping they could escape.

Corbin rode the bike out and along the paved area to the left. Beyond a chain link fence bordering that road were train tracks. He slid to a stop. This paved area at the back did not connect to a road on the left end.

They couldn't get out.

Evidently, that did not faze Corbin, who made a tight U-turn and raced back the way he'd come. As he passed the still-open trash garage door, a man wearing an SCIS uniform ran outside shouting at their backs.

At the other end of the building, she could see a sort-of outlet that wrapped around to the front.

A trained ninja would have known every exit point.

She should never play craps with her kind of luck. She called out, "Sorry. I didn't know."

He patted her hand on his stomach, and she stopped worrying. Leszek and others had criticized her every move if it didn't suit their goals, but Corbin blew off a bad decision by moving on.

When Corbin closed to within fifteen yards of the corner, he went wide left and leaned into a sharp right turn.

When they rounded the end of the building, a black sport utility drove slowly toward them and stayed close to the building as if trying to sneak around without alerting anyone.

Too late for that.

Corbin had a narrow gap between that vehicle and a continuation of the tall chain-link fence.

He moved the bike as far left as possible.

She shut her eyes. She believed in Corbin's ability to

split that space but couldn't watch with her heart hiding in her throat.

The bike leaned right again. She held onto him for dear life.

When the lean ended, she peeked around his shoulder. They had passed the sport utility, but police cruisers, an SCIS vehicle, and four officers were between them and their exit point to the road.

They spread out. What were they thinking?

That Corbin would wreck trying to weave between them, which might have worked if he hadn't hunkered down and ridden the bike up a flower-landscaped embankment that sent them airborne over the driveway.

Corbin landed the bike on the rear tire.

Rubber squealed, the front dropped down, then he sped away.

She felt dizzy from the terror and hope that hugged each other until the bike stabilized.

If she ever did a reality show, this would be the man she'd want as a partner who had quiet confidence under pressure. He didn't yell at her for making a mistake on which way to go. Her confidence grew by staying calm, trying not to distract him in a hairy situation.

He called over his shoulder, "Did I scare you?"

Lying would be useless. "A little."

His hand dropped down to pat her knee. "You did great."

She hadn't realized she'd been waiting on someone who could share the good and bad of her life, but she never believed she could trust another male enough to open her heart again after losing Corbin.

In hindsight, she'd been right.

Sirens filled the air—more than one.

Corbin yelled, *"Lock your hands at my waist and don't loosen them for anything!"*

Oh, no. That didn't sound good, but she did exactly what he said. Her heart hadn't slowed down from that last stunt. Pounding frantically now, she wondered if a shifter had ever died of a heart attack.

She refused to allow that to happen and distract Corbin.

He took two turns, then another one, then one more to emerge back on the road they'd been on heading away from the theater group's building.

Now the bike was pointed back the way they'd come.

What was he doing? Sirens were getting louder.

Cars ahead were peeling off to each side of the two-lane road. The police cruisers had nothing slowing them down.

Not police cruisers. Those were SCIS. A rifle poked out from a rear passenger window on the right side followed by the upper body of a man pulling the weapon up to take aim.

Corbin shouted, "Keep your head down!"

She felt his shoulder move with him pulling her denim bag free before he twisted his neck and gave a quick glance back before looking forward again. He gripped the top of the bag in his left fist as the motorcycle screamed toward the guy with the rifle who held it pointed at Corbin.

A bullet struck a sign they passed. She clamped her mouth shut to keep a scream caught inside.

The bike roared closer to the attacking vehicle, clearly passing on the shooter's side.

She heard another crack from the rifle but had no idea where that bullet went.

In the next seconds, Corbin swung her bag, knocking the rifle upward, which smacked the shooter's head. Then he yanked the bag back and shoved it over his shoulder. "Put it between us."

She fumbled with the one task he had given her but managed to stuff the bag into her lap and locked her arms around him again.

He made multiple fast turns right and left, leaving her confused about where they were until he rolled onto the interstate. When he rode north on Interstate 26, she let out the breath that had backed up in her lungs at leaving Spartanburg.

Safe, for a minute.

How far could they go before someone found them again?

Chapter 21

CORBIN RODE THE bike as fast as he could without drawing attention. He'd taken the Interstate 85 west exit and hoped he guessed correctly. Before escaping, Eirene had indicated that her trustee, the infamous Leszek Moore, probably had a financial deal with SCIS.

That he might even be paying off cops.

Leaving South Carolina for Georgia could be a giant mistake, but if Leszek knew he was with Eirene, then her trustee likely knew about Adrian, who had a direct line to his badass boss.

Riding to the compound would put Jaz and the others at risk.

With them as far from him as possible, he was willing to stake his life for Eirene's protection, but he would not impose that fate on anyone else. Not even Adrian. He'd call Adrian as soon as they stopped for fuel to let him know what was going on, and that while his boss carried weight with a lot of people, Corbin's actions with Eirene could put a target on his entire organization.

No alpha wanted that kind of trouble and certainly not from someone with Corbin's past with the Romanian.

Could Vlad be involved in any of this or working with Leszek? That made no sense. Why would Leszek put Eirene in jeopardy if she were his golden goose, as she'd put it? Still, Corbin could have been tracked if someone tagged his motorcycle. Based on things Adrian had said about using special phones his organization used, he doubted that someone could track his phone.

Since Adrian's people possessed highly sophisticated equipment for hunting criminals and finding their people, SCIS might have an equally advanced level of electronics to support their jackal shifters.

But how had Leszek figured out Eirene was with him or where her secret apartment was located?

Corbin tried to fit it all together, but he kept finding holes in his theory.

If Leszek knew about Eirene's warehouse, why hadn't he simply sent his security team to pick her up before now? That would mean she'd done a great job of keeping her rescue work away from him.

If that was the case, where had those two freak jackal shifters come from? Would they be working with SCIS when other shifters could smell the difference and see it when they shifted?

That didn't hold water, which would mean someone else sent those two jackals.

His head hurt from trying to sort out so many things at once while lacking the necessary information.

His fuel tank would be on fumes soon. Watching for an exit, he pulled off on Highway 17 for Lavonia, Georgia, and easily located a place to gas up. Pulling in under the fuel station canopy, he cut the motor and let Eirene step off first. With the bike on the stand, he turned to see how she was doing.

She pulled the helmet off then started fussing with her helmet hair. "I need a cap. I hate what that does to my hair."

He chuckled and kept his voice soft for her ears only. "We do a mad dash from police and SCIS, plus get shot at again, and you're worried about how you look?"

She pushed her nose up at him. "I do not want to die looking like a crazy woman."

Reaching out, he brushed a hand over her hair. "No matter the condition of your hair, you will always look adorable."

She gave him a smile that melted his heart. How had he lived all those years without her? He leaned down to kiss her sweet lips, intending to simply let her know how glad he was to have her.

Eirene, he was starting to realize, went all in when she wanted something.

She pushed up on her toes, deepening the kiss and waking every part of his body. He lifted her up, finished the kiss, then eased her back. "Keep that up and we'll be here awhile making a public exhibition."

"Don't threaten me with having my way with a hot male."

"You'll be the death of me, and I'm gonna love every minute, but we can't stop until we find a safe spot." Placing her back on her feet, he said, "Hungry?"

"Starving. I've got some cash in my bag, but not much. I gave the sisters all but fifty dollars thinking I'd run by the bank today."

"We're good. I've got some money." Not enough for him to run for long, but after thinking about who had sent the jackals, he'd decided to locate a safe place for her. Then he'd lead those monsters away from her. He assumed they'd keep sending monster jackals after them. Maybe he could keep one alive long enough to find out who had sent them and how they'd found him.

SCIS would be his first guess for who held the leash on those jackals, but … it could be the Romanian.

"I'm going to the bathroom," she announced, pulling the denim bag strap onto her shoulder.

He dug out a fifty-dollar bill. "Would you give this to the cashier with our pump number?" While Corbin filled the bike tank, he came up with what he'd tell Adrian. It might sever his last tie with a man Corbin held in high regard, but he would never harm anyone when he could avoid it.

Eirene came hurrying back to him as he hung up the nozzle. Why was she rushing? His heart went into overdrive. How could he have let her go in there alone?

He looked around for the threat.

"Crap. Look what I found in the bag." Out of breath

as she stopped, she lifted two mobile phones. Both had chunks missing. "Had to be that SCIS shooter in the car. I didn't know where that second rifle shot went, but I guess we do now."

Ah hell. He took both phones. "The good news is no one can trace your phone, but I only had one way to contact my people."

"No one could trace my phone. It was not on any network. Like some people call a burner phone."

He considered that. He could grab one of those phones that were not on a network, but he had no idea what numbers had been programmed into his. "Mine could not be tracked directly to me. It had some kind of relay or such that sent a tracer to my people's headquarters. They had their own way to find my phone."

His stomach growled. Much as he wanted to take off again, he had to be more careful now. The jackals and Leszek might not be able to track them, but they had far more resources at their fingertips than he and Eirene.

They loaded up, and he rode a half mile to a steak restaurant with plenty of business an hour before noon. He and Eirene should blend in with T-shirts and jeans. Seats at the bar were available, which meant faster service in his book.

Eirene gave polite smiles to the perky red-haired female bartender with heavily made-up green eyes, but he could tell his woman worked to hide her nerves. He reached under the counter and squeezed Eirene's thigh lightly.

She turned an electric smile his way. That was her truly happy smile.

They ordered the largest steaks offered, baked potatoes, broccoli, corn, and bread. Shifters burned calories easily. Shifters on the run ran through huge amounts of calories. He hoped to find food again without having to send their wolves hunting.

While chowing down quickly but not so much to draw anyone's attention, Corbin noticed Eirene had been staring at the end of the bar where a waiter and two waitresses were huddled. They talked excitedly as if sharing juicy gossip on someone major.

He ate the last of his potato and pushed the plate away, downed his iced tea, and asked Eirene, "Did you eat enough?"

She tore her gaze from the gossip corner and nodded. "I'm good. Considering the condition of our phones, I'm happy to report the energy bars I'd packed made it through."

He grinned at her attempt to find humor in the loss. "Good news as this may be the last normal meal for a while."

When the bartender called to one of the females talking at the end of the bar, that waitress hurried down to pick up her drink order on this end. The bartender reached out and stopped the waitress with a touch of her hand. She asked, "What's going on?"

Glancing at the two she'd walked away from, the waitress said, "Ernie's brother-in-law is a highway patrolman. He says between here and the next exit heading west, they're setting up a roadblock on the interstate."

"That's nuts. They'll back up traffic for miles."

The waitress nodded. "I think that's the plan. They'll close all our exits here coming and going. They're hunting …" She leaned in and whispered, "Dangerous shifters."

The red-haired bartender stood up quickly. Her face turned chalky white.

Nodding to show she agreed, the waitress lifted her tray of drinks and walked away.

Eirene turned a grim face to Corbin. He placed more than enough cash for the food and tip on the counter. "Let's go."

Hooking her hand on his arm, Eirene stared straight ahead as they calmly left the restaurant. He strapped her helmet on and tucked the denim bag into a saddle bag, then stood up the bike for her to climb on.

With each little action, he struggled to decide where to head then started the bike.

Eirene leaned close to his ear. "I looked at a map inside the gas station store. If this bike is as good off-road as you showed me earlier, and we're looking for a remote location, we should take 17 north. That might offer better escape routes."

"You may be right." His gut twisted at what he had to ask her. "I think these people could be after me more than you. Whether it's SCIS or the Romanian, we have to expect more dangerous jackals coming after us. If you called Leszek and said you were coming back, would you be safer in Spartanburg?"

She gripped his shoulder and pulled him around. "No. I believe Leszek killed my father to take over as trustee of my life and finances. Someone has been killing security guards. I can't finger anyone who would do that, not even him. But he's the only person I fear in all this. He might try to force me into his mental hospital involuntarily to make me sign a form making him my permanent guardian. I'm done running scared. My vulnerable shifter females are safe. I'm staying with you."

He had no idea how much she'd shouldered on her own. Wrapping his fingers around her small fist clutching his shirt, he held them and swore, "I will not let that bastard near you."

Her fingers relaxed. "We'll fight him together."

"Don't ever tell me you're not dominant. It only takes something you want to fight for to draw out your alpha side."

"That might be the nicest thing anyone has ever said to me about being a shifter." She blinked her watery eyes.

He lifted her hand and kissed it. "I need you to listen to me even if I tell you to run or hide. Staying safe is the greatest thing you can do to help me."

"I don't want to agree to that." She struggled to continue but said, "I will do as you ask and not let you down."

"Thank you. Let's hit the road."

He kept the speed even on Highway 17 as they cruised by the gas station they'd stopped at earlier. When he rode north across the interstate overpass, he could feel Eirene tense.

On the interstate west of the exit, law enforcement

vehicles, including a SWAT van, had already restricted all but one lane of traffic in each direction.

Personal passenger four-wheel vehicles and over-the-road trucks were allowed to keep traveling on the one open lane closest to the median. He spotted a police officer approaching a pair of motorcycles caught up in the stopped lanes.

Corbin looked forward.

He'd been on the run before with fewer resources and knew what to do, but he'd been alone. His plan to keep Eirene safe by hiding her crumbled under her last admission.

When running from predators before, his only goal had been to escape or die trying. Now he had to focus entirely on survival.

Could he keep the two of them alive?

Chapter 22

V LAD WATCHED A spider web outside the window of the cheap motel that he would leave soon. He enjoyed fine foods and better lodging, but he wanted no one in the United States to learn he'd been on this soil.

Fairly easy to remain under the radar in a country of idiots.

Jackal shifters topped that list. The one talking too much on this phone call tried to justify failure.

Mitch's voice shook as he rushed through what had transpired while Vlad traveled from Chicago to Charlotte, North Carolina, last night. "SCIS had a tip this morning that a rogue wolf shifter was hiding in Spartanburg with that singer Eirene Givenchy. Once they had the pair chained inside an SCIS prison van, I would have sedated the driver at the last minute and replaced him. It would have been so simple to deliver the wolf to you and sell the female."

Mistake number two for Mitch. "You would have offered the woman to someone else?"

"I, uh, thought you only wanted the male."

That was the problem when simpletons like Mitch tried to think for themselves. "I have a very successful network for unloading shifters."

"Sorry, I didn't know."

He was not supposed to know. Vlad pinched the bridge of his nose. "Finish what you have to say in the next sixty seconds."

Talking even faster, Mitch explained how SCIS lost the

two shifters who escaped on a motorcycle going west out of Spartanburg. "Roadblocks have been set on every primary road with warnings about the two of them being dangerous. The reports have not mentioned Givenchy by name. Authorities may be trying to return her to Leszek Moore."

"Who?"

"Her trustee. Powerful physician in the shrink business, among other things. Not a man any shifter wants to cross. He has a direct line to SCIS."

Vlad had heard enough from this dog. "Do you know where the male wolf shifter is right now?"

"Not exactly, but I'm east of Lavonia, Georgia. They were spotted going north after leaving that area fifteen minutes ago. I'm very close and bringing no one with me. There might be someone inside SCIS leaking information. I'll call you as soon as I've got your wolf in hand."

Could this jackal find Corbin as he claimed?

Vlad had his doubts, but the jackal might be closer than anyone else if his information was correct. "Call me immediately."

Mitch's relief washed across the phone line. "Yes, sir. I will. I won't let you down. I'm glad you're allowing me—"

Vlad disconnected the call to end the dribble. He had something else he needed.

Placing a call to the top man in his shifter trafficking business should result in better news.

Iso answered with his usual, "I am at your service."

Vlad had liked Iso from the minute he stole the boy at seven years old. "Have you found a shifter capable of performing the service I need?"

"Absolutely. This one has been well-fed until now. I currently have him chained in animal form with live food tied up six feet away. He will give you a show you won't forget."

"Very good, Iso. Take him close to where you have the helicopter and wait for my call to load and fly him immediately."

"It will be done."

A successful enterprise depended on compiling the best humans in the business.

Chapter 23

EIRENE LOOKED ALL around them, expecting police or SCIS to jump out from behind one of the many trees bordering Highway 17. Not a realistic possibility, she hoped, but she'd gotten to the point of expecting the unexpected.

She could tell they were going up gradually, but there was not enough elevation change to cause her ears to pop.

An average number of cars and trucks passed them heading south.

No one had gawked as if they'd heard about two shifters riding a motorcycle who were being hunted like vicious predators.

Had Leszek and law enforcement kept her identity and Corbin's description out of the news to lull her into thinking they were safe so long as they avoided SCIS or cops?

She wished she could guess what game Leszek played. He would not have sent SCIS after her unless he'd decided she no longer had value. Since he'd spent years getting his hands on the strings to her life and money, that didn't make sense.

He could be trying to destroy Corbin to make her heel at his side.

No more.

She had finally broken out of the emotional and mental chains Leszek had wrapped around her. She'd worry about the financial ones later.

Corbin had taken a wide curve to the left when he called

back to her. "I'm seeing traffic slow to a stop up ahead. Could be a roadblock. I'm getting off this highway."

She took note of them turning onto Highway 23. "Good idea." No point in sharing her worry that they might find SCIS and possibly police waiting for them on the new highway.

Riding for another twenty minutes with heavier traffic, she could see how Tallulah State Park drew so many visitors. The area was as soothing for the soul as the landscape was gorgeous for the eyes, or it would have been if not for her realizing cars were slowing to a stop yet again. She saw no safe exit point.

If they turned around near a roadblock, that would be a red flag to send law enforcement after them.

Before she could ask Corbin what he thought, he showed her. With the traffic ahead of them becoming bumper-to-bumper, he kept the bike upright until he dropped out of the sluggish traffic to take a dirt road off to the right that ran between two wooden posts.

Brilliant. He'd made that change so subtly, the drivers behind them probably thought this had been their destination all along.

Still, she held onto his hips and twisted to see if anyone had caught their deviation from Highway 23. Not yet, but at the roadblock, some of those drivers might volunteer that they saw a motorcycle with a couple leave the main road.

She hoped by the time anyone could alert police to seeing them, they'd have a decent head start.

Moving adroitly as when he'd woven their way through traffic on paved highways, when the dirt road ran out, Corbin began maneuvering around saplings and larger trees. Her fingers might not open after clenching them so hard to hold on and not disturb the balance for him.

It wasn't long before Corbin broke free of the woods to cross an undulating open space.

She slipped into a mindless time when she could do nothing to help and allowed the landscape to fill her thoughts. She'd dropped her head against his back and had almost fallen asleep when he patted her leg.

Shaking off the drowsiness, she watched as he rode the bike through thinning trees and the land climbed slowly. When he reached a small open area, he stopped. "Let's get off and take a break."

She stood on the back highway pegs, proud to remember what they were called, and clutched his shoulders as she stepped down. Her legs ached from being bent so long. Taking the helmet off again, she held it by the strap.

Corbin unzipped his tank bag and pulled out a black plastic disk six inches in diameter. He rolled the bike forward to a more level spot and leaned over to toss the disk on the ground where the kickstand hit.

Oh. That would keep the bike stand from sinking into the ground and the bike from falling.

He walked over to her with a stiff gait and pulled her to him, smothering his face in her hair. "I love your helmet hair."

She expected anything but that and started laughing. "Don't waste your time trying to convince me I'm hot with helmet hair."

Lifting his head, he smiled. "But you are."

He sounded so tired. It wasn't riding the bike. Corbin had a body built to go hard for long periods.

The strain of trying to keep them safe was weighing on him. She went along to keep from adding to his worry. "Want a picnic?"

"Great idea." He sounded excited when he knew they had almost nothing left for food.

While she dug out two bars for each of them, Corbin walked farther up the slight incline. Over the years, weather had worn dirt off the boulders.

Pixie had been quiet for a long time but came to life with a tingle of energy. *Ohhh, water. We should take a swim.*

Eirene listened. Water moved not far from them. She told Pixie, *There could be more jackals like Ares fought last night chasing us. May not be able to swim right now.*

I see, her wolf sighed, then went silent.

Finished pulling out what she and Corbin needed, she grabbed a bath towel that would have to do for a tablecloth. Not that they cared about getting dirty, but she wanted to treat Corbin and take his mind off everything for a while.

She followed where he'd hiked and found him standing next to a tree with six feet of land between him and a drop-off. Now she heard the roaring water. Looking over the cliff, she found white water rushing down below the way it had for probably centuries, wearing down the rock and dirt of a gorge.

"Pixie loves water. It's hard to keep her out of it. She'd dive in from here if we weren't running for our lives." Would this be near Tallulah Gorge? Wasn't it a series of waterfalls? She'd heard snippets about this area and had thought Tallulah River was more of a stream, but that rolling water appeared sort of deep.

"Ares hates water," Corbin admitted. "He'd face another bear rather than walk into a stream."

She found that almost amusing when considering what a beast Ares was but didn't comment. Everyone had fears. She'd never make light of his.

Leaving the relaxing scene to avoid teasing Pixie when they couldn't swim, Eirene found a pretty spot in the shade. She spread out the towel and put the snack bars in the middle with one bottle of water. They only had one more bottle left and had to be conservative.

Sitting cross-legged, she looked up to find Corbin headed her way with his everything-will-be-okay smile.

He dropped down next to her, pulled his boots off, and leaned over to kiss her cheek. "Should I expect fine dining like this all the time?"

"Probably since I'm not the best cook." She opened her eyes wide in challenge.

"I'm pretty decent with a grill. We won't starve."

She loved it when he talked like they were going to be together forever, but now was not the time to add anything new to his burden. She could be like Pixie and go along to get along until the time was right to talk about the future.

Placing her fingers on his cheek, she held them there. "I have never thought farther ahead than the day I woke up, but I would enjoy figuring out recipes. I would love to wake up with the windows open and chimes singing. I would love spending time together watching movies and reading."

He toyed with a lock of her hair that would probably never return to any civilized look and spun it around his finger. "I want to see you happy, morning, noon, and night. I want to feel you near me every minute we can steal and hold you close after we make love. I would love a life in a simple home with you, something I've never had."

"That's a pretty picture." She noticed he watched her closely as if wondering if that suited her or not. She held firm to her decision to let him set the pace. If he left it up to her, she would have him married, mated, whatever, so long as she could keep him.

Tearing the first bar open and handing it to him, she shuffled the conversation. "Just don't think I'm a princess. I did grow up in luxury, but all I wanted was to be free to do what other girls did. I couldn't date. My father feared some guy trying to take advantage of me and how I would react even after I assured him Pixie and I were not dominant. I had never been so excited as when you reached out to me. I'd scented you in the two classes we shared but feared speaking first because of my bodyguards."

He chewed the last of his first bar and took a gulp of water. "I was so shy it took me a month to get up the nerve to write the note once I carved the wolf."

She hoped Leszek would not bring someone into her apartment and take her things, but the one item she would fight him for was in a safe. "We never got to talk back then. What was your life like?"

"Not quite as cherry as yours. My dad married my mother with no idea she was pregnant, but he loved her and said he'd accept the child even if it was not his. He never thought he'd have to raise a shifter's pup."

"What about your real father?"

"By the time I could walk, I figured out my mother was mentally off. Crazy. She never said anything about my blood father. When she died, her husband who I claimed as my father, got drunk one night and ranted about the slut he married who had been a shifter groupie."

That was a horrible life. Eirene had an urge to hug him, but she wanted him to keep talking while she ate her bar. "What happened to your mother?"

Corbin had stopped eating the second bar in his hand and dropped it back on the towel. He stared down so long that Eirene thought she'd pushed too hard for more from him.

Washing a hand over his face, he said, "When I was two, she tried to kill my wolf. Ares had become a large pup, but he'd stepped into the tub filled with water thinking she was going to wash him like she had one time before. She leaned in, gripped his head with one hand, and flattened her other hand on his back, shoving him down beneath a foot of water. She had caught him by surprise with no time to suck in a breath. He screamed in my head. I panicked. Think I told him to shift. I'm not sure, but we did and squirmed out of her grasp when she had no fur to grip." He breathed deeply. "I screamed for my father. She jumped up and ran away. My father was appalled and dried me off, then put me next to his chair where he could watch me."

There had to be more. Eirene couldn't absorb the words he'd spoken. What mother would drown a child? Even a pup? No wonder Ares wanted nothing to do with water.

"When bedtime came, he went out to our old rickety garage and found her hanging from the center beam."

Eirene covered her mouth with her hand.

His sad eyes drifted to hers. "It was a long time ago. Other than Ares fearing water, we learned to live with it."

He could say that all he wanted, but no one gets over being almost killed by the one person meant to protect him.

"What happened to your mother?" Corbin asked, effectively shifting the attention to her.

"She died from complications during childbirth. My father had the best physician on standby, but she had a stroke during delivery. They almost lost me. Had I not been a shifter, they might have. She lived for two days. I grew up without her and felt bad for my dad who had lost the woman he loved."

Corbin tensed. He stood up.

"What's wrong?" she asked.

"Ares said he caught the faint scent of a shifter on the wind." She got to her knees and rolled their trash and empty bottle into the towel, then walked over to stuff it back into an open saddlebag.

"Eirene, come here."

She dropped the towel in the bag and swung around. "What's up?"

"Just come here now." Corbin wasn't speaking loudly.

Rushing forward, she kept her gaze on Corbin. He headed for her and dove at her as an explosion blasted. Rocks and metal hit her back.

Chapter 24

ADAMN JACKAL SHIFTER in human form had found them. He tried to make his five-foot-eight height seem taller by holding his shoulders back and jutting his chin forward. He might be forty or more with a butt-ugly face stuck on a bald head. The black cargo pants and a camo shirt looked out of place on this clown.

The jackal ordered, "Stay where you are until I tell you to move."

Corbin held Eirene in his arms. She was alive with a strong pulse, but she had scratches on her arms and neck from debris.

That wouldn't stop him from killing this bastard as soon as he saw an opening.

Walking closer to Corbin, the jackal shifter looked down his pointy nose and said, "Everyone is looking for you, but I told the man paying me I was the only one who could track you down. Me, Mitch the Snitch, known for my investigative skills."

Corbin dismissed his stupid introduction, wanting to know one thing. "How did you track me to the warehouse and here?"

Grinning like an idiot dying to brag on his limited skills, Mitch said, "I have eyes in the sky, and I had a tracker stuck on your bike at her apartment. You wouldn't have found it if you'd looked."

Eyes in the sky? A bird shifter. That's why Corbin hadn't picked up a strange shifter scent around his bike. He had never heard of SCIS having an airborne resource. "Who's paying you?"

Mitch clammed up. "Stop asking questions. I'm the one running this show."

"Doubtful," Corbin scoffed. "You're so afraid of me, you stink of it."

That wiped away Mitch's smirk. "I'm not afraid of you. I have another fun toy." He lifted what looked like some kind of C-4, but Corbin didn't think that material would explode without a trigger.

He still had to give the gray chunk respect so this fool would not harm Eirene again.

She moved around, regaining consciousness. "What … happened?"

Corbin hugged her to him. "This jackal asshole blew up the bike."

She turned her head away from Corbin to face Mitch. "What does SCIS want?"

"Do not confuse me with those bottom-feeding jackals at SCIS. I do unique work for high-dollar clientele."

"Just who is this client of yours?" Corbin asked. Had to be the Romanian.

Ares came forward hard inside Corbin, yelling, *Bear!*

Corbin stood and pulled Eirene up.

"Where do you think you're going?" Mitch asked in a shaky voice while frantically digging in his pants pocket. Did he carry small bombs on his body all the time?

Now Corbin smelled the bear heading for them.

Eirene trembled. "We can't kill it."

Mitch finally drew a deep breath and turned around, muttering, "What the hell?"

Ares demanded, *Give me the body or we die!*

Corbin replied, *I will as soon as I get Eirene and Pixie set.*

Corbin dragged Eirene away from the jackal. "Follow me. Get out of your clothes when I tell you and start changing. Tell Pixie to hide behind us. I'm turning Ares loose."

He pulled her into the woods and said, "Now."

While he ripped his clothes off and started shifting, a ginormous grizzly pounded toward the jackal.

Mitch screamed and tried to run, but the bear was on him instantly. Massive paws as wide as Corbin's head with long claws tore into the jackal.

Then the bear began eating him.

Ares ripped free in a blast of energy. He turned to where Eirene and Pixie were still in their shift. It allowed him to ignore the grizzly shifter eating another shifter in human form.

Corbin told Ares, *Watch the grizzly. Pixie should back away and hide.*

Yes. Ares turned back as the grizzly had paused and stared at him with blood dripping from his long fangs. That jackal had been a momentary distraction. The intelligence behind those almost black eyes of the bear confirmed they faced a shifter.

When the grizzly stood on his hind legs, his head reached over twelve feet tall, bigger than any natural bear, which removed any lingering doubt. His yellow eyes weren't even natural for a shifter.

That bear had been sent for Corbin and Ares.

Corbin said, *This bear has probably been tortured and may be jacked up on drugs. Kill him as fast as you can.*

I will. Ares said less and less when he went up against impossible odds.

Ares made no move, waiting on the bear to come for him. That could be a good strategy, or it might end with one fatal swipe of those deadly paws.

The bear started forward, not dropping down.

Hell. Corbin wondered why. Bears were so aggressive that they didn't take the time to dance around in a fight.

Ares took a step forward, then another.

Corbin had no idea what his wolf had in mind, but he would not distract Ares.

Then Ares turned to walk off to the left of the bear and into the trees, pausing to swing around and howl as if he'd taken down the giant.

The grizzly opened his wide maw and let out a roar of fury that chilled Corbin, then he dropped and went hard after Ares.

Ares waited, waited, then dove into the woods and spun to run around a thick area of underbrush.

Roaring the whole way, the grizzly's claws ripped up ground, lumbering after Corbin's wolf, who slowed for the bear to catch him. When Corbin could smell the putrid breath of the cannibalistic bear, he feared Ares had cut it too close.

Halfway around the thicket behind Ares, the grizzly stopped to swing a paw at Ares' hindquarters.

Ares leaped up and flipped back around, hitting a small tree with his shoulder. Ouch.

Before the bear could push up taller, Ares jumped on its back and did his buzz saw routine to rip a large gash through the thick fur. He dove off as the bear stood.

Corbin still recalled the bear Ares had attacked the same way, rising quickly to slam Ares against a boulder. This time, Ares had been ready. With the grizzly standing upright, Ares now attacked the bear's ankle—one of the only weak spots on a Goliath animal.

His wolf clamped down and shook his head, trying to rip out tendons.

The bear dipped down and swatted Ares, catching him across the face and knocking him away.

Corbin tried to breathe past the agony of the head strike. He lost track of Ares and the fight. Forcing his vision to clear, he looked through his wolf's eyes at a towering bear coming down fast to crush him.

Ares rolled away and stood, wobbling.

Corbin said, *I felt that hit too. Move. Don't stand still.*

Without replying, Ares started pacing around the back of the bear, who turned to protect his backside. This would not last long.

Ares walked on shaky legs. Corbin had no advice. Warm liquid poured down his wolf's face. They were bleeding profusely.

If the grizzly simply waited, Ares would lose consciousness, and this would end immediately.

A high-pitched growl interrupted Corbin's thought.

Oh, no. No, no, no. Pixie had come to help.

The grizzly huffed in surprise, then turned to the reddish-golden wolf, forgetting Ares.

A rush of panic exploded inside Ares, almost blinding Corbin with so much power at once.

Pixie started barking.

That bear kept walking upright toward her. He would try the same thing he'd tried on Ares. To crush her.

Ares lunged at the ankle he'd started tearing into before, this time with claws slashing fast. When blood and tendons broke free, Ares grabbed a chunk and dragged them out.

Pixie quieted, staring up at her death. She had to be in shock, unable to move.

Ares growled at her.

She jumped back then spun around and ran twenty feet.

Good thing, because the grizzly fell face-first in her direction. Its long arms came down beyond the head, reaching for Pixie.

Ares ran around and clawed the second ankle, destroying it. Any other time, he and Ares would agree to take off to live another day. Not this time. Ares would not leave until he ensured the bear could not get up and reach Pixie.

The bear's outstretched body had landed outside the woods, not far from the destroyed motorcycle and Mitch's mangled corpse. While the bear lay there whining in pain, Ares sat down hard. He fought for breath after breath.

Corbin gave the words his wolf deserved. *That was the most powerful fight I've ever seen you execute. You are one hell of a wolf, and I am honored to share my life with you.*

Ares had nothing to say, which was encouraging for Corbin. Maybe his wolf really heard him this time.

Pixie waited beyond the bear's reach. It would take a while for this one to die, but Ares had done his best to end it quickly. He could not risk getting close enough to rip out the bear's throat.

Adrenaline could push the monster to kill Ares with one slap.

Besides, this bear did not live in this park. Someone had brought him.

Corbin told Ares, *We should leave as soon as we can before whoever brought this bear shows up with weapons and titanium rounds. They'll see the bear the minute they get into this clearing.*

Ares stood, sidestepped, then shook off the dizziness. He made a wide circle around the bear and exited the woods on the left of where Pixie stood. He gave a huff, and she came running to nuzzle his neck.

Corbin had never seen Ares smile since the attempted drowning, but he could swear his wolf was happy now. Ares licked Pixie's muzzle then angled his head away from the bear.

She nodded and followed him. When they reached the woods beyond where Corbin and Eirene had picnicked, Ares froze.

Water roared far below them.

Corbin said, *We're out of sight of the bike explosion and the bear. Take a moment to rest, and we'll figure out what to do next.*

Turning until he had a spot shielded by underbrush, Ares dropped all the way down with his front legs extended as he faced the carnage.

Corbin would like to talk to Eirene, but Pixie was being a trooper. She dropped to the ground next to Ares.

A minute later, Corbin found out who had paid Mitch to find them.

The Romanian walked in, surveying the destroyed bike and the dying grizzly. He rolled his eyes. "I pay for best. How did the wolf defeat this one?"

Behind him, two vicious human men with high-powered rifles stepped out from Vlad's left and two more on his right. That cut off any exit they had except one.

Ares said, *I kill them all.*

Corbin replied, *I have the greatest faith in you right now, but we can't battle four men armed with titanium-loaded weapons.* His wolf must have agreed. He didn't argue, and Ares would argue with a sock.

Finally, Ares asked, *What is plan?*

Try to trust me. We only have one way out, and it's behind us.

Panic flared in Ares. *Water? No!*

Give me the body and I'll go into the water. I can keep us alive.

Not shifting, Ares argued. *No energy to shift again soon. If we fight new beast, we die.*

Corbin's heart broke for his wolf. *You're absolutely right.*

Vlad ordered, "Find the wolf. Do not kill him. That is my right only."

Corbin pleaded, *Please do this, Ares. If we can escape now, we will never hunt for the Romanian again. If he captures us, he'll torture us and keep us alive to do horrific things to me as a human and you in wolf form for as long as he can.*

Ares shook with agitation. Corbin's wolf had never backed down from a fight, but his terror of water couldn't be more real.

One of the men holding a rifle called out, "Let's clear the easiest area between us and the cliffs."

They would find Ares and Pixie in minutes.

Pixie leaned her head toward Ares and nuzzled his neck.

That was Corbin's only hope. He rushed to convince Ares. *Pixie loves the water and will stay with you. If we do not get up and run, the Romanian will capture Pixie. You remember how he treated all the female shifters, right? He would torture her to hurt us. Then he'd sell her to some monster.*

Ares continued to shake. His bones should be rattling by now, but he stood. Pixie followed his action, giving Corbin hope they could pull this off.

Turning to Pixie, Ares pushed her behind him and began backing up. With every step back, Corbin questioned what Ares intended to do.

Was his wolf moving Pixie back until she had to jump first? She would, too, because based on what Eirene had said, Pixie loved the water and had no fear of heights.

He wanted all four of them to live, but if saving Pixie was the best Ares could do, then at least Eirene would survive.

By the time cool air blew over his wolf's coat, Corbin prepared for Pixie to leap into the water.

She didn't. Instead, Pixie had planted herself at the edge of the cliff, but to the side of Ares. Eirene might have figured out what Ares was doing and discussed it with her wolf.

Ares swung his head around and gave a deep huff at Pixie.

She lifted her chin and ignored him.

One of Vlad's men shouted, "I see them. Close in now."

He raised his rifle and pointed it at Pixie.

Ares swung around fast, knocking her off the cliff. A shot rang out, then Corbin felt Ares backpedal, but his paws were slipping. Ares went flying off right behind Pixie.

The dam must have been opened. A wall of water rushed through the deep mountain gorge. The high water would make rapids difficult for rafters, which might be why he had yet to see any on the river.

Turned headfirst toward the water, Corbin saw what was coming at them fast. As Ares fell through the air with wild paddling movements, Corbin silently admitted that raging froth scared him too.

Chapter 25

ARES PLUNGED INTO icy water, thrashing his legs around.

Corbin lost direction for a moment.

A reddish-golden wolf's head came into view, then Pixie got under Ares and pushed him up.

When Ares broke through the surface, he was coughing and terrified.

Finally getting his wits back, Corbin started talking to Ares. *You're doing good. Pixie is right here with us. She will not let anything happen to you. She's an extremely strong swimmer, so this is her element. Try to calm down and relax. You will have an easier time keeping your head above water.*

Ares still floundered and slashed his paws like he was trying to claw the water to death.

That could be true.

Pixie bumped into him, and he jerked around to face her. She paddled smooth strokes.

He wouldn't even try to mimic her and started sinking.

Pixie growled at him and shoved her muzzle under his head to keep it above water and allow him to breathe.

Corbin told Ares, *She's working really hard to keep you safe. You could help her by relaxing and moving your legs with smoother strokes. Do that and you'll be swimming.*

Ares said, *Too heavy. Drowning.* Then he coughed up water.

Pixie is a big wolf, and she isn't sinking, Corbin argued.

Trust her. Our mother was sick in the head. Pixie and Eirene are smart and good.

Once again, Pixie swam closer, but this time she licked his muzzle, an intimate motion for a wolf.

Ares still didn't know what to make of her, but he did calm down. He moved his legs in less erratic motions. His shoulder muscles flexed without being tight.

Hope surged in Corbin again. Ares was beginning to swim!

Pixie slyly watched Ares, then floated away from him.

Ares made a loud bark, then paddled over to her.

Corbin laughed. Pixie was playing with a dangerous wolf half again her size who was acting like a love-sick puppy.

Once Ares calmed down and churned his powerful legs more like Pixie, he began making progress. She had no problem keeping up with him.

They'd made it probably two miles by the time dark began to settle fast with the sun hiding behind tall trees once they'd left the gorge. Corbin searched the bank until he found muddy skid marks likely made by people who had camped and then put kayaks into the water.

Ares, see that muddy bank on this side of the river?
Yes.

Guide Pixie there. I think we'll find a good place to rest for the night.
Good.

His wolf sounded calmer, even relaxed. Corbin had never thought he'd use those words to describe Ares before now. His wolf would still blast out to kill anything in sight when needed, but he had been gentle around Pixie even after hitting the water.

Once both wolves reached the bank, Ares pushed Pixie out first. They shook off water and then sniffed the area. Yes, someone had camped here recently. The grass had been flattened where they'd raised a tent to sleep in.

Ares said, *Need food.*

Corbin couldn't argue with that, plus the wolves eating something easy to find like a rabbit would be simpler than him trying to feed Eirene anything decent. They didn't even have energy bars.

Ares killed a rabbit and gave it to Pixie after he realized she was not much of a hunter. Then he found one for himself.

Corbin had to see Eirene soon. He'd been patient through everything his wolf needed because Ares had faced his fears and overcome them. He'd also shown more desire to be a partner today than before. Corbin wanted to cling to that and not lose it.

Once the wolves had drunk their fill of water, Corbin said, *Please give me the body.*

Instead of a sharp no, Ares gave a long sigh and started the shift.

Pixie noticed, and she began shifting.

Pushing up to his feet, Corbin moved over to pull Eirene to him. "Are you okay, babe?"

Her pretty hair stuck out in different directions. She looked up at him for a few seconds and started laughing.

He didn't know if he should be happy or worried at that reaction. "What's so funny?"

"Surviving all that and hours in the water to finally shift so I can see you, and my second thought is how much I want a hot shower. Maybe I am a bit of a princess sometimes."

He hugged her to him, holding her close. He would give her all the hot showers she wanted if he could get her to safety.

She squirmed closer to him like the minx she was and asked, "What would you want if we could snap our fingers and make it happen?"

"Given that both of us being naked is opportune, I wouldn't need a genie to grant my wish, but … I think we need rest."

"Sadly, I agree."

He walked her over to the flattened grass and stretched out on his back. "You lie on top of me. That's the best I can offer for comfort."

"My favorite bed." She snuggled down on top of him.

He muttered, "Keep moving like that and your bed will be bumpy."

Her laugh sounded like a bell tinkling in the wind.

He loved how easy she was, even at the worst of times. He had no intention of sleeping so he could keep watch over her. She started humming a tune that sounded like a lullaby. He closed his eyes to absorb her wonderful voice, looking forward to the day he could hear her sing a real song.

After a while, her voice trailed off and her breathing slowed. She was falling asleep.

He forced his eyes open, but he'd almost been lulled asleep. He listened for any threatening sounds, only to hear crickets and frogs chirping and croaking. He thought she would sleep like the dead, but after two hours of snoozing, his sexy ass female started running circles around his nipple with a finger.

Then she ran her tongue over his other nipple.

He grabbed her hand. "Last night, when I said I wanted to make love to you in many different places, this one hadn't been on the list."

"Good time to add to the list," she said against his chest in a sleepy voice.

"Are you sure you're awake, babe?" Because she'd brought his dick to full attention.

"I won't go back to sleep with you poking me."

"Hey, you're the one who played with my nipples." He smiled.

"You're complaining?" she asked and pushed up to prop her chin on her folded arms.

"Not a bit. But I want to give my princess a more comfortable place than this."

"It's a good time for us to be creative," she challenged. "Got any ideas?"

He considered everything and started grinning. "Just so happens I do."

"Really?"

Ha. He'd surprised her. "I need to get up from here first."

She scrambled off him and stood, bouncing on the balls of her feet with excitement. As soon as he reached his feet, he swung her up in his arms.

She made a squeak. "Where the hell are you going? We don't have a bedroom."

Striding across the muddy strip, he walked straight into the water.

"Whoa, that's cold," she yelped.

He was laughing so hard that he waited for a breath to speak. By then, he was in the water up to his chest with her tucked against him. "You're warmer now, aren't you?"

Chuckling, she said, "I am now, but that first dip took my breath away."

Pulling her around to let her body hang in the water in front of his, he said, "You take my breath away. I feel like that shy kid in school who had a massive crush on the sweetest girl there."

She'd been holding onto his shoulders and leaned in to kiss him. He answered her invitation with a soft brush of his mouth, then kissed her sincerely for a long time. No light made it to this part of the river, but it was as if they'd known each other their whole lives. He knew her body, and she knew his.

There would never be another for him.

He moved his fingers to her waist and slowly massaged his way up to her breasts. She had the perfect handful and pert nipples begging for attention. With her suspended in the water, he had easy access to both.

Rubbing his thumbs under the plump weight, he moved up to roll her nipples with his thumb and forefinger.

She dropped her head back and moaned. "I had been lying there thinking not to wake you and take care of myself."

His hands stilled. "Show me."

She moved a hand from his shoulder. He slid his hands down to cup her waist.

Sliding her hand down his chest, she played with his nipple again, then moved farther down to where his dick had recovered from the cold dip. She ran her fingers over the head and stroked him twice.

He growled at her, and she laughed, then her hand disappeared. He felt her arm moving. Then she made a needy sound and arched back.

Stupid idea on his part.

He'd ached even more to drive into her. Still holding her with one hand around her waist, he pulled her hand away from her folds. He caught her fingers and brought them to his mouth, licking them.

She slapped her hand on his shoulder again and complained in a teasing voice, "Back to me. I need to feel you."

Releasing her fingers, he returned to where she'd left off and stroked her folds slowly.

She begged, "More."

He changed the tempo and worked her into a slick heat, then plunged his finger inside. She rode his hand, and he brushed his thumb over her sweet spot, pushing her closer to climax. Her fingers dug into his shoulders, and he loved it, moving his finger inside her faster until he paused and stroked her nub.

"Corbin!" She clutched him to her as he kept her on that high until the last second, then she slumped against him. Her legs hung loose.

He cupped her bottom, pulling her to him and slowly rocking her back and forth in the gentle water.

She caught her breath and lifted her head, kissing his neck, his chin, then his lips. His tongue poked at hers, and she loved on his.

When they broke apart, she sounded dazed. "I thought I could give you time, but I can't."

What the hell was wrong? He stayed silent and waited.

"I love you, Corbin, with all my heart. This may be too soon for you, but I don't ever want to lose you."

His heart felt as if it had started expanding with each breath. He said, "It's not too soon. I wanted to wait until my life was simpler and I felt I had something to offer you, but you are my forever. You are all I have ever wanted and will be until my last breath."

She lunged and wrapped her arms around him. "Does this mean we get to be mates, married, or what?"

He smiled into her hair. "We get to do whatever we want. You are my mate, and I will happily marry you if you want that too."

"Mate." She pulled back, and he couldn't see her, but he could hear the thrill in her voice. "My mate. My man. I like the way it all sounds."

"Keep in mind that I have some problems to sort out," he admitted.

"I can probably match you in problems. We'll sort out everything together if mine don't scare you off."

"Nothing and no one will scare me away from you." He leaned down to kiss her, happier than a man deserved to be. He hadn't wanted anyone as a mate after losing her and figured no female wolf would want Ares, but his wolf had proved himself worthy of Pixie. She had shown him she could hold her own even if she wasn't dominant.

He didn't give a damn what the world threw at him because he was mated with the greatest female on Earth.

Her legs moved up around his chest. He thought she was getting closer for a hug, but she shoved herself down on him.

Tensing at the incredible feel of being inside her, he choked out, "A little warning next time, babe."

"I thought this would be a good way to celebrate our mating," she said as if she were explaining how the river flowed. Then she broke into giggles. "Consider yourself warned."

"Don't ever change. I love you." He put both hands under her bottom and began to move her up and down. So easy in water.

"I won't as long as you always love me."

"Bet on it."

She took over the pace and rode him with more enthusiasm than she had his hand.

When she reached underneath them and cupped his balls in her cool fingers, game over.

He came harder than the last time, which was saying something.

She flopped her arms over his shoulders. He wrapped her in his arms, content to stand here for as long as she wanted, but she stirred and began cleaning them both.

"Think you can sleep now?" he asked, trudging through the water to the shore.

"Oh yes. I might not make it back to the grass."

He wrapped a hand around her wet hair that she'd wrung out and pulled her forehead to him, kissing her. She gave a contented hum.

Once they were settled again, he rubbed her shoulder muscles and down her back until she slowly dropped off to sleep again.

This time, she snored a little. Cute.

Hours went by while the water lapped at the bank and nature sang its tune. He fought to keep his eyes open again and again, sure that sunrise would be in an hour or two. He could make it and grab a nap while she kept watch before they struck out again.

Sounded like a plan, but with the tension in his body, he was spent.

Exhaustion pulled at him, dragging him under.

Daylight began to peek over the trees and brush away the darkness. He forced an eye open then immediately ran a hand along her back, just to let him know she was breathing and safe.

She kissed his chest and mumbled, "I want waffles this morning."

Someone answered, "That will not be possible this morning."

Corbin rolled her over beneath him, but he had no hope against this threat.

Vlad and four heavily armed men stood above them.

Chapter 26

IRENE FORCED BILE back down her throat to avoid drawing that horrible Romanian's attention. He carried his bulky body around on two short tree-trunk legs. Black hair slicked back over his blob-like head looked unwashed. His narrow eyes looked black above a bulbous nose. Garlic odor oozed from his skin. She was thankful that for a moment, he ignored her and Corbin while talking with his men.

Being naked didn't bother her as a shifter.

No, it was fear for Corbin. After Vlad, the Romanian Corbin had told her about, had announced his presence, he'd opened his fisted hand to reveal a small red device.

Corbin had leaped off her the second he saw what that evil man held. One quick press of the button and Corbin arched into a hideous shape. His body contorted with pain. He yelled in agony.

She screamed, *"Stop hurting him!"*

Her words meant nothing to that pig.

It was all over quickly, leaving Corbin sucking in air.

Something must have been put in his body that could be activated by a remote device. What kind of horrors had he and Ares suffered at that man's hand?

Pixie shouted in Eirene's head, *He hurt Ares too.*

Sighing in despair, Eirene said, *I know. I wish I had a way to stop that monster.*

Ares had a rough day in the water, Pixie fretted. *He*

proved he could do it, but this man will destroy the nice Ares who does not scare me.

Eirene hoped that would not be the case. *We can't shift and save them, but we will find some way to help Corbin and Ares*, Eirene told Pixie. *I hate this too. Try not to panic. I can think better when you're calm.*

Not calm, but I will be quiet.

Thank you.

One of the armed men held out what appeared to be a satellite phone to Vlad. "The call you have been expecting."

Vlad took the phone and stepped away from everyone, deeper into the forest. His men followed him, arrogantly sure she and Corbin would not move. Corbin struggled to sit up next to her. She moved her hand slowly to cover his fingers, which felt like ice.

He barely spoke, his words only loud enough for her to hear. "Can you swim as well as Pixie?"

"Yes. I'm good."

"Please listen to me and do what I ask. I don't have much time. Vlad rarely talks long on the phone."

She squeezed his hand. "Go ahead."

"Be ready to scurry to the water when I distract them."

"No!"

"Please, babe. We're running out of time. You're my only hope."

She heard truth, but he held back something.

He continued, "I will always love you, and Ares wants Pixie to know he'd be thrilled to have her as his mate too. For my wolf to make that admission is amazing for me."

"Pixie wants Ares, too, and is upset that he is hurting. We want both of you."

Turning his hand to hold hers, he squeezed her fingers to give her comfort as his world crashed down on his head. "I will only get one chance at this. You must leave, or our misery will be ten times worse if we can't save you both."

He'd given her an impossible task. She didn't want to leave him, but if she could not save him here, then she'd do as he asked on one condition—that she could free him of this man. "I'll go only so I can find a way to save you."

"No." He shook his head. "If you make a peep, the Romanian will find you. You won't be able to save Pixie or your females. Don't toss your life away when you can't stop these people. Don't destroy your reputation with the public finding out you've been with a lone wolf because, without the pack I had, that's what I am. I won't drag them into this hellhole either." He licked his lips, which looked dry. "But don't worry, Ares and I will find a way to escape again."

Her heart shattered. His last sentence had been a blatant lie.

He expected her to leave and forget him.

That was not happening.

His breathing hitched, and he gritted his teeth. "I want to kiss you so badly, but any move I make will bring them back over here. You only have one chance to escape. Get ready to hear me say stuff I'd cut my arm off before I'd say for real. Stick with my plan. Don't look back for any reason. Make it to the other shore, shift, and run. Please do this for me."

Tears ran down her cheeks.

Corbin stared ahead, blinking hard. "None of these humans can keep up with you. Always know that I love you so much that I can't even put it into words."

He was telling her goodbye. She couldn't do this.

Then he grimaced.

"What?"

"Ares said he doesn't want to lose Pixie. I understand, but I reminded him how Vlad abuses the female shifters he traffics. Ares is hurting but said he wants Pixie to be safe too." He tensed. "I hear Vlad ending the call. Get ready."

She couldn't believe she was going to leave him here.

What could she do if she stayed? Make him watch them do awful things to her? She would only add to his suffering.

This wasn't the way it was supposed to be.

She had no choice, but that wouldn't stop the feeling of having her heart ripped from her chest.

When Corbin eased up into a crouch, she told Pixie, *We're going to swim faster than we ever have and go for help.*

Corbin whispered, "Now." He shoved up fast and ran through the armed men facing their boss. He rammed into Vlad, knocking him backward.

Crying, Eirene hurried to the water and dove in with the smoothness of a knife's blade. She stayed underwater, sparing her from hearing Corbin's voice scream at being hit by that red device again.

When she'd made it as far as her lungs could take, she eased up to break the surface and spun. She'd reached halfway across the river.

Out of the chaos, Vlad shouted, "Where is the female? Get her!"

Corbin was not in sight. He had to be curled up on the ground shaking.

Two guards took off into the woods.

A third ran to the bank and lifted his rifle.

She gulped air and dove at an angle, going deep. Bullets zinged through the water, but they were to the left of her. She continued swimming until she could put her feet on solid ground and slowly pushed up to peek again.

The same guard still held the rifle pointed at where she'd gone under.

Looking around, she spotted tree limbs overhanging the water on the bank near her.

She swam slowly underwater again until she came up by those branches and pulled herself through them, gritting her teeth at the deep scratches and jagged cuts over her bare skin.

Yet she made it out of the water with that one guard still searching the surface.

Once she'd wiggled her way through the thicket to a more open area, she stood and held onto a tree to catch her breath.

I will heal us, Pixie said.

Eirene's wolf was hurting as much as she was and wanted to do her part. *Thank you, Pixie. We will rest for one minute, then shift. Starting now, the only thing I care about is saving Corbin and Ares.*

I agree.

If Eirene were discovered to have joined up with a lone wolf, SCIS would come for her. Leszek might not be able to stop them. Worse yet, Leszek would use that scandal to turn the courts and the fans against her unless she handed him her future.

She'd never find her father's killer.

Nothing mattered more to her than Corbin's freedom.

What she had in mind would likely blow up in her face, but she was done playing defense.

Corbin and Ares had no one else but her and Pixie.

Chapter 27

STRUGGLING TO BREATHE and stay conscious, Corbin rolled his head until he could look out over the water.

Eirene surfaced halfway across. She'd be safe.

He and Ares would never know what the word safe meant ever again, but they had saved their mates.

"Chain the dog and take him to the van," Vlad ordered. He stepped closer, knowing from experience that Corbin would be in no shape to hurt a fly for another hour. "When I find your woman, I will show you what I do to female shifters who try to defy me. I will enjoy watching her beg to be killed."

The three men put a chain around Corbin's neck and connected it to where his hands and feet had been cuffed.

I'm sorry, Ares. I hate that this is happening to you. Corbin was sick over Ares finally facing his darkest fear and coming out on the other side not as the wolf he'd known as a child, but a much greater version. *I am so proud of what you did in the water and how you fought that bear. I would never want another wolf.*

Ares made a pitiful moan. *Want Pixie.*

I know. I want Eirene, too, but we did the right thing by getting them out of here. I never want Vlad to touch either of our mates.

Vlad's men were dragging Corbin through the woods, letting his head bang against tree trunks. He didn't care about blood oozing from his head or low bushes or broken branches digging long cuts into his body. Not after being hit twice with Vlad's remote control then kicked around by his men.

That was merely a taste of how much worse it would be now that Vlad had no desire to use Corbin and Ares as part of his operation.

When Ares spoke again, he sounded vicious. *We fight our way out.*

Corbin would not try to change his wolf's mind. Ares knew fighting would end in their deaths. His wolf understood the raw pain of having what he wanted within his grasp, only to lose it as much as Corbin did.

We will fight.

Chapter 28

STARS FLEW THROUGH Corbin's vision during lucid times before he'd eventually black out. Neurological damage from Vlad's sadistic beatings. He peeked through the slit in one swollen eye past the tiny lights flickering through his vision to determine if it was daylight or nighttime. The barn door stayed open continuously.

He might have been here three days or more. He couldn't say for sure.

After flashing a permit showing they had captured a rogue wolf shifter and were delivering it to Canada's version of SCIS, Vlad's men drove off with no one thinking twice to check their story.

They drove for an hour before taking a dirt road that went on forever. Then the van entered the yard of a farmhouse with an aging barn. They'd killed the elderly human couple living here.

Vlad arrived right behind them, warning his men to be vigilant because he needed time to replace the bear before they departed this continent.

One of the guards confirmed their contact in Canada had found this location for them because the couple that had lived here for over twenty years had stayed away from others. They basically lived off the grid, making this an ideal place to wait.

Two of Vlad's men had dragged Corbin into the barn before one left to meet with the person supplying Vlad's replacement shifter. Having three guards gave Vlad two to watch his back while one grabbed a battle nap.

Then payback began for pissing off the Romanian.

Corbin tried to roll over and stopped. He'd forgotten he had multiple cracked ribs plus broken bones in his swollen face. One foot would not work correctly. His hands trembled nonstop from his beaten head. He'd developed a twitch in his cheek.

Ares had wanted to blast out and kill them.

Corbin asked his wolf to stay put and let him take the abuse. He didn't want to think about what they might do to his wolf once Vlad found a replacement for the dead bear.

What would the Romanian bring in? A rhinoceros?

He tried to smile at that thought, but his facial muscles couldn't make that happen.

The Romanian had hit him with so many electrical charges over the first three days that Corbin had become numb.

Ares had not.

He broke free and killed the last one to strike Corbin. That left the Romanian two men, one of whom shot Ares with a titanium load before the Romanian could stop him.

Vlad threatened to kill the next guard who shot Corbin or Ares with titanium and robbed him of his pleasure in abusing them.

The other guard had withdrawn a dart gun and shot Ares with a drug.

Losing consciousness, Ares gave the body back to Corbin. The titanium burning his leg from the inside out kept him awake.

The Romanian grumbled about Corbin dying too quickly because he had no one to take the titanium out without exposing his presence in Canada with a captured shifter. Evidently, the Black River wolf pack in the states was to deliver a jacked-up replacement shifter to make up for their bear's failure to produce the desired results.

Ares said, *Bear should have killed this man.*

True, Corbin agreed. Once Vlad had his new shifter, he'd

fly all of them to Romania, where he owned more people of power than Corbin could count. Few criminals possessed his capacity for blackmail.

Corbin whispered, "Want water. A sip." Not for him, but Ares, who needed water after that tranq shot.

The garbage in that shot made you beg for a trickle of water.

Corbin opened his eyes and looked through the foggy air that cleared as a bucket of cool water came into view. The bucket tipped and poured over him.

He told Ares, *Ah, that's refreshing, isn't it?*

Ares moaned. *You see ghosts again.*

No, Corbin had not seen ghosts since they escaped Vlad. Had Ares not gotten enough to drink?

The bucket vanished, and dark swirling air returned. Corbin hadn't moved a muscle since hitting the hard-packed dirt after Ares shifted back to human. Everything felt familiar in a sick way—even being naked.

Corbin hadn't worn clothes for years under the Romanian's rule. The reason had been to remind him daily that he would never be more than an animal.

Screw Vlad. Corbin had better things to think about.

An image of Eirene came floating into his mind for the millionth time. That's how he'd made it through nonstop torture. Her pretty face smiled. Wind tossed her strawberry-blond locks around. From time to time, he had fleeting moments of heaven until his heart ached with losing the woman he'd wanted forever and beyond. The woman he'd planned to wake up with every day, so he could see her face and hold her warm body.

He'd feel the same a hundred years from now.

His thoughts were lucid again. She was not here but safe far away.

No regrets. This time, he'd chosen to walk back into hell for the most meaningful cause in his life. How had he become numb at times to the vicious pain inflicted by Vlad? Because nothing would ever match the agony of feeling his heart split apart, one slow piece at a time.

What could the Romanian do to him now that he'd lost Eirene?

She had to be safe.

Darkness closed over Corbin again. He welcomed leaving here.

Ares brought him back awake when he spoke up in a rough voice hurting for water. *Someone coming.*

Huh? A guard looked down at Corbin. Had he said that out loud? He moved his good eye to find Vlad sitting on a chair someone had brought here. He scrolled his phone.

Be quiet, Ares said.

Never had Corbin's wolf sounded beaten, but he did now. Corbin asked, *What is coming? Is it the shifter Vlad is waiting for?*

Maybe. I do not scent anyone yet.

A tear worked free of Corbin's swollen eye. He didn't want to hand Ares a broken body for his last fight. They'd had no food and little water. His wolf couldn't heal them.

A loud explosion erupted outside.

Vlad yelled at his guards. They yelled back in their native tongue. The two heavily armed guards slipped out the back end of the barn by opening a door held in place with a bent nail.

A strange hush fell around the building.

Corbin tried to hear what was going on. Shouldn't they be shooting?

A scream outside jolted the Romanian.

Corbin smiled. That had been a human scream. Deep sounding as if from a male. Who had Vlad pissed off now?

Were the strangers here to steal his broken wolf shifter?

Corbin hoped not. He knew this monster. Why trade for one with more evil ideas?

The barn door hanging half open yanked wider.

This could be interesting. Corbin tilted his head to see more with his half-closed eye.

In came Adrian with a badass pistol raised. He fired twice.

Corbin had to be hallucinating, but he looked at Vlad.

The Romanian dropped his rifle and stood there for a

second with two bullet holes in his forehead, and then he fell backward.

Better than hallucinating. This was a dream come true.

Ares had been right. Corbin must be seeing apparitions again. He turned back to Adrian to enjoy this moment for as long as he could before Vlad zapped him.

Adrian shouted over his shoulder, "Cole! Call in the chopper and send Rory in here." He rushed to Corbin's side and dropped to one knee. "I'm so sorry we didn't arrive sooner. The Guardian has teams all over this part of Canada searching for you."

"Is this real?" Hope sent relief zinging through Corbin.

"Yes, it is, buddy." Adrian's face distorted with a look of horror for only a second. Then he tried to smile but failed. "Oh, man, they did a number on you. Wish I could have saved you from this. Jaz will fix you up. Hold on while we get you to the chopper and out of here."

Was Adrian taking him out of here? Did that mean the Romanian was dead?

Ares said, *Good people. Let them fix us.*

His wolf thought this was real too. Corbin had no fight left in him. Even if it wasn't real, he decided to go along with all of it for a moment of peace from Vlad's red remote.

"Thanks, Adrian," Corbin rasped in case Adrian was here. He'd failed to let Adrian know when he left that building with Eirene. "I would have called …" He drew in a painful breath of air that gurgled on the way out. "My phone. Broken."

"Forget about it and stop trying to talk. I think you're bleeding internally. Please stay still."

Outside, the sound of helicopter blades whomping grew louder and louder.

In strode another shifter whose scent Corbin did not recognize. He smelled of wolf.

Adrian said, "This is one of our medics. His name is Rory. Do whatever he says."

Corbin mumbled something even he couldn't understand but came alive when he saw a syringe in Rory's hand.

"Nooo Jugo stuff!" Corbin protested, but it came out in a scratchy voice.

Adrian carefully held Corbin's arms down. "This is not Jugo Loco."

Rory said, "Nah, man. We would never do that to you. This is to help with pain. Take it easy and you'll be thanking me."

The needle pricked his arm. Felt like a tiny mosquito bite.

Adrian called over his shoulder, "Bring the stretcher and hurry the hell up."

Rory complained, "I don't know how much of this Jaz can fix."

The last thing Corbin heard was Adrian shouting at Rory, "Do you *always* have to be so negative?"

Chapter 29

CORBIN LICKED HIS lips. A tiny bit of water dribbled into his open mouth. He mumbled, "More."

"Not yet, tough guy." Confident female voice. A woman in charge.

He mentally swam through fog to get his brain working. Where was he?

More water dribbled. He needed to wake up and get a real glass of water. His eyes fluttered. Determined, he forced one eye to open. That seemed easier than two.

An attractive face surrounded by wild short black hair.

"I know you," he said. "Jaz."

She chuckled. "I hope you do. If not, I missed a head injury, which is unlikely since I spent a significant amount of time making sure you didn't have permanent brain damage."

He thought back to the last time he was cognizant of his surroundings. "That was real after all, huh? Adrian and a guy named Rory. They truly showed up to rescue me." His voice held wonder he could not hide.

She put the back of her hand to his forehead and no longer joked with him. "Yes, it was real. Rory did a great job of keeping you alive. Even with how badly you were injured, it wouldn't have been so difficult, but you'd been shot with titanium. It was slowly killing you and prevented your wolf from healing your body."

"Ares. How is he?"

"I haven't seen him yet. I'm hoping he's in a deep sleep to heal."

Air whooshed from Corbin's lungs after a deep inhale, but with only a small amount of pain. "Thank you and Rory. Will I see him again?"

"I'm sure. He's with our local headquarters. I believe the Guardian, our eagle shifter boss, wants you to meet the rest of our Gallize shifters in this area."

"Gallize? Is that what you and Adrian are?"

"Yes. We have said little about that to the pack, but Bosse knows, and you've gone through as much as any Gallize would have. Our Guardian said it's time we bring all of you up to date, but only you right now. You'll find out everything about when he's ready to share that information."

Corbin struggled for words that would express how much this meant to him. "What an honor to be brought into your group. That alone is huge, but to be alive and not tossed off the compound means the world to me." He paused, thinking of all that had happened. "And I'm still a pack member. You're the best."

She gave him a reluctant smile.

"What? After all that, you're going to give me bad news?" Corbin smiled. Good to know his facial muscles worked again.

"I don't think it's bad news, but I did something without your permission. Adrian said the Romanian guy had been electrocuting you through that chip in your back."

"That's right."

"When I put you into a deep sleep, I took it out."

Nausea rose in Corbin's throat. Was he paralyzed? He wiggled his fingers and toes. They worked.

"You're fine, Corbin. I have unusual powers, as you're aware, which I tapped into to move through your body. What I had to do caused some minor bleeding, but once I finished removing that chip, I closed those cuts."

Thinking of what she did for him was sobering. "You're far more than a healer. Thank you for doing that. You and

Adrian are both amazing. I owe you a huge debt for all you've done."

She released a sigh. "You're welcome, but that's not how it works here. We're all a pack. We do for each other. I am extremely fortunate to have Adrian for a mate. One day, you'll be just as lucky, I'm sure."

Corbin froze. How had he not thought of Eirene? He tried to sit up, gasped, and fell back onto the bed.

"Don't you dare screw up my hard work," Jaz stormed at him.

"Sorry, but I have a mate."

She had reached to recheck his temperature and stayed her hand. "Adrian said you told him Eirene Givenchy was your mate."

"She is. Do you know if she's safe?"

Jaz stared at him slack-jawed.

Adrian strolled in with a bounce in his step. "You look a hell of a lot better than two days ago."

"*Two* days?" Corbin turned to his side, grunted in pain, but kept working toward standing.

"Didn't you hear me?" Jaz demanded. "Don't you dare get up and fall."

Adrian said, "Hang on, Corbin."

Corbin tried to make them understand. "The Romanian caught Eirene, too, but I made her promise to escape. Then I distracted Vlad so she could get away. I've got to find out if she made it back safely."

"She *is* in Spartanburg. Give me a minute." Adrian turned to Jaz. "I've got to talk to him and maybe get him up to go with me."

Jaz swung her anger at him. "I told you he can't get out of bed for another day."

Putting his hands on her shoulders, Adrian said, "He could use some fresh air badly. I won't let him fall."

She flipped her hands up as if dismissing them both and walked out.

Corbin called, "Thanks a lot, Jaz. I promise I'll rest later."

Glum at making her unhappy, he turned to Adrian. "Sorry she's angry."

Laughing, Adrian said, "You can't fix that. When anyone messes with her healing, stay out of her way."

Once Adrian had him up and helped him with putting on workout pants and a loose T-shirt, Corbin felt better. He spoke to his wolf. *Ares, are you okay?*

Ares sighed and grumbled, *Hungry.*

Corbin had never been so happy to hear his wolf speak to him. *I'm getting on my feet for the first time. Let me move around a little to see what kind of shape we're in. Keep resting, and I'll get some food for us. I'm excited to be alive and never having to face the Romanian again.*

Yes. We have good friends.

Hearing Ares sound genuinely happy about the people around him gave Corbin hope that they could have more than a peaceful existence. They could become the brothers in heart they should have been from birth.

By the time he made it to the porch, Corbin dropped onto a wicker loveseat, exhausted from that small effort. Jaz had a point. That short walk had wiped him out. "Thanks, Adrian, for more than getting me out of here without Jaz strangling me. I never expected to escape Vlad or be entirely free of my past."

"You're welcome. Jaz does not like her people to be in pain, but she does like them to be happy."

"How did you find me in that barn?"

Adrian shrugged and only said, "We had some help."

These people were connected way better than the Romanian's criminal organization.

"I'd like to get a message to Eirene." In truth, Corbin wished he could shift and run to her, but she'd come close to being killed more than once since they found each other. She might have initially been happy to see him but could have come to her senses about how dangerous being with him would be.

He still wanted to talk to her about taking risks by trying to save female shifters all by herself.

"Let me grab you some real food and then we'll talk," Adrian said over his shoulder as he went back inside and let the screen door swing shut.

Corbin wanted another glass of water but not enough to bother Jaz.

Adrian returned and seemed jumpy. He put a tray down on the table in front of Corbin filled with four loaded hamburgers, a double pile of fries, half an apple pie, and a large glass of water.

The aroma alone had Corbin salivating. When was the last time he'd had real food? Too many days to count, but … he couldn't eat without knowing how Eirene was doing.

Putting his hands on his hips, Adrian said, "Go ahead and eat. I'll fill you in on Eirene."

"I can't talk to her?"

"Give me a chance to catch you up."

Ares rumbled, *Eat. We need food now. I want Pixie.*

Corbin sent back, *Okay, okay. I'm eating fast so I can talk to Eirene. If she's okay and they both still want us, then we're going to them.*

Ares asked, *Pixie not want me?*

Damn. His wolf sounded pitiful. Corbin lifted a hamburger and chomped down while explaining to Ares, *Sure she does. That was awful and dangerous with the Romanian. I need to be sure they both still feel safe with us.*

His wolf made a snort sound. *Pixie wants me.*

Corbin didn't doubt that, but life as the wolf part of their body was less complicated than the human side. He leaned back with a napkin in his lap and kept working on the pile of food in front of him. "I have the feeling something has gone on while I was unconscious that I need to know about. Is that correct?"

"Shit fire. I'd like to wait until Eirene can tell you."

"Well, I'd like to know what you know right now," Corbin countered.

"Okay, but don't jump up or try to move around. I want to keep the peace with my mate." Adrian tapped his fingers on the arm of the chair. "When you and Eirene vanished,

Leszek went on the news saying a rogue wolf shifter had kidnapped her."

Corbin put down the last half of his hamburger and worked past his aches to sit forward. "How bad is the fallout?"

"SCIS found me after Beckham called me to find out what was going on. I told him she was with you. I did not tell anyone you said she's your mate."

"That's good. I want it to be up to her to announce something like that. I have to admit, I'm not sure how she feels about being my mate after what she went through with Vlad. She and her wolf are not dominant."

Ares said, *You are wrong. Pixie strong.*

Adrian said nothing. He erupted into laughter and couldn't catch his breath.

"None of this is amusing, Adrian."

"I know. Give me a second." He wiped his eyes and propped his forearms on his knees when he leaned forward. "Eirene showed up in Spartanburg a day after you two disappeared and called a press conference. She said you were not a lone wolf, and a shifter trafficker from Romania had captured you. She called on anyone who knew anything about this Romanian and where he might be holding you to come forward and offered an expensive ring as a reward. When one of the reporters asked about her relationship with the lone wolf, she said you were her mate, and you were a member of a pack. She warned her fans not to listen to lies floating around the media."

Heart bouncing around his chest like a gerbil on cocaine, Corbin would never be able to wipe the grin off his face. She still wanted him as a mate. "That's my girl."

Ares added, *Our girls.*

Yes, they are ours, Corbin replied to his wolf.

Adrian lifted a hand. "Now that you know the good part, stay calm while I tell you the rest."

What could be bad after that? "Lay it on me."

"At the end of that press conference, SCIS showed up to arrest her. To her credit, she already had an attorney standing by who stepped in and argued that SCIS had no cause to arrest her if you were truly with a pack. SCIS did arrest her and threatened to have police arrest her attorney."

"*What?*" Corbin moved to stand and cursed.

"Sit back down or I will stop talking." Adrian turned stern. "I promised Jaz I would feed you and keep you still."

The food had been important. Corbin felt a lot better after eating, and energy began flowing through him, thanks to Ares. He wanted to shift and run to her. "I can't stay here with her locked up at SCIS."

"She was only there for half an hour and is not there anymore. Let me finish."

"Oh." Corbin could barely sit still. Adrian needed to give him fast bullet points, but to say that would be unkind after all Adrian, Jaz, and their people had done for him.

Adrian kept explaining. "By then, my people had seen the news conference. My boss called to let me know he had people hunting for you and he'd sent one of our attorneys to Eirene, which is why she did not stay at SCIS. The best way to gain his attention is to either harm or protect one of ours, especially when someone puts our shifters ahead of their own well-being."

"I didn't want her to wreck her life for me." Corbin began to think about how detrimental all this would be to her.

"Would you have wrecked your life for her?"

Corbin snapped, "Without question."

Adrian's eyes lit up with his grin. "That's what mates do for each other. She has convinced everyone from my boss to the other Gallize shifters that she's your mate."

Emotions swam through Corbin, threatening to take him under. He'd never felt so loved in his life. He had never expected to have a female so selfless and strong to go to bat for him and Ares.

Pixie strong, too, Ares told him.

Yes, our mates may not be dominant, but they are powerful in their own way, Corbin agreed. But now he worried they were in danger up to their necks.

"I know you're getting anxious about Eirene, so let me

finish," Adrian said. "When our attorney arrived at SCIS, Eirene's trustee, Leszek Moore, was shouting about locking up one of the most celebrated shifters in our country. He held his own press conference, rallying fans around a young woman who had bridged the gap between humans and shifters, only to make a mistake by trying to help a rogue wolf."

"What a bastard," Corbin groused. "He's taking advantage of his position as trustee. She told me she hates how he rules her life and fears him. She said she thought he was behind her father's death and cut a deal with SCIS after her father died to allow her freedom so long as he remained in charge of her life. She thinks he may be giving them hush money."

"That explains what happened next. Leszek announced that her concert would be postponed while she had time to rest from her ordeal. SCIS agreed to free Eirene if Leszek could ensure that she would not see you again for any reason."

Corbin tried to make sense of what Adrian was saying. "She's been ordered to stay away from *me*?"

"Yes."

Ares asked, *What is wrong?*

Corbin replied, *I'm not sure, but I will find out.* Then he told Adrian, "She worried about Leszek doing this, that he's been looking for a way to hold onto her trust beyond the time limit set. To remain the trustee forever. This could be a move where he's using this incident to blackmail her into agreeing to things she never would have agreed to before now." What was Corbin going to do? He would not give up Eirene after the declaration she made in public. "I need to talk to her."

Adrian became quiet.

"Don't stop there, Adrian. I'm awake and need to know everything going on."

"You can't talk to her."

"Why not?" Corbin roared.

"Please, settle down. Leszek told our attorney that he

was jeopardizing her safety, and her label had full control of defending her. My boss called him back to take pressure off Eirene, but he told me that it changed nothing when it came to protecting her. Part of her agreement for being released into Leszek's care was that all communication from here on had to go through Leszek's office. If she's caught with a mobile phone of her own, SCIS gets to take her back into custody."

Those words would not compute in Corbin's mind. "How could he do that? How could anyone do that?"

"Leszek has assigned a bodyguard to stay with her twenty-four-seven."

Corbin argued, "She's gone from being a free shifter celebrated by humans and shifters to a prisoner with no hope of freedom." Corbin's voice broke. "I destroyed her life."

"Does that mean you're giving up?"

Lifting his gaze to Adrian, he said, "Not a chance in hell. I do need some help. I don't know where to start."

"That's the way to think." Leaning forward, Adrian's eyebrows lifted. "The injured guard, Archie, woke up this morning. My boss sent an attorney to be present when the police questioned Archie. We still had a guard outside his hospital room door. I requested that right after you left the theater to tail Givenchy … uh, I mean Eirene."

"Thank you." Corbin meant that for the guard and in respect for his mate.

"Archie said while Eirene was in her dressing room, Brody knocked him down, then must have had the steel structure set to fall easily, because that crashed down next."

"Damn! That clears Eirene from being a suspect."

"Exactly. Our people grabbed Brody before the cops could get him. We pulled information out of him."

Chills rushed up Corbin's arms at what that might mean. He hoped they waterboarded Brody before the cops got to him. "Did he give us anything we can use to save Eirene from Leszek?"

"That will depend upon Eirene. We could release what

we found out from Archie and Brody, but there is no legal chain of possession. My boss is all about following human laws, but when it comes to humans harming shifters, my boss has his own rules. In the interest of gaining the truth, we had to act fast. However, if Leszek has SCIS and some law enforcement in his pocket, he may have judges on his side as well. He could argue that as a sticking point. If he dragged out the investigation for a long time, he could still possibly skate free. The only way this ends now is if Eirene can trap Leszek into confessing. But if that attempt goes awry, she'll lose any battle in court about his trustee position."

Corbin considered the risk to her. He wanted to be the one to step between her and danger, but he'd told Ares that their mates were strong. With no other option, he had to respect their strength no matter how sick to his stomach he felt about her stepping into a battle alone.

Nodding at Adrian, he asked, "How do we get this rolling?"

"The first hurdle is the most difficult. We have to get a message to her without Leszek's bodyguard finding out. Leszek is sending her out on tour in a week. It will be virtually impossible to get to her once she's on the road with more security."

Everything raced around in his mind. None of it sounded possible, but Corbin refused to let despair kill a plan before getting started.

He and Ares had no life without Eirene and Pixie. He said to Ares, *We're going after our mates.*

Yes. Kill anyone in the way.

For once, Corbin said, *Agreed.*

Chapter 30

EIRENE STEPPED OUT of the ride-share car wearing khaki slacks, a long-sleeved peach-colored T-shirt, and comfortable walking shoes, all purchased from local retailers who served middle-income patrons.

Ivarson no longer had a front row seat to her every move. She'd terminated him after Leszek had shared details during an argument only her driver would have known. No wonder Ivarson hadn't taken time off in recent years.

He made too much money by sticking to Eirene like glue and feeding information to Leszek.

She justified ridding herself of Ivarson to Leszek by saying her bodyguard could drive her. Leszek had liked that idea and acted as if she were finally coming around.

Funny how the bodyguard had gotten held up trying to get her sedan to start for the trip here.

Gremlins could be found in any engine if a person knew what they were doing. She'd been ready to ask the nice man at the front door of her apartment building to call a car for her the minute her bodyguard lifted the hood to see if he could fix the problem. She had given the bodyguard no trouble and acted meekly around him so he would not expect her to slip away.

She might not be a black ops ninja, but she had plenty of experience sneaking around.

Corbin would be proud of her.

She paused at the elevator inside Leszek's building and breathed slowly to calm her nerves. Every minute of the past five days had been hell, first waiting to see if Corbin had escaped, then signing the agreement that gave Leszek free rein over her forever to make SCIS leave Corbin alone, and now … today.

Five days of no Ares and no freedom, Pixie griped loudly inside her.

This whole thing had taken a toll on Eirene's wolf. Her sweet Pixie had never been crabby, but she hadn't shifted since escaping that Romanian. The bodyguard said Leszek would not allow her to shift every day. He expected her to act more like the humans whose world she lived in.

I know, Pixie. I'm doing my best today to fix all that.

Pixie made a sighing sound. *I am not a friend today.*

Yes, you are, but you're just like me. You hurt. You could help me by staying quiet when I meet with Leszek.

I will.

A bell pinged, and the elevator door opened. Show time.

When she exited on Leszek's floor, she slowed only long enough to tell Alexandria, "I'm going to see Leszek. You can tell him or not."

His receptionist had half risen and stared at Eirene as if she'd spoken in tongues.

When she encountered Leszek's true gatekeeper, Timothy, she brushed past his desk without a word. She heard his angry sputtering behind her as she opened the door to Leszek's office and slapped it shut after stepping in.

Her trustee held up his mobile phone, speaking to someone. He slashed a furious glance at her and politely ended the call. Then he stood up and shouted, "What do you think you're doing barging in here like that?" His gaze raked her from head to toe. "And what are you wearing?"

Ignoring his questions, she went forward hard with her first verbal assault. "You knew my father would be home waiting for me the day of his accident. You set it all up."

"What the devil are you talking about?" Confident in the center of his empire, Leszek stood tall, ready to decimate her.

Regardless of what he threw at her, she would have her say. She'd practiced over and over at night when the bodyguard watched television, then slept on the sofa.

Clearing her throat, she said, "I found a photo of me and my father in the disaster the shifter made of our home after killing him. The scent on that photo and the rest of the house matched the one I smelled on my father's body." Her heart crumpled every time she brought that awful image to mind, but she pushed it out of her thoughts. She had one chance to nail this bastard, and it was slim.

Leszek crossed his arms, listening to her as a defense attorney would to a star witness.

"I'm thinking you didn't expect the shifter you hired to go crazy after attacking my father and destroy the house."

The eyes of her trustee shifted slightly, enough to know she'd surprised him.

He laughed dismissively. "You're obviously suffering from emotional trauma, Eirene, by making up a story to soothe your guilt for leaving your father alone to have some time to yourself."

Time and again, she'd regretted the week she'd taken off by herself with no guards. She'd raged at herself for not being home when a shifter broke in. The weight of that anguish eased once she'd realized her father's death had been a foregone conclusion.

She held her chin high. "I'm not the one suffering from delusions. You are going to pay the price for killing my father as one of your criminal acts."

He calmly asked, "If this were true, which it is not, how do you plan to prove it?" He shook his head and waved a hand at her. "Get out of my office, little dog. Threaten me again, and your whole world comes down. I can have you put in my institution with one phone call. Even humans who adore you would believe you were merely another shifter who had snapped."

No one was sending her away. "When I was a child, I thought you were a wonderful uncle. As I got older, I began to see your creepy ways. I wonder if my dad figured that out and that's why you sent the shifter to kill him. Maybe he opened his eyes after you suggested having him add you as the co-owner of my label so you could turn me into a superstar. My dad had always respected my ability to sing and understood I didn't want fame and fortune. He knew I wanted to teach others to sing and perform for those who couldn't afford tickets as well as those who would pay."

"You were always too stupid to think big," he spewed in a nasty tone. "Your father wouldn't push you. You both needed me. You should thank me for what I did to help you."

"I will never thank a psychopath for killing the only family I had. My father was something you can't comprehend. A decent man respected by all."

Leszek started walking back and forth behind his desk.

She could hear his heart rate rise. Now for the next little bomb. "I recently found out from my father's attorney that my father had intended to change his will and replace you as trustee over my trust fund with his attorney. To do this, he had hired an investigator to determine if your business dealings were above board and you were an upstanding citizen."

That stopped Leszek, who lifted an eyebrow. "All he learned was that my businesses and reputation with money are above reproach. That makes me the perfect candidate to be the trustee."

"What they found out was that while your financial life shone, you brought young, underage women from third-world countries back to the States on your private jet. The first two disappeared without a trace, leaving no sign they were still alive. A third one was photographed through a window, bruised badly. That's why he was going to remove you as trustee. He feared for my life. I wish they'd gone to someone to save the woman in your house, but I can understand how his attorney feared crossing you after that shifter killed my dad."

"Again, you make wild accusations without any proof." However, this time, Leszek's words lacked confidence, and his fear stunk up the room.

Unable to stop her hands from fisting as she related all the sordid details, Eirene relaxed her fingers and slowed her breathing. She wasn't done yet.

He had to be pushed harder.

"As for evidence, I have plenty. I may have been isolated from other shifters, but they have found me."

"You mean that rogue wolf? One word from me, just one word, and SCIS will track him down. They'll drag him to their prison and make an example of him. His death will be broadcast to prevent other shifters from making his mistake."

Her throat tightened at Leszek's warning. He'd held an iron fist over her head for so long that she could not easily ignore his threat.

Corbin had been through so much misery in his life.

Her words today could shatter the world he'd built with his pack. She suffered a moment of panic at not having broken through Leszek's hard shell. She couldn't stop halfway. "Do not threaten my mate. You have no idea of what terrifying power you'll bring down on your head."

Leszek's hands shook like she'd never seen before. His skin paled, but he did not fold. He jabbed a long finger in her direction. "That's it. You've made a huge mistake."

She held her breath, hoping she'd stomped on his defiance enough for him to capitulate.

He stabbed a button on a polished mahogany box sitting on his desk.

The door lock audibly clicked behind her.

In the next second, he lifted his mobile phone and punched a button. "This is Dr. Moore. My ward is having a psychotic episode. I need you to pick her up and deliver her to my institute."

Stunned silent, she stared at him.

When he placed the phone down, he explained, "Acting calm won't work when security arrives from my clinic."

He raised a revolver. "This carries titanium bullets if you try to attack me or refuse to cooperate."

She didn't so much as flinch, but her blood pressure shot up like a geyser erupting. She couldn't back down. If she lost today, it wouldn't be because she failed to throw everything in her arsenal at him. "You're done, Leszek. You won't need a titanium bullet. I wish I had it in me to kill someone like you, but I don't. You will face justice, though."

He withdrew a small white box from a pocket in his black suit jacket, the size of an unmarked container of mints, and placed it at the front of his desk. "Take one of the pills inside and swallow it. You will not die, but you are going to wake up wearing a straitjacket. If you don't take that pill in the next thirty seconds, I'll shoot you and claim you had gone mad and tried to attack me. Then I'll personally oversee your care." His eyes lit up with madness. He grinned like the crazy monster he was.

She changed her voice from antagonistic to soothing. "I will do as you say if you'll simply tell me one thing."

He cocked his head at her. "What would you like to know?"

"Once I take that pill, I have no way to ever convince anyone of anything I believe you've done. I'm only asking for one thing. Answer that, and I will take the pill without fighting you. How did you find the shifter to send into our home that night?"

Maybe it was her submissive tone or the need for a maniac to brag about his deed. Either way, he beamed the confident smile of a man comfortable in his position of authority. He put the gun down and shoved his hands in his pockets, walking around the desk as if to casually discuss a dinner reservation.

When Leszek reached the corner of the desk, he bragged, "I have a secret wing in my clinic where I treat shifters. An SCIS recovery expert, a jackal shifter, delivers particularly disturbed ones there to use as test subjects. The jackal shifter admires what I've done with you and hopes to see if other shifters can be trained to follow orders. He has a resource in another country who pays well for strong workers. I chose a shifter that had shown a lot of promise, but when he finished your father, he had blood lust and went crazy." Leszek shrugged as if the shifter had only broken furniture.

Tears burned the corners of her eyes. Her father had been protective and overbearing, but she didn't believe he knew what his security had done to Corbin or that he deserved a horrific death. She blinked them away and drew in a cleansing breath at having finally gotten an admission from Leszek that she had doubted would ever happen.

She lifted her voice and announced, "I'm done. I've said all I want to you."

"Good." Leszek rubbed his hands together and walked back behind the desk. "Hurry up and take the pill. I don't wish you to be in pain while being transported. Once you've gone through treatments, I'll announce that you voluntarily entered my clinic after an emotional breakdown due to the rogue shifter who tricked you, but you are healed and ready to sing again. That album will be priority number one for you."

The lock on the door clicked on its own, sounding like a gunshot.

Leszek frowned at the noise and picked up his handgun.

The door opened, and Corbin walked in, stepping between her and Leszek.

She loved his protective nature. She would always protect him equally. She'd come to learn that she and Pixie might not be dominant, but they would fight for their mates.

The tall man with strange eagle eyes, she now knew as Corbin's boss, stepped inside next. His mere presence filled the room. He wore an expensive-looking suit that had to be custom-made for a muscular body of that size.

His eagle-shaped eyes zeroed in on Leszek, who stood with his mouth open. Spoken in a voice with old-world sophistication, he ordered Leszek, "Put the gun down."

Leszek had become so shocked that he seemed to have

forgotten he held a gun. He jerked it up and leaned a hand on the desk, probably to steady himself.

The gun went right back down, crushing his fingers against the desktop. He screamed in pain, but the gun never moved.

Corbin's boss quietly said, "Send in law enforcement." Two men in SWAT gear filed in but quickly realized Leszek was no danger to anyone. They walked over, and the gun slid out of his hand to the desk surface. Leszek grabbed his ruined hand and cried.

One of the SWAT officers looked back at Corbin's boss with a surprised glance. When his boss said nothing, the officer jerked the hand with bleeding fingers behind Leszek's back, then the other hand, and cuffed him.

That same one read Leszek his rights, adding, "In addition to being suspected of killing this woman's father, you are also accused of having played a role in killing two Beckham Security guards and severely injuring a third. Additional charges may be filed later."

"You can't accuse me of that. I had nothing to do with Beckham's accident-prone guards." His wild gaze swung to Eirene. "She's behind all this. She didn't want security guards."

Ignoring Leszek's rant, Corbin said, "Yes, they can charge you. It so happens that Brody submitted a signed confession to the police this morning in exchange for leniency for his part in your deadly plan. Our organization has handed over the shifter you paid to kill Eirene's father to law enforcement. We tracked him down from the scent on the picture she provided. He will testify against you at your trial in exchange for life in prison instead of being handed over to SCIS. Archie, the third Beckham guard, remained protected until he came out of his coma when he fingered Brody for trying to kill him, which clears Eirene of any suspicion. Brody confessed to his actions and showed evidence that you paid him to perform those attacks and killings. He also faces life in prison. The list goes on. As you can see, the evidence is insurmountable. A court will terminate you as the trustee over Eirene's trust fund the minute you are booked."

Leszek threatened Eirene in a vile tone. "You will pay for this! You cannot hide from me. You will not survive today."

Eirene stepped up next to Corbin. "You're done. I am free of you." She would never be standing here if Corbin's people hadn't sent a massive hawk to her bedroom window one night. She couldn't believe it had sat there tapping slowly on the window. When she'd lifted the old-fashioned window, the hawk flew in and dropped two rolled-up sheets of paper on her bed. It waited until she read them and told the hawk her answer was yes.

She had been ready to go to war with Leszek right then.

"You're not dominant, Eirene. You can't stop me," Leszek warned.

Corbin must have had all he could take. He stepped forward, warning, "If you aren't sentenced to die for your crimes, which I think you will be, you will never come near her again, or you'll face me. I'm not sweet like Eirene. I spent years in hell and have no compunction about terminating any threat to her."

Red flooded Leszek's face. He shouted, "You will all pay a price for this. I hold power over SCIS and law enforcement. No judge will—"

His words were cut off as he passed out.

The officer who had been walking him from behind the desk grabbed one arm. His sidekick caught Leszek's second arm. They lifted him between them. As they neared Corbin's eagle shifter boss, one said, "Thanks."

"You're welcome."

Chapter 31

BACK AT THE compound, Corbin helped Eirene step out of a big black vehicle that reminded him of a Secret Service SUV.

Bosse had driven him, Eirene, Adrian, and Jaz back from Leszek's building. All but the eagle shifter, who first thanked Eirene before walking away.

On the ride to the compound, Jaz and Adrian had spent time making Eirene feel welcome.

Corbin held Eirene's hand as they followed Jaz and Adrian to the big house, as everyone called it. He had waited through terrified seconds while Leszek threatened her. Adrian's boss had quietly instructed him to be patient.

As they approached the house, a familiar man with eagle eyes, wearing a sharp suit, waited on the porch.

Why Corbin had a moment of panic, he had no idea. He couldn't help watching for something to fall from the sky and destroy his happiness.

The Guardian stepped down to where the rest of the pack walked up to greet them. Bosse clamped Corbin on the back first. "Now I won't be the only one with a mate. The rest of these idiots can envy you for a while."

"I can take it." Corbin's worries lightened.

Ladrón stepped up next and shook Corbin's hand. "Congratulations on winning the heart of an angel." He turned to Eirene and kissed her on the cheek before Corbin could stop him, laughing loudly.

Corbin grumbled, "How is it you manage to compliment me and piss me off at the same time?"

"It's a gift. You're welcome."

Badger stood thirty feet back and yelled, "When's dinner?"

Corbin sighed and murmured, "I told you we had some problems."

"He can't be as bad as Vlad." Eirene's laugh floated through the air like a perfectly tuned chime. Heads turned her way.

Shocked into not moving, Hammer lowered the sunglasses no one was allowed to touch and stared at her in awe. "It's really you. I heard you sing once and … I have no words to describe something that amazing."

"I'm flattered," she stammered. "If anyone wants me to, I'll be happy to sing for all of you."

Silence fell over the crowd.

The Guardian walked over and politely took her hand in his. "I, too, have heard your melodic voice and would love to hear it again. The greatest gift I ever receive is for any of my shifters to bond with a worthy mate. You and Corbin have proven yourselves more than worthy. I am honored to have you join our group. Jaz and Adrian have indicated they welcomed you to become a pack member."

She nodded.

Corbin understood she had likely choked up at all the adulation, unable to speak. He said, "Thank you and everyone else who saved both of us. To have Eirene and Pixie with me and Ares is a gift we can never repay. I promise all of you in the pack that I'm going to work hard to help finish your cabins."

"Me too," Eirene chimed in. "I heard about what you're doing. It so happens I have an album coming out soon, and that means I have disposable income I can put toward the projects."

Corbin turned a shocked look at her. "I thought the album wasn't ready?"

"That's what I told Leszek. It's been finished for a while."

The men cheered.

All except Badger, who yelled, "Food and beer. Is that so hard to do?"

Jaz rolled her eyes at him, then asked Corbin and Eirene, "Will you two join us for dinner at five tonight?"

Corbin looked at Eirene, "I'm good if you are, but I want to take you for a bike ride through the country."

Eirene nodded happily at Jaz and told Corbin, "I'd love it."

He turned to Adrian and then shifted his gaze to the Guardian. "Will it be acceptable for me to leave the compound on occasion with her?"

"You have proven yourself trustworthy in many ways. You are free to come and go so long as you inform Jaz or Adrian first. That way, we will know when to become concerned if you fail to return when expected. As you've discovered, there are some unsavory individuals in SCIS. Bosse and his mate have already been told they may do the same." Moving his gaze to the other shifters, he added, "Adrian is determined to take each of you with him to develop your skills in the human realm and prove you are ready to be independent as well. Work with him and you will benefit."

Eirene drew the Guardian's attention when she asked, "Will I be able to continue my work helping vulnerable female shifters?"

Corbin hadn't thought to ask about that and worried at the Guardian's answer.

"Yes. I'd like to introduce you to Scarlett, who is mated to one of our shifters. She's been involved for a long time in locating vulnerable female shifters who need support and aid. She has quite a network and is very experienced. She is the reason we were able to locate the shifter who killed your father after taking the photo you supplied to a wide number of women in her local shelters. One of her ladies recognized the scent as the male shifter she had escaped. Scarlett would welcome someone like you on her team and said she'd like to discuss Nova with you. She seems to have knowledge of Nova and has questions about the woman."

"I definitely want to meet her," Eirene said, sounding surprised at this news. "I have zero ninja skills and would be happy to learn from Scarlett and help her save others. She might have some insight into finding Nova's daughter. I also want to thank her for finding my father's killer."

In his meticulously polite way, the Guardian assured her, "I shall arrange the meeting. Thank you again for what you did to save Corbin. You and your wolf will always have the protection of our entire organization should you need it."

Overwhelmed by the incredible community he and Eirene now belonged to, Corbin stayed quiet until a pause stretched. He asked the eagle shifter, "Is there anything else you want to talk to us about?"

"Not at this time." He told Eirene, "I'll look forward to hearing you sing after dinner."

Corbin noted Adrian and Jaz's surprised looks at learning their boss would stay for dinner. But they appeared to be pleasantly surprised. With plenty of time to catch up later, he turned to Eirene. "Ready to go for a ride, babe?"

"Absolutely. Do you still have a bike?"

"Yep. Adrian had a replacement for mine delivered here." He took her hand to pull her away from everyone.

She called over her shoulder, "See you all tonight. Thank you, Adrian, Jaz, and Mr. Guardian."

Corbin snorted at that. When he reached the bike parked inside the bunkhouse, he rolled it out and climbed on. "I'm taking us on a ride, then back to a private area on the far side of the lake on this property. I think it's time we give Ares and Pixie a relaxing, long visit before we come back.

Ares said, *Thank you. You are best human.*

Corbin sent back, *You're welcome. You are my better half.*

Eirene said, "Pixie is excited. She can't stop talking about seeing Ares."

Corbin could feel happiness spread through him from Ares.

———◆———

This is book two in my new Wild Wolf Pack series, which is a spinoff of the League of Gallize Shifters. I hope you enjoyed this story, and I *would appreciate a review* wherever you shop for books.

To keep up with new releases and be the first to find out when the next book will be available, please join my **https://authordiannalove.com/connect**. I send very few newsletters, and I *never* share anyone's information. I hate to have mine shared.

Wild Wolf Pack from the world of Gallize Shifters
Book 1: Bosse
Book 2: Corbin

LEAGUE OF GALLIZE SHIFTERS
Book 1: Gray Wolf Mate
Book 2: Mating A Grizzly
Book 3: Stalking His Mate
Book 4: Scent Of A Mate
Book 5: Wild Wolf Mate

RAVES ABOUT DIANNA'S OTHER SERIES:

Belador **Urban Fantasy:**

"When it comes to urban fantasy, Dianna Love is a master." Always Reviewing.

"There is so much action in this book I feel like I've burned calories just reading it." D Antonio

"There are SO many things in this series that I want to learn more about; there's no way I could list them all." Lily, Romance Junkies Reviews

Slye Team Black Ops **Romantic Thrillers:**

*"...suspense, thrills, excitement, danger and a super romantic couple...****Dianna Love*** *writes romance suspense so well, as I consider her one of the best at creating believability and hooking us in from the start all the way to the exciting climax."* ~~ Barb, The Reading Café

"Dianna never disappoints! ... would have give it a 10 if they would let!!! Very enjoyable read, can't wait for the next one :-)." ~~ Amy, Goodreads

Red Moon **Young Adult Sci-fi/Fantasy Series**
by Micah Caida (pen name of collaborators Dianna Love & Mary Buckham):

"Time Trap is amazingly original and unexpected...I loved every second of reading it!"* ~~ Alexandra F, 15, who has read *The Book Thief, The Hunger Games,* and *Anna Karenina.*

"Reading this book is like riding on a roller coaster, getting to the top and not knowing when the next drop is." ~~ Alex B, 12 years old, has also read all of *Rick Riordan's* books, the *Hunger Games*, the *Chronicles of Nick*, and the *Rangers Apprentice* series.

To contact Dianna – email her
assistantATauthordiannalove.com

Websites: AuthorDiannaLove.com and
DiannaLoveSignedBooks.com

Facebook – "Dianna Love Fan Page"
"Dianna Love Reader Community" Facebook group page
(You're invited.)

AUTHOR BIO

New York Times **Bestseller Dianna Love** once dangled over a hundred feet in the air to create unusual marketing projects for Fortune 500 companies. She now writes high-octane romantic thrillers, young adult and urban fantasy. Fans of the bestselling *Belador* urban fantasy series will be thrilled to know more books follow with the new *Treoir Dragon Chronicles*. Dianna's Slye Team Black Ops romantic thriller series wrapped up with Fatal Promise, but also launched the *HAMR Brotherhood* spinoff series. *League of Gallize Shifters* paranormal romance series continues with spinoff *Wild Wolf Pack* from the world of Gallize Shifters. Look for her books in print, e-book, and audio. On the rare occasions Dianna is out of her writing cave, she tours the country on her BMW motorcycle, searching for new story locations. Dianna lives in the Atlanta, GA area with her husband, who is a motorcycle instructor, and a tank full of unruly saltwater critters.

Visit her website at www.**AuthorDiannaLove.com** or www.**DiannaLoveSignedBooks.com**

A WORD FROM DIANNA...

Thank you for reading *CORBIN,* and thanks also to all the readers who have written wonderful notes about my Gallize Shifters. I appreciate your feedback so much! I'll keep expanding the Gallize world in the Wild Wolf Pack series. I also have more of the original Gallize books planned.

Without my amazing husband, Karl, I could not write my stories. He's the best.

A special thank you to Judy Carney, who gets better with every book she goes through, and Stacey Krug, who has a critical eye for catching continuity errors. Also, I appreciate Tina Rucci, Jennifer Cazares, and Sherry Arnold for being terrific early beta readers who catch small things missed by all of us even after multiple editing passes.

I want to send a huge thank-you to my Super Read-and-Review Team peeps, who read early versions and then share their opinions—you rock!!

Sending a shout-out to Candi Fox and Leiha Mann, who work hard to support me in so many ways. Thanks to Joyce Ann McLaughlin, Kimber Mirabella, and Sharon Livingston, too.

As always, the amazing Kim Killion creates all my covers, and Jennifer Jakes saves my butt time and again with great formatting just when I need it. Much appreciation to both of you.

Thank you to my peeps on the Dianna Love Reader Group newsletter list and on our Facebook group page where I love visiting with you.

Dianna

www.ingramcontent.com/pod-product-compliance
Lightning Source LLC
Chambersburg PA
CBHW071243190726
48292CB00007B/2389